CARDINAL
HOAX

KARL BOZICEVIC

CARDINAL HOAX

FLOW FOCUSING
press
San Francisco

Library of Congress Control Number: 2011935017
ISBN: 978-0-615-51767-4

Cover illustration: Jeff Wack
Cover design: Anton Khodakovsky
Interior design: Anton Khodakovsky
Production editing: Lydia Bird

FLOW FOCUSING PRESS
San Francisco, California

Printed in the United States of America

Dedicated to my former law partner Carol LaSalle, who consistently encouraged me to write this book and who passed away in 2011. She was not only my partner, but a dear friend to me and to so many others. We miss her adorable quirky smile.

CHAPTER 1

Do you want to know who you are? Don't ask. Act!
Action will delineate and define you.

—Thomas Jefferson (1743–1826)

On a crisp autumn afternoon, Herbert Sedlack and his friend Thomas Freeman headed into the woods surrounding Herbert's home on the upper Michigan peninsula. They each carried BB guns fully loaded with copper BBs poured into their guns from a small tube Herbert had bought that morning. Herbert was nine years old and filled with a sense of adventure.

About one hundred yards into the woods the two boys stopped, looked up, and spotted a cardinal sitting on a pine-tree branch thirty yards away. The bird was bright red, singing, and facing directly toward them. Herbert raised his rifle to his shoulder.

"You'll never hit him from here," said Thomas. "He's out of range."

What Thomas didn't know was that Herbert had taken his gun apart, put in a stronger spring, and lubricated the piston to make a tighter fit. He could smell the gun oil as he aligned the sight toward his target. He fired. The BB flew in a slight arc from the barrel to a point well above the target, then dropped and hit the bird directly in the center of its chest. A few small feathers flew into the air around the point of impact, and the bird fell.

"You got him! I can't believe it, you got him!" Thomas shouted.

Immediately Herbert felt sick. He never expected his gun modifications to work so well, and never wanted to kill the bird.

The scene flashed through his mind almost fifty years later as he sat nervously in a high-end restaurant on the edge of San Francisco's theater district. He picked up the empty plate in front of him, examined the intricacies of the design around the edges, and put it gently back on the table. Generally a happy person, he was feeling anxious and using the plate to stall. He picked it up again and smiled at the reflection of his overweight face. He wondered how much he would reveal tonight, and just how to do it.

He'd accomplished a great deal as a particle physicist, and acquired a degree of wealth from companies formed based on practical applications of his work. His success flowed from his ability to focus his intellect in a way few others could.

He studied the abstract art on the walls to avoid eye contact with Korin, a tall, attractive venture capitalist ten years his junior. A large brass impressionistic statue dominated the center of the room, surrounded by tables that were spaced apart to provide diners with a degree of privacy. A small cluster of yellow flowers in a simple silver vase caught his eye next, and he noticed how they contrasted with Korin's stylish deep purple dress—a dress that left one of her shoulders bare.

Korin had asked the waiter to decant an '82 Petrus she'd brought to entice Herbert to meet with her. The sommelier returned the filled decanter and empty bottle to their table. Herbert picked up the bottle, examined the label, and ran his thumb back and forth across the Petrus name. He looked forward to smelling the wine, tasting it, and drinking every drop.

"So, where did you get an eighty-two Petrus?" he asked. "This is an amazing find. Did you find a new dealer? Someone in Saint-Émilion?"

"I bought a case in the original box when I was in Bordeaux last year. The dealer had just picked it up from a local who needed the cash. But I'm not here to talk to you about wine."

"But I really enjoy talking about wine," Herbert said.

"I know, and we'll get to that. Right now I need to understand why you didn't show up for the dinner on Saturday. I had fifty people there. Those people expected to see you. They invested in your ideas. You never even called. What happened?"

The previous week, Korin had invited a group of wealthy investors to a celebration dinner. They had put money into a company she'd formed based on one of Herbert's inventions. The company had gone public, and their originally risky investments had paid off well. Some of the guests knew Herbert, others were expecting to meet him, and Korin had promised he would be there.

Herbert continued to direct his attention to the wine label. "I don't like big events with lots of people. I don't want to be the center of attention. It was just too difficult for me."

"That's a start. But I know there's more to the story. I set you up with a date for the dinner, and this isn't the first time you've stood up someone I arranged for you to meet. We've known each other a very long time, and think I deserve more of an explanation." Korin gently removed the bottle from Herbert's hand and placed it to the side, which Herbert understood to mean that the wine would come later, but for now she needed his attention.

Herbert wasn't quite ready to answer. Perhaps some wine would help, he thought. He picked up his glass, swirled the wine, smelled it, took a sip, and held this amazing complex Bordeaux in his mouth with his eyes closed and enjoyed himself.

"I know this wine deserves a more sophisticated compliment, but I'll just say it's really yummy. What did you pay for this stuff?" he asked.

Herbert knew Korin was becoming increasingly frustrated as he avoided answering the very questions he wanted to answer. He knew she prided herself on her interpersonal skills, which included her ability to get others to talk openly. He admired this skill, in part because he believed he lacked it. At some point, he hoped to unburden himself about his deepest secrets. But perhaps not tonight.

"I paid about a hundred thousand dollars for the case, when you make the Euro-to-dollar conversion. But you're still not talking to me. I have feelings too, Herbert. I was hurt when you didn't come—not just embarrassed. I thought we were more than business associates. I thought we were friends, and I deserve to know what happened last Saturday night and why you never seem to care for the women I introduce you to. I'll give you the rest of the case of Petrus if you'll tell me."

"Well, it's not as though I'm seeing someone else," said Herbert with a slight laugh.

"On the one hand, that's good to hear," said Korin. "But I was almost hoping you'd tell me you were getting back together with your high-school sweetheart. At least I could understand what was happening."

"I never had a high-school sweetheart," said Herbert. He knew why that was. He also knew that he didn't regret the lack of a high-school romance. Many people had never had a meaningful romantic relationship in high school. But Herbert knew that most people had wished for one. He had not.

"Was that a disappointment for you at the time?" asked Korin.

"No. It wasn't a disappointment," said Herbert.

"That's fairly unusual. Is that because you were focused on your studies?"

The waiter arrived with their meals and provided Herbert a chance to think. He cut a piece of roast beef and lifted it to his mouth. He chewed slowly, savoring the tender meat, and then spoke.

"It's actually the opposite of what you're proposing. I focused on my studies because I had no interest in romance."

"Well, maybe you were too young at the time. People mature at different rates. Did that change in college?" asked Korin.

The direction of the conversation was making Herbert uneasy. "We're not here to talk about my lack of dates in high school. I was working on a new breakthrough the night of the dinner, last Saturday night. I just couldn't leave my lab," he said.

"How many times have you told me there was some new breakthrough you were working on? Dozens of times over the last fifteen years you were making a discovery that was going to completely change the world of electronics. Why should I believe you now?"

"Because it's the truth. It's really important, and I got so involved I forgot about everything."

"Well, I've known you to be an incredibly driven and focused guy when it comes to your science. What were you working on?" asked Korin.

"I was working on a way to make electrons much smaller," said Herbert.

"One thing I know is that electrons are very small. So why is it important to make them smaller?" asked Korin with a smile and a slight laugh.

"I know you don't want a long scientific explanation. I also know you've heard me get excited about my work in the past. Just trust me when I tell you this could be the most important scientific discovery of all time. Last Saturday I made an important breakthrough, not just on the science, but on a practical application of what I'm doing. You need to see what I'm doing to appreciate it," said Herbert.

"Why would you want to show me? I'm no scientist. I won't understand it."

"It's not complete, and I don't need you to understand the science behind it. I've put a lot of my time and nearly all my money into this project. I've put millions of dollars into it so far. It's far enough along now for me to show someone, but I don't want to disclose it publicly. I need more money now, and I'd like you to invest in further development."

"Invest in it? If it's as important as you say, why don't you keep using your own money and reap all the rewards?" asked Korin.

"I'm not poor, but unlike you I don't have ten million dollars lying around. I know there's still considerable risk, and I've already spent a great deal of what I have. Much of it was spent going in the wrong direction. I'm on the right path now. After you've seen it, and I tell you what I want to do, I'm sure you won't be able to resist being a part of the project."

Herbert knew his interpersonal skills left much to be desired. He also knew Korin well, and thought it best to say very little at this time and let his accomplishments do the talking for him. He had great confidence in his work and enormous excitement about the possibilities he knew would flow from it.

"I'm intrigued. When can I see it?" asked Korin.

Herbert smiled. He had interested her in investing, and this was his primary goal. He'd said what he wanted to, and not said what he wasn't ready to tell.

"How about tomorrow morning at eleven, my place?"

Korin removed her iPhone from her purse and checked her schedule.

"That works—and this evening has worked as well. I'm glad you told me what was going on. You're an interesting guy, Herbert."

"You have no idea how interesting," said Herbert with a wink.

Their dinner proceeded, and he could tell that Korin was more focused on his invention than his having missed her dinner party. He had assumed she would react this way. In fact, he'd counted on it. Dessert wine was ordered and the evening wound down.

"Let's finish off our d'Yquem and I'll see you tomorrow morning," said Korin.

"One more thing. To make sure you show up, I'll promise you something. I know you like jewels. Tomorrow morning I'll tell you something about diamonds you never even imagined. It fits into the story about my work," said Herbert.

"Fascinating," said Korin. "I can't wait."

Herbert left the dinner feeling very satisfied. He had someone who was very wealthy interested in investing, but Korin wasn't just any investor. He liked the way she saw things differently. Korin made her own rules. This was, in part, why he felt she could help him move forward with his project. He had in mind a plan that would break all the rules.

CHAPTER 2

It is neither wealth nor splendor; but tranquility and occupation which give you happiness.

—Thomas Jefferson (1743–1826)

Korin Prentise stood in front of her bedroom mirror assessing what she saw, a tall, athletic woman approaching fifty. Her features carried traces of both her Italian mother and her British father. Her flawless white skin with the faintest hint of brown contrasted with her bright green eyes, and her thick, wavy brown hair hung just below her shoulders. Korin understood the importance of appearance and knew she had a classical beauty. She would look good without even trying, but she did try to look her best. She wanted to look fabulous, while appearing as though she wasn't even trying. She also knew it was her inner energy, more than anything, that attracted men and women to her.

As she headed downstairs, she paused to admire an original Marc Chagall that hung on the landing. The dreamscape made her reflect on just how fortunate she was.

Half an hour later, she was driving north on Highway 280, looking forward to seeing what Herbert found so very interesting—and wondering how it might be connected to diamonds. She exited off 280, passed through the small commercial area of Woodside, and headed west toward Herbert's.

Trees lined the winding two-lane road and hid most of the homes from view. Woodside was one of the wealthiest small towns in America, and its residents paid generously for peace and privacy.

Herbert had more than once exaggerated the importance of his work. Sometimes his exaggerations and enthusiasm served to convince others to invest. Herbert had, to an extent, made her wealthy, or at least her work with his inventions had. Some of his inventions and those of others she had handled with were little more than minor modifications of the original pioneering inventions. She'd been able to take those slightly modified inventions, market them, build companies around them, and sell those companies for many multiples of the original investments. Building another company and making more money was a way to have more influence. She wanted the power and influence that came with money, but she also wanted something more from life. She wanted something that really challenged her. She suspected that what she was about to see would do just that.

She arrived at the large black iron gate in front of Herbert's estate, pushed the intercom button, and waited.

The speaker came to life. "Is that you, Korin?"

"Yes, it's me. Who else would it be, your high-school sweetheart?"

The gate swung open. She drove up the driveway and saw Herbert leaving his house with his yellow Lab, Quark. He gestured for her to park by the building she knew to be his laboratory. He and Quark followed on foot. As soon as she turned off the engine and stepped out of her car, Quark bounded over to greet her. She hugged him and pressed her cheek against his as Herbert approached.

"So Herbert, what kind of quark is Quark?" she asked, pulling a handkerchief from her purse to wipe her face.

"As you know, quarks are subatomic particles," said Herbert, breathing a little hard. "There are all kinds of quarks—red, green, blue, up and down. But he's none of those. I liked the name because of its first appearance—in James Joyce's *Finnegans Wake*."

"Interesting. I never thought of you as a reader of Joyce. I brought you something." She handed him a pink box containing the jelly doughnuts she knew he loved.

"Thank you," said Herbert. "I knew you'd remember. Do you mind if I eat one now? I haven't had breakfast."

"Please do," Korin said.

They headed toward the lab. Large oak trees shaded the area, their trunks bent in intriguing ways. The ground was covered with small smooth pebbles that crunched beneath their feet as they walked. Quark trotted at Herbert's side, looking up in hopes of falling doughnut crumbs.

The door closed behind them with an electronic click and buzzing noise, and Herbert gave it a tug to confirm it was secure. The lab was brightly lit and filled with electronic equipment, most of which appeared to be new and partially disassembled. Instead of conventional artwork, boldly signed photos of scientists were mounted on the walls, supplemented with glass cases containing old models of patented inventions. She couldn't identify all of them, but some looked to be miniature steam engines and others were railroad cars.

Herbert seemed a little uneasy as he looked around the lab. "So, Korin, I know you're always telling me to simplify my explanations. So I'll try. Have you heard of Moore's law? I'm sure you have, right?"

"I have, actually. I think most people dealing with computers in Silicon Valley know it's got something to do with the capacity of computers to double every two years or so."

"Well that's right," said Herbert, offering Quark a small piece of doughnut. "One of the cofounders of Intel was a guy named Gordon Moore. In the sixties he noted that since the development of the integrated circuit, the number of transistors that could be placed on a given chip was doubling every eighteen to twenty-four months. He wrote a paper about this, and then around 1970 or so a guy named Carver Mead read Moore's original paper. He did further calculations and coined the phrase 'Moore's Law.'"

"I'm guessing you're telling me all this for a reason," said Korin.

"Just give me a chance. I'm trying to give you some background. I'm not good at this. So you know that until now Moore's Law has been shown to be true. Most people think it will continue to hold up for maybe another decade or two, and they're still focusing on making silicon transistors smaller. But at some point those transistors will be as small as they can get, and something different will have to be used to get more and more information onto a given space."

"Whatever mainstream researchers are working on, I'm sure you're working on something different," said Korin.

Herbert looked up with a smile and some powdered sugar around his mouth. "You know me well. The reason the silicon transistors can only be made so small is that at some point the electricity running through them will melt them."

"So you figured out how to cool them down?"

"No, but that's what some folks are working on. It turns out that diamonds conduct heat very well. You remember I told you I'd work diamonds into this?" asked Herbert.

"Of course I do. Go on," said Korin.

"Although diamonds conduct heat well, they don't conduct electricity at all. That is, most diamonds don't."

"But some do?"

"Yes, blue diamonds conduct electricity," said Herbert. "The Hope Diamond is the most famous. Take a look as this."

He led her to a large curved black table with a rough textured surface. Three computer screens were positioned side by side on the table just behind a keyboard. Herbert sat down, activated the center screen, clicked on an icon, and brought up a photo of the Hope Diamond. The stone was brilliant blue, cut with dozens of facets and surrounded by sixteen clear diamonds of varying shapes. Its size was difficult to judge, but unmistakably huge.

"Quite beautiful," said Korin.

"If you shine ultraviolet light on a blue diamond then turn off the light, it will glow. Here's what the Hope Diamond looks like in the dark." Herbert clicked on the photo. The white diamonds dissolved and the blue diamond emerged as a brilliant red glowing stone. It looked completely different from before, at once opaque and translucent. The facets were barely visible, and the diamond reminded Korin of red-hot metal.

"The glow you see comes from electrons. It shows that the Hope Diamond is conductive. Others are working on ways to make diamonds conduct heat and electricity. It has some promise. I decided to take a completely different route. I decided to see if I could make the electricity itself different," said Herbert.

"Different electricity? That sounds strange."

"I'm a strange guy. Simplifying, what I did was try to make electrons smaller. I generated an electron flow and used positively charged energy around it to focus the electrons to a smaller and smaller stream. This produced effects that I never predicted."

"What effects?" asked Korin.

"That's what I brought you here to see."

He led Korin to an elongated black-marble-topped lab bench. At one end was a large crude-looking machine, with a tube leading from it to what looked to be some small pedestals at the other end.

Korin was all but certain none of this involved a computer, but she had no idea what it did involve. She was hoping Herbert wouldn't start writing equations on his white board, and that whatever he did show her would be something she could understand.

"I'm sure you know what this is," said Herbert, pointing to a gumball machine next to the bench.

"Yes, but you didn't bring me here to show me a gumball machine."

Herbert put a coin in the slot and pulled the lever. Out rolled a green gumball. He handed it to Korin.

"Take a look at this. I just want you to know that it's an ordinary gumball," said Herbert.

"Yes, it looks like an ordinary gumball to me."

"Take the gumball and put it on that pedestal at the end of the tube on the bench," said Herbert.

Korin placed the gumball as directed, then looked at Herbert. "Now what?"

"Just stand over here behind me and keep watching the gumball," said Herbert as he walked over and switched on the power to the equipment on the table. Quark began to bark. Herbert turned a large black dial that looked as though it belonged on a large safe.

"Just keep watching the gumball," said Herbert, "and stay behind me until I've switched this off."

Korin suspected a trick of some sort. She stared intently at the gumball and the pedestal where it was positioned. As Herbert turned the dial, the equipment hummed quietly. Quark barked anxiously and moved back behind Korin. Then, without fading, without moving, the bright green gumball simply disappeared.

A pulse of adrenaline shot through Korin, followed immediately by a wave of excitement, nearly sexual in its intensity.

She swung her gaze to Herbert's calm face. He switched off the power, then sat on the floor to hold and comfort Quark. If this was a trick, the dog was playing some role, but all seemed so genuine.

"Where is it?"

"Go take a look," said Herbert, stroking Quark.

Korin moved quickly to the pedestal, touching the surface where the gumball had been. She checked the bench, the floor, even the ceiling.

"It's not here. What happened to it?"

"Nothing happened to it," said Herbert. "That's the whole point. It didn't go anywhere I can detect, but it's gone."

"That makes no sense. I think even Quark would understand that if it's gone it went somewhere."

"I've lost a gumball machine full of gumballs. Every time I turn this on, Quark barks. He detects something, and then the gumballs appear to be gone. I've tried, but I haven't been able to get them back."

"Is your machine here somehow vaporizing them?"

"No. If they were vaporized, they'd be here, simply in some other form. It would be gaseous. I've checked, and there's no gas from the gumballs. I even tagged some gumballs with transmitters and searched for a signal, but nothing. The whole thing just completely defies conventional physics," said Herbert.

Korin didn't answer right away. She knew without a doubt that she'd just witnessed something very important. If Herbert could replicate his results on larger objects, perhaps his invention could be used for waste disposal, or maybe even tunneling through mountains. Instead of demolishing old buildings, you could remove them in their entirety. The possibilities would be endless.

She made Herbert rerun the demonstration three times. Each time, she changed some variable of the experiment. First, she put the gumball in a glass. Next, she filled the glass with water. Lastly, she put the gumball behind a block of lead. But each time, the gumball disappeared, leaving everything else in place.

After the final experiment, Korin left Herbert and Quark in the lab and took a walk around his property, her head spinning. When she got back, she asked, "So what kind of investment were you thinking about?"

"You came here today thinking I was exaggerating, didn't you?" said Herbert.

"Okay, I admit it. You've done it to me in the past and I had the same expectation this morning. But I was wrong. I'm a little disappointed I'm not getting a diamond, but this looks very important."

"I want more than your money," said Herbert. "I want a serious commitment from you."

"What kind of commitment?" asked Korin.

"I'm sure you've already thought about the possibilities, if I'm able to develop this technology. One of the first things I thought of was using it to dispose of nuclear waste, assuming the objects that disappear don't just end up somewhere random. Then I envisioned ridding the world of nuclear weapons."

"I know you have strong antiwar sentiments. But if the nuclear powers found that their weapons were disappearing, they might get very nervous. You could end up creating a war," said Korin.

"We're getting ahead of ourselves. There's no way to know where this might go. I need more money to develop it, but I don't want you in on this just for the short term, in order to sell it to make some quick money."

This was something that Korin and Herbert could agree on. She didn't want another project she would promote and sell quickly. She wasn't sure Herbert had shown her everything, and she knew that people often had a strong subconscious component to what they really wanted out of a project. Understanding the influence of that component is what she believed to be her best asset. She was certain that Herbert's subconscious was suggesting to him what his discovery might be used for, even if he didn't consciously admit it. She needed to explore this further.

"It always concerns me when people say they're not interested in quick money," she said. "I wonder if they're being realistic. It usually means they have poorly formed ideas, or simply want to do something that makes them feel good. That's not what makes the world work. To create a successful project, you need a lot of greedy people working very hard together with the goal of making lots of money," said Korin.

"Maybe my idea to rid the world of nuclear weapons isn't workable. But it's the kind of idea I'm thinking of. Something that will shake things up. We'll get back to that later. For now, I want you to invest ten million dollars. I'll use the money to move the project forward, and I want you to have some skin in the game. I need you helping me to come up with possibilities for using this. Something very different from what we've done before—not just cashing out with a profit on the low-hanging fruit. I need you to give me time to develop this, and I need you to keep it a secret," said Herbert.

"I'll keep it a secret. But the legal rights need to be locked down. Have you filed for a patent?" asked Korin.

"If I tell some patent lawyer, he and everyone in the office will know about it. That's not what I want. I might want to use this in some truly unconventional way, and the fewer people who know anything, the better. I'm not saying the use would be illegal, but others might not agree with it."

Korin was already excited about this project, but his mention of an "unconventional plan" upped her level of interest. Risk was what Korin was all about. She thrived on risk. She'd been enormously successful by taking huge calculated risks.

"Does anyone else know about this?" asked Korin.

"Not a single person."

Korin actually liked the idea of keeping the invention secret for now, although the idea of not filing for a patent made her uncomfortable. She knew she could lose her entire investment if someone else filed for a patent before Herbert did.

"Are others working on the same idea?"

"As far as I know, no one in the world is working on anything like this. Others are focused on making smaller semiconductors or artificial diamonds. No one is trying to make smaller electrons," said Herbert.

"That's what everyone thinks. Everyone thinks no one else has the same idea, and then two different people invent the telephone on the same day. What makes you think that won't happen here?" asked Korin.

"Others would announce it. They would need publications to get funding. I'm not announcing it because first, I don't need to publish and second, I'm getting all the money I need from you. Third, I want to do something I may not want to tell others about. Those three things are extremely unusual, and all three would need to be present for someone else to have this idea and not announce it," said Herbert.

"You make some good points. Still, I'm not sure I agree with you. Others could be working on it, but be less far along than you. From what I'm hearing you may have a long way to go on your own invention. You don't even know if the technology will work on something bigger than a gumball."

"That's why I need your investment. To build the system you're looking at bigger. And before that, to figure out where the gumball goes, and how to get it back," said Herbert.

"Why would you want to get it back? Getting rid of something could be an end in itself. Bringing it back defeats the purpose, doesn't it?"

"Not at all. Eventually, I want to be able to make anything, including people, disappear from one place and reappear in another," said Herbert.

"You really think you can do something like that?"

"When you came in here today, I'm sure you never thought an object could just disappear. Now that you've seen it work you see things differently. Korin, I know I can figure out the science behind this and make it work. And I'm convinced you won't regret this investment."

She knew he was right. "Even if you never figure out how to get the gumball back, it's an amazing invention. So what's next?"

"I want you to put an agreement together. You'll get an ownership position. I'm suggesting ten million dollars for ten percent. That's enormously generous. I'm doing it because it's you. I don't want just your money, I want your help in thinking through a plan and helping me carry it out, even if it could get us both into a lot of trouble. But first, I want you to go home and think about it."

"I'm not interested in getting in a lot of trouble," said Korin, though in fact that was the part that most intrigued her. "But I do understand that you have something very interesting here. I'll think about it. If I decide I want to invest, I'll see about moving money."

They both stood and said their goodbyes. Before she left, Korin looked under the bench one more time. She was all but certain this wasn't a magic trick, though she always enjoyed a good magic trick. She reflected on shows in Las Vegas where objects far larger than a gumball had disappeared at the deft hands of a magician. Herbert was a kind of magician, but a very different kind.

"You know something about those gumballs, don't you boy?" she said, stroking Quark gently as she left the lab.

CHAPTER 3

I never see what has been done;
I only see what remains to be done.

—Gautama Buddha (c. 563–483 B.C.)

Korin left Herbert's place, trying to make sense of what she'd just seen. Even in its current form, Herbert's invention was nothing short of amazing. She had every expectation that he would figure out where the gumballs went and how to get them back. Once this happened, the technology would be more important than anything she'd ever worked on. But she wasn't sure how it would be applied. Pollution could be a thing of the past, for example. If Herbert could make a gumball—or another object—reappear somewhere else, then the whole political and economic power structure of the world could change.

But, she wondered, would other things remain the same — the family she cherished, her husband and two children? Those relationships were enormously important to her, and for a reason unrelated to Herbert's project, she feared they might change as well. Even though the possibilities for change were exciting, she wanted her family to remain the same. For now, she pushed the fears aside, embraced the risk, and, for the first time in quite a while, became excited about the possibilities. The question she faced wasn't really whether everything would change. It would. The question was how she would control that change and make it happen in some directed way—not just a random unfolding.

Herbert enjoyed fooling others, and she continued to wonder if this could be a trick. He'd fooled her many times before, and as she drove south on Interstate 280, she wondered if he were up to an elaborate hoax. This seemed unlikely, because this time he was asking for money. He enjoyed a good hoax, but he was honest. As she contemplated the possibilities, she became so absorbed in thought that she missed her exit and didn't realize her error until she'd missed the following one as well. She regained her focus and headed back on northbound 280 toward home.

She lived on a densely wooded hill in Portola Valley alongside an eclectic mix of wealthy individuals. Some had made their money in start-up high-tech or biotech businesses. Others had just inherited it. The homes, as varied as their inhabitants, were generally not visible from the street. Trees shielded the view of her house from even her closest neighbor, while the home's rear windows looked out toward Stanford, the San Francisco Bay, and the bridges that spanned twelve miles of water.

Korin would keep her word and reveal nothing about what she'd seen, even to her family. She wondered, however, if they would notice something different about her. She felt different. As she drove up the driveway and into the garage, she was enormously excited and reflected back on coming home the night after she first had sex. Would her parents know? Could they tell she was different? Would they question her about where she'd gone and what she'd been doing? They often did. Not because they didn't trust her, but because they cared, and wanted to be a part of her life. The same was true now of her husband, to whom she'd been married for twenty-three years. The children might ask her questions for a different reason. They loved to hear a good story, and from time to time they asked her to repeat a favorite one. Whenever she retold a story, she added an interesting new twist here and there.

Korin opened the door from the garage into a large, brightly lit kitchen.

"Hey, guys. Look who's decided to pay us a visit. It's your mom," Jim joked, standing to embrace Korin with a short hug and a small kiss on the cheek. "Where have you been? It's five-thirty. I thought you'd be back by two o'clock to take a hike with me and the kids."

Korin felt guilty about not calling. She'd forgotten the time as she made Herbert repeat variations on the experiment. "Herb was showing me some of his work. He has a lot of equipment set up in his lab, and once he gets going, it's hard to stop him."

"Anything interesting at Herbert's?" Jim asked.

"Sure. You know Herb. He's always got lots of interesting things." Korin walked out of the kitchen toward the children. It wasn't that she was not telling the truth; she was. But she was very good at not telling the whole truth some of the time. It was very difficult for her to lie—almost impossible. Still, she'd found that people were usually satisfied with a short answer, even if it left out a great deal of important information. Part of her skill in dealing with others came from what she didn't say. She'd mastered the art of being brief when she needed to be, and she understood that a well-timed silence was more eloquent than any words could ever be. She intuitively knew that most people focused on what they themselves were going to say next.

"Hi, guys." Korin leaned over the couch where Camille and Evan sat. She pulled each of them against her face for a kiss. Although they were glad she was home, for the moment they were fixated on the television.

"What are you watching?" She looked at the screen to see something quite unexpected.

"This guy. He's a preacher. It's cool, Mom," answered Camille, age eleven.

"When did you get interested in religion?" Korin asked.

"Well, this preacher keeps shouting about Jesus," said Evan, eight. "Then the people shout back at him. Then he touches some of them, and they fall down."

"This is really amazing, Mom. I've never seen this before," Camille added.

This caught Korin by surprise. Her head was already spinning from her visit with Herbert. She kept wondering if what she'd seen was real, and if so, how it might change things. She hadn't expected this change in her kids. She couldn't fathom why they were suddenly interested in a tel-evangelist preaching Jesus. She had no use for religion and had never taken them to church, though she'd gone with her family growing up. She had little recollection of her child-hood thoughts on religion.

"Do you guys like this because you believe in Jesus?" Korin hoped they didn't want to become part of some orga-nized religious group.

In response, Camille and Evan both turned toward her with a look of confusion, as though they didn't know how to answer. She stared at them, not knowing what to say or what they might be thinking.

"What do you mean, Mom? Do we believe in Jesus? Wasn't there a person named Jesus?" asked Camille.

"Yes. There was a person named Jesus. But these people believe he was God, or the only Son of God," said Korin.

"So they believe Jesus had superpowers?" Evan asked.

"Well, yes. They wouldn't say 'superpowers,' but they believe he had the power of God. They believe he had omnipotent powers and could turn water into wine, walk on water, and rise from the dead."

"Mom, these people are adults," said Camille. "I'm sure they know Jesus didn't have superpowers or rise from the dead."

Korin thought about this, feeling some guilt that she hadn't exposed the children to knowledge about religion. At the same time, she was pleased they hadn't been indoctrinated with ideas she felt were not based on reality. "You'd be very wrong about that, sweetie. That's exactly what they do believe."

"Well, if they believe that, do they believe in Santa Claus and the Easter Bunny and things like that?" asked Camille.

"People, at least some people, would be bothered by you asking a question like that," Korin replied.

"Why? I just want to know," Camille said.

"There are a lot of reasons. You're comparing their religion to things most people don't take seriously. Most Christians would be very offended if you compared Santa Claus with something they hold sacred and believe is real. They see Jesus very differently because he's part of their religion."

"We thought they were all just having fun, playing along and singing with the preacher. We didn't know they thought there was something serious about this," said Camille.

"Oh, they're quite serious." Korin sighed with relief that her children weren't becoming "Born Agains." She reflected on how her children could, without effort, refocus her thoughts. No matter how the day had gone—and this had been a most unusual one—something the kids said or did invariably made her focus on them and forget the work world. Without realizing it, she always found herself in their world.

This innocent question from Camille made Korin wonder why so many people subscribed to something that small children thought was make-believe. Why, she wondered, had people gone from believing that the sun was their god to accepting Jesus as the only Son of God? It seemed illogical to trade a sun god for a Son of God. Certainly the sun didn't want to be worshiped. The sun had no wants. She thought that Jesus had not wanted to be worshiped. If he were alive today, he would be confused and disappointed at how Christianity had developed.

Korin wondered if perhaps people believed in religion simply because their parents told them they had to. Very few people grew up to join a religion other than the one their parents had believed in. Was there, she wondered, some kind of Darwinian survival value involved in religious belief? When parents told a child he would be eaten by a saber-tooth tiger if he ventured out of the cave, he would listen. If he didn't and he was eaten, his genes would not be passed on. Under this theory, children who obeyed their parents' serious instructions would survive, and people always spoke of religion in serious tones.

Camille interrupted her thoughts. "Mom, let's play Monopoly."

"I'll go get the game," Evan said, running off to find the box.

"What do you think, Jim?" Korin looked back toward the kitchen where Jim sat reading a magazine.

"Well, I had something else in mind for you and me, but that can wait." He got up and embraced Korin.

"That's something I was looking forward to as well," Korin said softly in Jim's ear as they hugged. "Let's play with the kids now, and *we* can play later."

"Put it down here," Camille said to her brother as he arrived in the living room with the game. She pointed to the coffee table.

"I'll be the banker." Korin sat down on the floor and rested her back against the couch. She could reach the game board from this position.

"No way, Mom. You cheat," said Camille. "Let Dad be the banker. He sticks to the rules."

Some friendly back-and-forth followed as they set up the game. Korin did, in fact, cheat at Monopoly—not so she would win, but so that one of her kids would. She did the same from time to time in her work environment. Korin enjoyed taking risks in life and broke the rules just to make the game—any game—more interesting. To Korin, a game of throwing dice, moving a piece to the correct square, and collecting the correct amount of money was incredibly boring. Although at first she always denied that she cheated, she corrected the wrong and secretly took great pride whenever the kids caught her. Her approach to Monopoly reflected who Korin was: She didn't see herself as a cheater, because in her mind she would never break the rules to hurt others or simply benefit herself. To the contrary, she bent the rules to make sure others got more than their share, to her detriment. It was sometimes important to let others prevail. Winning at Monopoly wasn't important to her. She disliked rules, particularly those that served no real purpose. From early childhood, she had enjoyed figuring out new ways to break them—sometimes just because it was interesting to do so.

They played for hours and ordered pizza in for dinner. Korin's thoughts reverted to what she'd seen at Herbert's. She still wondered what he was up to. For certain, he wasn't sharing everything.

As time passed, Korin sensed they all wanted the game to be over. "It looks to me like Evan has the most money and property," she said finally. "Let's say Evan's the winner, and you guys go brush your teeth and get ready for bed."

No one objected. Evan was delighted and held up a large stack of Monopoly money and property deeds with big smile. Evan hadn't won in a while, and she had "cheated" a bit to help him win this time. It pleased her to know that she had a role in making him look so happy.

"So, are *we* going to play now?" Jim asked as soon as the kids had picked up the game and gone to their rooms. He pushed Korin's hair aside so he could kiss her softly on her neck.

Silently, Korin reached her hand out to Jim and led him to their bedroom.

"It's been a while." Jim closed their bedroom door.

"Well, three days. I guess we're just getting old," Korin joked, unbuttoning her shirt.

Once naked, they never talked much. Neither found a need for conversation in bed. They often held and caressed each other until one of them took the initiative for sex. Tonight that was Korin.

When it was over, she lay there wide awake. This had been one of the best days of her life. Herbert's work was nothing short of amazing, the kids had fun with Monopoly, and she and Jim had just had great sex. Almost anyone would have been totally content, but she wasn't just anyone. She was restless, and needed to burn off energy.

Jim reached over, grabbed the remote, and turned on the TV.

"Do you want to watch the tube for awhile?" asked Korin.

"Yeah. I just want to see if there's anything on the news."

"Okay. I'm going downstairs to use the treadmill. Go ahead and go to sleep if you feel like it. I didn't get a chance to hike with you and the kids today, so I need some exercise." Korin quickly rose from the bed and put on a loose-fitting top and a pair of tight black stretch pants that she often wore for working out.

"Your ass looks great in those pants."

"I gotta try and keep it that way." Korin laughed and headed down to their workout room. She couldn't focus on working out, however. Her mind was on where the gumballs went, and how Herbert's work might lead to a huge return on her ten-million-dollar investment. Sometimes the treadmill helped her focus her thoughts and come up with creative ideas. She hoped for that tonight, but for now would settle for something to keep her mind from racing, tire her out, and let her get some sleep.

She also kept thinking that she hadn't told Jim what had happened at Herbert's. Yes, she had promised Herbert not to tell anyone, but that didn't completely explain why she'd kept it to herself. Perhaps if no one else knew about this invention, the possibilities for what might be done would be greater. If the secret got out, they might have to limit the options and perhaps keep them from doing something very important. Herbert wasn't going to agree to just any plan. It had to be a bold plan that somehow fit with his idea of something meaningful.

CHAPTER 4

Whenever you do a thing,
act as if all the world were watching.

—Thomas Jefferson (1743–1826)

Korin awoke the next morning with a new set of questions on her mind. Had Herbert really spent all his money on this project? Did he really need ten million dollars to develop it further? Most importantly, was he keeping what he really wanted to do from her? She called him and arranged to meet at his place.

"What? No doughnuts?" joked Herbert, as he invited her in.

"I brought them. Just two. They're in a bag in my briefcase. First things first." She put her briefcase on Herbert's desk, opened it, and handed him a white bag containing two raspberry jelly doughnuts. "I brought some paperwork. It's based on an investment I made a few years ago. It gives me ten percent of the company you've formed around your latest work."

"There always seems to be too much paper. I never understand why."

"I agree. But when things get reduced to writing, everyone has a clearer picture about what's agreed to." Korin trusted Herbert, but she couldn't just turn over ten million dollars without something in writing. She wasn't a lawyer, but she knew more about corporate investment documents than most attorneys. Besides, she had another motive for presenting the documents to Herbert.

"I don't think I need to read these." Herbert flipped through the papers. "Can I just sign, and we'll move on?"

"While I appreciate your trust, I'd prefer that you read them. For one, I want to be sure we're on the same page, and I'll need you to help me fill in some of the blanks. For example, what are you calling this technology?" asked Korin.

"I made up the term 'nanotron technology.' The term 'nano' describes things that are very small, so I thought it sounded like a term for very small electrons."

"Nanotron technology works for now. We'll call the company Nanotron Technology, Inc. Does that work for you?"

"Sounds good," Herbert said.

"We'll need to put together a short description of what 'nanotrons' are. These agreements generally just incorporate some patent numbers. I'd like to put those numbers in here, but since you haven't filed for a patent, we'll need to explain your invention. Do you have anything written up?"

"I knew you'd ask for that. I put a nonscientific description together. Take a look at this." Herbert handed Korin some printouts of a series of slides in a Power Point presentation.

After reading the first few printouts, Korin looked up at Herbert with a puzzled expression. "'Merging the worlds of classical physics and quantum mechanics...' That isn't clear to me. You merged two types of physics? What does that mean?"

"The idea of merging the engineering technologies used in the main two areas of physics came to me after I read a paper by a Spanish physicist studying fluid dynamics."

"Herbert, this is partially why I need you to go through this with me. When you throw around a lot of names and terms I don't know, you start to lose me."

"Not to worry," said Herbert. "I've got some graphics on all of this. I'll show you what I'm talking about."

Korin kept asking questions in an effort to determine how confident Herbert was with his work. She had dealt with all types of scientists and inventions she never really understood. However, she firmly believed that those who could explain their work at a level she could understand were the ones who truly understood it themselves.

Herbert showed her some drawings of what he described as tubes extruding electron flow. He explained that by forcing a huge amount of positive energy toward the negatively charged electrons, he was able to create a much narrower stream of electrons. These tightly focused electrons were the "nanotrons."

Korin finished reading the last slide. "Let me see if I've got this. You're using a nozzle or tube that produces the electron flow so you can make the electrons as small as possible?"

"That's right," said Herbert.

"So if the electrons were a stream of water, you would use air around the stream coming out of the nozzle to compress the stream."

"Well, not exactly," said Herbert. "The stream of water, as with a stream of electrons, comes out of the nozzle. However, it's very hard to compress water and more difficult to compress electrons, so the stream is not compressed. Rather, it's focused at its end to a narrow point, and surrounding energy draws out the focused end into a very narrow stable jet. It's as though you sharpened a pencil to a point and then drew the point out in a long thread, but you don't compress the pencil or the lead in the pencil."

"Okay. I'm following you now."

"Now, for the really interesting stuff," said Herbert. "These nanotrons are a completely new type of particle."

"Why is that important?"

"At first I thought it was important just because I was making a new kind of very small particle. I figured that alone would win me a Nobel Prize in physics — and it would. But then I figured out the really amazing part, which is what these particles could do. These particles can generate a field, and whatever they surround does not operate in accordance with any laws of physics that we've known — not classical physics *or* quantum mechanics. By directing this focused stream of particles, which began as electrons, it's possible to create a nanotron field around an object. That field allows any object within it to slip out of our time/space. That's why the gumball disappears...the nanotron field allows it to slip out of our dimensional space."

"Does that mean the gumball is now somewhere in outer space?" Korin asked.

"No. Not in outer space as we know it. It's no longer in our universe. It's in some other dimensional space."

What Herbert said completely stunned Korin. For her, it was like the feeling when she first found out what sex was all about. She'd been told something new and wonderful about how the world worked. She didn't understand it all, but she knew that her newfound knowledge was about to provide many exciting possibilities. It was scary and exciting at the same time. Now she was all but certain Herbert wasn't tricking her about the disappearing gumballs, and she wondered again how this discovery would change her life. "I don't think I understand. No, I'm sure I don't understand. But I know it's amazing," she said at last.

"It's not done yet. It's far from done."

"What's next?" asked Korin.

"There are two parts. First, I need to figure out how to get the gumballs back. I'm pretty sure it involves interdimensional movement."

"What does that mean? And don't give me a lot of science talk. I want you to tell me what it means in layman's terms."

"If I could describe the physics, I'd have the answer. I can't. In layman's terms, imagine the gumball on a sheet of paper. A sheet of paper is two-dimensional. If the gumball rolls off the paper, and all you can see is the paper, you think the gumball is gone. But it's not gone. It's just not on the paper. If the paper is all you can see, the gumball isn't somewhere you can see it."

"So you're sure the gumball isn't gone? It's not gone; it's just off the paper?"

"I'm positive of that. The field has very little power. It can't move a gumball. It doesn't even have the power to move something much smaller than a gumball."

"But it has to move it. It has to move it because the gumball is gone," Korin insisted.

"Yes. It appears to be gone," Herbert responded. "But it hasn't moved in the sense that we normally think about things moving in the same space/time we're in. It's something that our minds can't grasp. We only think in terms of three-dimensional space. We can't think in terms of two-dimensional or four-dimensional."

"I can think of a sheet of paper. That's two-dimensional space," said Korin.

"Yes, but you can only think of the sheet as it exists in our three-dimensional space. That's the problem here. I believe the gumball is in another space/time or dimensional space, and that's the part I need to figure out."

"Okay. You said there were two parts. What's the other part?" asked Korin.

"This stream of focused electrons or nanotrons can be used to make a computer work much faster. The over-heating computer problem I told you about is what I started out to solve. I was trying to figure out a way to keep Moore's law working. There has been a fair amount of concern that computer power wouldn't double in the next eighteen to twenty-four months. With this focused stream of nanotrons, we'll be able to increase computer speed one-thousand-fold or more."

"So you've developed some kind of new computer with this?"

"Not me. I haven't done it," said Herbert.

"Well, who then?"

"Alan Wierman is working on it. It's been a few years, but I'm sure you remember Alan from the video game venture we worked on together. He knows about the nanotrons, but only as a way to make computers work faster. He hasn't even seen what I've done with the gumballs. I gave him a device I made that generates the focused stream of nanotrons, but the nanotrons run in a stream, not a complete field. I asked him to see if he could use the stream to make a micropro-cessor run faster."

"I might have figured you would work with Alan. What's he been able to do?" Korin asked.

"Quite a lot, he said. I haven't seen it yet. He wants me to go there tomorrow to show me what he's got. Do you want to come?"

"Of course I want to. Let's finish this contract."

Korin used Herbert's slides to describe the technology merging his description into her agreement. They added and deleted sections and printed out two copies. Although it was a fairly simple contract, it meant a great deal to them. They each read the printed copies and made some edits for clarification. Korin entered the changes and printed two final versions. They signed them, shook hands, and made plans for meeting tomorrow morning.

"Before I go, do you want to tell me anything more about what you think you'd like to accomplish with this?" asked Korin.

"I'll work on the science. I'm good at that. You work on a plan to do something."

Korin had hoped for more of a hint from Herbert. She sensed that he wanted something in particular but didn't feel comfortable expressing what it was. "That's good enough for me," she said. "We're partners on this venture now. I've agreed to put ten million dollars into it. I need to know what you're thinking. You're always hiding behind the science."

"Science is what I do," said Herbert.

"Yes, but you've thought of other things, as well. At dinner two days ago, you told me this project was what kept you from coming to the celebration. I knew there was more to the story then, and now I know there's something you're not sharing."

"What do you want to know?"

"You're working with Alan. I know Alan is gay. Are you gay? Is that why you never want to go out with the women I set you up with?"

The words were barely out of Korin's mouth when she saw the impact they made. Herbert was emotionally shaken. He backed away from her, looked toward his computer screen, and tried to speak, but he couldn't. She waited until he began to talk.

"No, Korin, I'm not gay. I'm asexual. I have no interest whatsoever in sex—not with women, not with men. Just no interest." Herbert was unable to look at Korin. "I've never told anyone. I've imagined telling others and contemplated what they might say. But this is the first time I've ever said this out loud."

"That actually explains a lot to me," Korin said. "When did you first realize this about yourself?"

"My family was Catholic. I was an altar boy, and from the age of nine until almost eleven, I was sexually molested by our priest." Herbert was still unable to look at Korin. "I've known many others who were molested, but I haven't met anyone who told me that they later became asexual."

"Oh my, I'm so sorry, Herb. I never imagined. That's awful. Do you think your experience with the priest is what made you asexual?"

"I don't know," said Herbert. "I never had any sexual desire before, during, or after the priest. I certainly wondered whether, if I hadn't been molested, I would have developed sexual desires when I went through puberty. I'll never know the answer to why I am the way I am. After years of not knowing, I just gave up trying to figure it out. Now I believe I was always meant to be an asexual person."

"This isn't something I'm familiar with. Are there other asexual people?"

"Yes. Of course. It's not publicized, perhaps because most of the world is overly preoccupied with sex. It's estimated that the population is probably about one to three percent asexual. It's not studied much, so no one knows for sure what the percentage is, but it's small. There will never be an 'asexual pride day,' but there are other asexual people. I'm not unique in that respect. Everyone fits along a spectrum for all characteristics. A person can be totally consumed by sex, moderately interested, or as with me, completely uninterested."

"Issues about sex are all around us all the time, but I've never thought about it that way," Korin said. "I just thought that there were heterosexual people and homosexual people."

"Some cultures recognize five sexes or sexual preferences. The first two are men who are attracted to women and women who are attracted to men. The second two are men who are attracted to men and women who are attracted to women. The fifth is made up of people who may be biologically men or women but are attracted to both."

"I hadn't thought of it that way before, but you don't seem to be in any of those groups. You're telling me you have no desire."

"You haven't quite understood what I'm telling you," said Herbert. "I am asexual, but I have very strong desires. They're so overwhelming that at times I can't control them. It's just that my desires are for doing my work. When I'm in the middle of an important experiment, I can no more stop and do something else than a sex addict can stop having intercourse and go have tea. I needed to finish the work."

"So that's the rest of the story on why you didn't show up for my dinner party?"

"Yes, and I'm sure you'll understand when I ask you to keep what I told you to yourself. Sharing this with you was difficult for me—very difficult. Now that we're working on this project together I somehow felt I had to tell you."

"I won't tell another soul," Korin said. "But I think you should talk to someone professionally about this. It could help. You're missing out on a great deal in life. Tell me how you feel about it all."

"I know sex is a part of life. I know I'm missing something important—something that others see as all-important. I've had a lot of time to think about it, and I know that I can't fully appreciate something I've never known. But when I see how sex—and thoughts about sex—so dominate the lives of others, I wonder if it's really *their* lives that are restricted and not mine."

"Herb, as always, you make a good point, and, as always, I'm not sure I fully understand or agree," said Korin. "When you talk about science, I know you're correct, even though I'm not sure why. But this isn't science. It's emotion; it's love, it's raw animal sex and there's nothing logical about it."

"I know it's not logical, and I know I'm missing something. But I do feel emotions, very strong emotions. I just don't want to have sex with anyone. Why is that hard to understand?"

"Well, it's just that most people integrate sex and emotions. I think of not wanting sex as not wanting strong emotional attachments. But I hear you saying you still want the strong emotional attachment, but not the sex."

"For me sex and emotion are separate. I'm sure you can understand having one without the other," said Herbert.

"Now you're sounding like many of the guys I knew in college—except they wanted the sex with no emotion."

"So you understand that people separate the two," said Herbert. "Men generally tend to separate sex and emotion more than women do. But nearly everyone recognizes that having sex doesn't necessarily mean strong emotions are involved—and having strong emotions doesn't mean sex is involved."

"Give me an example where you have strong emotions— something I can relate to."

"I love my dog Quark dearly. If anything happened to him, I'd be very sad. Having him around makes me happy. I know you have a dog, and I think you feel the same way."

"Okay, that works. I love Smokey, and I know you love Quark. But they're not people," said Korin.

"The concept I was trying to convey is still there. People are capable of completely separating sex from a relation- ship and still having a very strong emotional bond. I actu- ally think the emotional part can be stronger without the sex part."

"Well, that's not easy for me to understand in a normal man-woman relationship. Why would you say that?"

"I know the sex part is important to others," said Herbert. "But when one important component goes away, other com- ponents can be strengthened. Think about human brain function involving blind people. They can't see, and seeing is important. But their other senses—hearing, touch, even

taste and smell—are more developed. It's not that their ears
work better; it's that their minds are more focused on hearing. Being asexual, I've gained something in terms of my
ability to focus and use my mind in ways that others cannot.
Most people are distracted by sex, thoughts of sex, wanting
to have sex—and they're often overwhelmed by it. It's not
an issue for me. I'm completely blind to it."

"I came over today thinking I could use this agreement
to learn more about you. I never would have guessed this is
what I'd learn," Korin said.

"I hope I didn't overwhelm you. Let's call it a day."

Korin left wishing she'd been a bit more cautious about
what she asked Herbert, and now she was even more curious
about his subconscious motivations. There was no question
in her mind that Herbert had told her about his asexuality
for a reason, and she needed to find out what that reason
was.

CHAPTER 5

*The real voyage of discovery consists not in seeking
new landscapes, but in having new eyes.*

—Marcel Proust (1871–1922)

Korin got up the next morning just before six o'clock,
having slept on and off over the previous six hours.
A late-night workout and a double dose of Benadryl had
helped her deal with her allergies and ever-present insom-
nia. She went downstairs to the kitchen, turned on the TV
and the computer, and checked her email as she ate breakfast. Alan had sent directions to his place in San Francisco.

Jim walked into the kitchen. "Good morning, love."

They hugged, and each took the opportunity to reach
around and squeeze the other's butt. With some disappointment, Korin accepted that this had gradually, over the years,
become more of a handshake than a sexual touching.

"Don't worry about the kids this morning. I'll drop them
at school before heading up to Alan's," Korin said.

"What's going on with Alan?"

"He's working on something with Herb. Herb was going to
Alan's this morning and asked if I wanted to go along."

Korin understood that Jim had no real interest in what
she was doing. They'd met while Jim was playing college
football, and she was attracted to his athletic body and

rugged good looks. Unable to become a professional football player, but wanting to continue to work in the sport, he got a job in coaching and was now in management with the San Francisco 49ers. The work was seasonal, giving him more time with the children during the off-season. He often went places with the children and felt comfortable interacting with them. She regretted that they were much closer to him than to her.

Korin finished breakfast, confirmed her nine o'clock arrival with Alan, and printed his email. She left Jim at the table, kissing him lightly, and went upstairs to wake the kids, shower, and dress. She woke Evan first, as he was the more difficult of the two to rouse. She always woke him the same way. She leaned down, kissed his cheek, put her arms around him, and pulled him toward her. Holding him close, she whispered in his ear, "Time to get up, Evan." This time was the same, and as she kissed his cheek, she wondered how long she could continue the ritual. She couldn't imagine a time when his soft cheek would be covered with the stubble of whiskers.

Evan hugged her back, and she knew he was awake. She stood up with him in her arms and then put him down standing on his bedroom floor.

"Dad's downstairs. Go get breakfast. I'm going to get Camille up."

She went off to Camille's room and repeated the ritual.

"I need to drop you both off a little early this morning. I have a meeting in the city."

In what seemed like a blur of one routine after another, the kids ate, showered, dressed, and got in the car. Korin had drawn a mental map of her route to pick up Herbert before proceeding on to Alan's house. She'd decided not to bring up Herbert's asexuality, but rather to focus on how to develop the nanotron field technology.

Korin imagined how different her morning routine was from Alan's. His partner, Jeremy, would make him a breakfast of fresh fruit and poached eggs on whole-wheat toast. She would like that from Jim. She brought up a mental image of Alan's four-story home in the Russian Hill area of San Francisco with its view of the Golden Gate Bridge. Again, this was something she would like. Living in the secluded wealth of Portola Valley was comfortable, but often boring. She wanted a safe, comfortable, and quiet place to raise a family. But that didn't prevent her from wanting the restaurants, plays, music, and overall excitement San Francisco had to offer. She longed for the diversity of the city as she drove north on highway 280 to pick Herbert up.

"Do you feel ready to give your presentation?" Jeremy asked Alan while serving him breakfast.

"Herbert convinced me to give a different presentation. I've changed it completely, and I'm feeling—well, I'm feeling uncertain. I'm not sure Herb is right," Alan replied.

"What kind of different presentation are you talking about?"

"There's nothing in it related to aliens or spaceships," said Alan.

"I can't believe what I'm hearing. That's everything you wanted. How could you change that?" asked Jeremy.

"I trust Herbert. He doesn't believe I ever saw an alien spaceship, but he knows how important the issue of UFOs is to me. He understands that I don't want to be labeled as someone who's completely insane," Alan said.

"Alan, you know I'll support you in whatever you want to do. But I know how long it was before you could even tell your parents we were lovers. You know you have difficulty saying what you really feel. This is an opportunity for you to publicly express your thoughts. If you let it go by, you may not have another opportunity. Don't miss your chance."

"I won't. I just need to take it one step at a time. I've put together a new video. I like it, even though it has no hint of aliens. I'll show them that one," said Alan.

"Is this one perfect?"

"I could keep improving it forever. But it's better than anything I've done, and I'm sure they'll be impressed. Even though I wish he were wrong, Herbert is correct in saying it's more believable than the one with UFOs. When I finish breakfast, I'll go downstairs and run through some of the programs just to be sure it's all operating as it should be."

Korin and Herbert parked in front of Alan's house. The four-story structure was large by any standard, but enormous for a San Francisco home. It was an unusually clear and bright day, cool but not cold. Seeing the Golden Gate Bridge elicited an emotional response in Korin. She wondered if she could buy an apartment in this neighborhood and enjoy the city more. The area seemed so much more alive than Portola Valley. She wanted to stand there just looking at the Bay, but Herbert was already walking ahead. She rushed to catch up with him.

Jeremy answered their ring at the door and led them along a large, marble-floored entrance way. "The marble is quite nice. Is it Italian?" asked Korin.

"Yes, it is. Alan and I went to Italy to pick it out. We knew the colors we wanted but couldn't find anything just right in San Francisco." Jeremy seemed delighted that Korin had noticed, and he was eager to tell stories about the marble and the rest of the house. "We bought the carpet in Istanbul at a place near the Blue Mosque. I'll have to give you the name of the place later. Well, here we are." Jeremy opened double doors leading to an in-home theater. "I'll go tell Alan you're here. Can I get either of you anything while I'm upstairs?"

"I'll have a cup of Earl Grey tea," said Korin.

"Do you have any doughnuts?" Herbert asked.

"No, of course not," Jeremy answered, clearly proud of that fact. "How about some fresh fruit?"

"That would be great."

Jeremy left them in a room with no windows, nine large, velvet-covered, dark-maroon chairs, dim lighting, and a slightly domed ceiling. A signed photo of Isaac Asimov hung on a wall, inscribed, *"I do not fear computers. I fear the lack of them."* Movie posters on the walls were mostly from science-fiction films, almost all of them signed by a famous actor or director. The most prominent was a poster from *Contact*, signed by Jill Tarter and Jodi Foster. "Which one of them is the movie buff, and who is Jill Tarter?" asked Korin as she walked around the room.

"I think Tarter is the real-life character Jodi Foster played, and Jeremy is the movie buff," Herbert replied. "He's a stage actor. He's done a lot of work around San Francisco. He's actually quite good. I've seen him in a couple of plays."

"I didn't know that," said Korin. "I wonder why Alan never asked me to go to one of the plays."

47

"With a husband, two young kids, and a big home way down the peninsula, I'm guessing he may have thought you wouldn't be all that comfortable with the plays."

The answer made Korin think about how Alan perceived her. To Alan she must project an image of a wealthy white conservative, a person perhaps all too predictable. She had created that image, but it wasn't who she felt she really was.

"Well, I guess I'll have to do some things to change my image with Alan...and perhaps with you, as well, Herbert."

Alan opened the door and came in, followed by Jeremy carrying an ornate silver tray. "I'll just put this down here," he said. "If you'd like anything else, except doughnuts, just let me know."

Alan greeted his friends. "Thank you both for coming. I hope the traffic wasn't too bad this morning." Without waiting for a response, he added, "If you'll sit down, I'll get started." Dimming the lights, he began projecting a video on a large screen lowered from the ceiling.

The first image was of Alan's house and the surrounding area. "This will help orient you," Alan said. "That's the entrance you just came in. You'll recognize someone you both know arriving and getting out of a car in front."

The video projected a late-model black Mercedes driving up in front of Alan's house and stopping. The driver got out and walked around to open the back door. California Senator Dianne Feinstein got out. She walked to Alan's front door, where Alan and Jeremy greeted her. The camera followed the three of them along the marble flooring to an elevator, which took them to the fourth-floor living room. The camera focused on each of them as they spoke.

"Jeremy, I want you to know how much I enjoyed your performance last week. Thank you for inviting me to the play," the senator said.

"Jesus, does everyone go to Jeremy's plays but me?" interjected Korin.

"Thank you, Senator," said Jeremy. "That means a lot to me."

"What I'm really here for, though, is to talk to you, Alan, about your new software. The federal government is very interested in knowing more about it, and I've been arranging some meetings for you in Washington."

"Thank you," said Alan's image on the screen. "Despite my disappointment at the current administration's failure to follow through on campaign promises, I do love this country. Your help in making the right connections for me is much appreciated."

The film stopped.

"Before we go to the next clip," Alan explained, "I want you all to understand that it took a bit of work before we finally set up the meeting I'm going to show you now." He restarted the video.

Korin gasped as she saw Alan being escorted into the Oval Office of the U.S. president.

"It's an honor to meet you, Mr. President," said the onscreen Alan as he shook hands with Barack Obama. In the following conversation, the president repeatedly went out of his way to say that the resources of the federal government would be available to help Alan develop his software.

"I guess you guys didn't realize how well connected I was," Alan said, pausing the video once again. "I've just got a couple more clips to show you."

The video next showed Alan sitting in an office with Nicolas Sarkozy, the president of France. The meeting was carried out completely in French with English subtitles showing Sarkozy repeatedly complimenting Alan on his brilliant work.

The video switched to a different office. All those present except Alan were Asian, and Korin recognized General Secretary Hu Jintao, the current head of China. Alan spoke fluent Chinese, and a similar meeting ensued with English subtitles at the bottom of the screen.

Alan brought the lights up. At first there was silence as they looked at each other. Then Korin spoke. "Okay, we're all very impressed, Alan. If the testimonials are over, now maybe you can explain to us what you've done."

"There's nothing more to show you. You've seen it all," Alan said.

"They're all fake. Alan never met with any of them, and I know he doesn't speak French or Chinese," Herbert said.

"How could you say such a thing?" A smile grew over Alan's face. "You saw me interacting with them in person with all of them speaking as they normally would."

"Herbert's right, isn't he?" said Korin. "The sound, the lighting, the details all looked right, but you faked all of it. If that's your new software, it's very impressive."

"I won't bore you with the details," Alan said, "but I'll tell you that it works so well no expert can tell the difference between this 'created reality' and a video of real events. All video is simply made up of pieces of information. When the information is correctly arranged, the real and the fake are indistinguishable."

"Have you actually had experts try to tell the difference?" asked Herbert.

"Not with these videos. I didn't want to raise suspicions," Alan responded. "But I sent two other sets of videos to three different experts. Each set had five real videos and another five I had created with my new program. All three experts came back telling me that as best they could tell, all the videos were real and not digitally altered."

"That's impressive," said Herbert.

"What's *really* impressive is your nanotrons. Without the nanotron generator you provided, I wouldn't have been able to do this. I want you to know I really appreciate you giving me first crack at working on this," said Alan.

Herbert looked embarrassed. "There's no one I'd rather work with."

"I haven't explained how any of this works because I felt it was better to show you," Alan added. "I also haven't told you that by using the nanotrons and my new program, I can create these videos very quickly. Let me show you." He immediately focused a camera on his friends and began typing. Almost instantly, the three of them seemed to appear in the Oval Office talking with President Obama.

"That's impressive," said Herbert. "Do you need a real person to form the basis of the video?"

"It's a bit more difficult to do it without having at least some video of a real person to start with. But I have stored thousands of hours of shots of real people, and I mix and match them together to create virtual people who can't be distinguished from genuine," answered Alan. "The videos I sent off to the experts were a mixture of virtual and real people."

"Once this is out there, no one will be able to tell you what's real and what's fake. We'll go back to relying on what people remember as having happened as opposed to what's on the videotape," Korin said.

"I think that's right," agreed Alan. "All of us in the software field knew this was coming at some point. It was just a matter of time as to when we got there."

"It seems to me that there are two enormous opportunities to exploit. The nanotrons themselves and the new software," said Korin thoughtfully. "From what you've both told me, no one else knows about your work, Herbert. You haven't even filed for patents on it. Is that right?"

"Correct," said Alan.

"I've always been a great believer in the patent system," said Korin. "I've made a lot of money using the market exclusivity that patents can create. This all needs to be patented, or someone else will steal it once they figure out what you've done."

"I agree, but Herbert keeps saying he doesn't want to file for patents," said Alan.

"Until I figure out what I want to do with this, I don't want others to know about it," said Herbert. "I don't want to tell some patent attorney or the Patent Office. I don't want others involved."

"What if I look into it? Maybe there's a way to file for patents and not tell anyone all of what you have," said Korin.

"Do you have any ideas on that now?" asked Herbert.

"Nothing specific, but if you guys are comfortable waiting a while, I think we can come up with something."

"You work on that, but don't move forward until I hear your plan," said Herbert.

"Understood."

"Alan, I'll give you a call about coming over to my lab so you can see what I've been working on," Herbert said.

"Sure thing."

"Well, if I'm not going to get any doughnuts here, I guess I'll be on my way." Herbert stood up.

With a few closing pleasantries, they said their goodbyes. Korin and Jeremy walked ahead, leaving Alan and Herbert together.

"Thanks for showing that one. I know you wanted to show your alien video," said Herbert.

"I'm fine for now, but as I told you, I need others to understand the reality of aliens," said Alan.

"I understand. Just sit tight for now. The video won't get you the kind of acceptance you think it will. If you trust me, you'll get what you want and much more."

CHAPTER 6

All, too, will bear in mind this sacred principle,
that though the will of the majority is in all cases
to prevail, that will to be rightful must be reasonable;
that the minority possess their equal rights, which equal
law must protect, and to violate would be oppression.

—Thomas Jefferson (1743–1826)

Herbert smiled smugly as he left Alan's and walked out to join Korin. He wasn't surprised by what he'd seen. Korin had had no way of anticipating what Alan had developed. Seeing it would get her thinking, and he wanted to hear her ideas. His strong connection with Alan had developed through years of working together. During that time, Alan had shared an experience with him that he would not share with others, and Herbert appreciated what Alan wanted to accomplish. Herbert had just told Alan he could achieve everything he wanted and more. He wanted to make Alan happy while accomplishing his own goals.

"I know you're not much of a coffee drinker," Herbert said to Korin. "But I know a quiet place near here where you can get a cup of tea, and I can get that jelly doughnut I've been thinking about. What do you think?"

"You know I'm going to say yes," said Korin. "This just keeps getting more interesting. Get in and tell me how to get there."

"Excellent," Herbert said in a voice that imitated Mr. Burns of *The Simpsons*. "Just pull out and go straight. I think it's about five blocks. It'll be on the right."

Once Korin had her tea and Herbert his jelly doughnut, he asked her, "What are you thinking?"

"At first, the concepts of a gumball disappearing and a faked video seemed unrelated," said Korin. "In terms of their commercial uses, they're unrelated. However, it doesn't take much imagination to understand how the nanotrons can impact so many industries. By analogy, the television and radio businesses are huge, and they dominate advertising, entertainment, and culture. The different uses of nanotrons will change so many things. Where do you want to take this?"

"I know you'll want to focus on getting a return on your investment, and you will. But I need your patience for a while."

"When I first saw the gumball disappear in your lab, I thought it was some kind of magic trick," said Korin. "The videos that Alan put together have a similar air about them. Is there some kind of trickery going on here?"

"I'm not interested in performing tricks to make people believe in magic."

"I thought you liked magic," said Korin.

"Well, I do. But there's no magic, no trickery of any sort here. It's all very real." Herbert had both his own plan and Alan's in mind. He wouldn't share either with Korin at this time, as he needed to keep her interested, and he needed her money. There was no way of knowing how long the next step of his work would take.

"Hear me out, Herbert. The world is a mysterious place. For most people, it's so mysterious that they're always looking for someone to solve the mystery for them. Pick any area of life, and most people will admit they know nothing about it. For example, they know nothing about finance, so when Bernie Madoff told them he could make them a steady return of one percent per month, every month, they gave him their money."

"No!" Herbert insisted. "I'm completely uninterested in cheating people out of their money."

"That's not where I'm going with this, Herbert. I was just making the point that even without any real substance behind him, Madoff found it easy to get smart people to buy into an unbelievable story. He got them to believe he could repeatedly pay them a return of one percent per month, and do it month after month, year after year, regardless of the ups and downs of the market. He showed them something by sending them interest checks, and they wanted to believe it, so they did."

"So," said Herbert. "If you don't want to cheat people out of their money, what do you want to do?"

"If it's real and not some kind of trick, I want you and Alan to get to a good law firm and file for patents. This is too important not to patent."

"I know that's the right thing to do, and I will. I just don't want to do it now. Can you live with that?" asked Herbert.

"I don't like it. If someone else files for a patent before you, I'll lose my ten million and the opportunity to make so much more. It just seems way too risky," said Korin.

"I know it's risky. But before we exploit the commercial aspects, I need a chance to play with the technology a bit, and I need your help."

"What sort of help?"

"I've been involved in hoaxes of one sort of another ever since my days at MIT," Herbert said. "Along with some others, I formed a group called the Hackers. You might have heard of them. We put a car on top of a building once, and President Obama commented on our work when he was at MIT. The hoaxes are great fun, and figuring out how to do them is intellectually challenging."

"I might have figured you were an MIT Hacker. It fits with the way I've seen you behave. Exploiting the commercial aspects of your work should be enough for anyone. Why do you need to use it to accomplish some hoax?" asked Korin.

"It's important to me. I've told you I'm different from most people, and you know how."

"This has to do with your asexuality?"

Herbert wasn't sure how to answer or what he wanted her to know. He needed her money, and telling too much of his plan too soon could completely change her thinking. He stalled while enjoying a piece of raspberry jelly doughnut and carefully sipping his hot coffee. "Most things people do are based on their desire for sex. So it's not incorrect to assume that most things I do have a different motivational basis," he said finally.

"That doesn't even sound like you. What's your point?"

"I'm going to move forward with commercializing the technology. You can count on that," said Herbert. "You'll make your money back thousands of times over. But before that happens, I need to use the nanotron technology secretly. It'll be risky, and if you don't want to be involved, that's fine. For now, I need your money and your silence."

"How could I know if I want to be involved unless you tell me what you're planning to do?"

"You've heard of a cardinal rule. This will be a cardinal hoax. Something much bigger than anything I've ever done before. I haven't figured out just what it will be because my work isn't finished," he replied.

"I'm sure you don't want to use your invention just to send gumballs into deep space."

"Gumballs into deep space. You said 'gumballs into deep space.'"

"Yes, and so what?"

"I never quite thought of it that way, but now that I have, I think I know how to get the gumballs back!" Herbert said excitedly. "At least I think I can get back the ones I send from now on."

"Why? What did you figure out?

"You'll remember I told you the gumballs never moved and yet somehow they were gone."

"Yes, I remember," said Korin.

Herbert had tried everything he could to get gumballs back. He knew the nanotrons were far too weak to move the gumballs to a different place, but he couldn't quite imagine where they were in some other space/time, and, therefore, every attempt at retrieval had failed. "I sent the gumballs into another dimensional space. When I try to get one back, I always aim at putting it back where it originally was. However, that original space is somewhere in deep space by the time I bring the gumball back!"

"I don't follow you."

Herbert pushed his plate aside and put a piece of paper on the table. He started drawing as he talked. "Even while we perceive ourselves to be sitting perfectly still here, we're rapidly moving through space. The earth rotates on its axis, and, at the same time, it orbits the sun. The entire solar system is moving along an elliptical path through the galaxy, and our galaxy is moving in the universe. We don't feel it, but we're all moving very fast in several different ways."

"Okay, I see what you mean. But I don't get what that has to do with where the gumballs are and why you can't get them back." Korin frowned.

"I actually did get them back!" Herbert said. "It's just that the gumballs went back to their original location. However, we moved away from that location, so from our perspective, that place was no longer at the end of the table in my lab; it was in deep space. Think of it this way: The gumball is on a fast-moving train at point A, and then the gumball leaves. If we bring the gumball back to point A even a few seconds later, the train will have moved from point A to point B. If you're on the train, it doesn't seem that the gumball came back, but it did! The gumball is back at point A, but *you* are on the train at point B and not there at point A to see it."

"Why didn't you think of that until now?"

"I was still thinking in three dimensions. When the gumball left our three-dimensional space, I brought it back to the same position it was in originally. Now that I know what happened, I can adjust. We have to go now." Herbert suddenly stood up without finishing his doughnut.

"Go where?"

"Back to my lab, of course. If I can make this work, I can pull off any hoax I want." Herbert was now more excited about the new possibilities than he had ever been. He believed he could accomplish what he wanted, and at the same time surpass Alan's expectations.

CHAPTER 7

*Friendship is but another name for an alliance
with the follies and the misfortunes of others.
Our own share of miseries is sufficient: why enter
then as volunteers into those of another?*

—Thomas Jefferson (1743–1826)

Herbert tore up the papers on which he'd been writing, dropped the pieces into his half-drunk coffee, and headed with Korin back toward his lab. She shared Herbert's excited anticipation, but she recognized that his fixation on perpetrating some hoax could impede her ability to make money. She wondered what was so secret and why he didn't want to file for a patent. "What did you mean by making it easier to pull off any hoax?" she asked.

"I think I can adjust the particle beam to position any object anywhere!" Herbert said.

"Interesting. If it works, it would make the airline industry obsolete overnight." Korin knew his attention was focused on his experiment. She had never seen him leave part of a jelly doughnut uneaten.

"I'm sorry," he said. "I was thinking about how to recalibrate the experiment. What were you saying?"

"I was saying that if it works, it could change the way so many things operate."

"Yes. This will change everything. Nothing will be the same if this works," Herbert replied absently.

"We need to file for patents. It's the only way we can exploit it commercially. Don't you agree?" Korin persisted.

"I don't want others knowing what I'm doing. Why do we want to bring someone else into the group? That concerns me."

"I understand," Korin said. "It should concern you. The more people involved, the more possibilities that it will somehow leak out. But unless your ideas are protected, others will take them. You'll be left with nothing."

"I told you it would be risky, and I understand that you might lose your investment. But I have something else in mind."

"What else. What do you have in mind?" Korin demanded.

"I want to pull off a hoax, something that will fool the whole world. But not just any hoax. I told you what happened to me when I was child. Others knew of the priest's behavior but did nothing, and now they're dead and gone. But the Catholic Church is still around."

"So you want to pull a hoax on the Catholic Church? What kind of hoax?"

"I'm not sure. But it's something I need to do. I don't expect you to help if you think it's too risky, but I'd like your help," said Herbert.

"You know I'm a risk taker, and you might also know I'm no fan of religion of any kind. None of it ever made any sense to me. Because I don't know what your hoax might be, however, I can't say I'm willing to take a big risk on pulling it off."

"That's fair enough. Once I figure out how to get the gumballs back, we'll figure out how to devise the hoax. I'm not sure what we'll do, but I do know that to fool people, you need to know a lot about them. I'm not an expert in religion or the Catholic Church. Do you know anyone who is?" asked Herbert.

"I know a professor at Stanford who teaches the history of mythology and religion. His name is Oscar Cantor. He would be the perfect choice."

"Okay. Under two conditions. First, I need to do my experiment and confirm I can get the gumballs back. Second, I don't want you telling him about the nanotrons or any hoax until I know more," said Herbert.

"Agreed. I'm going to drop you off at your lab. I wouldn't be of any use to you there. I'll go over and talk to Oscar while you're working on the experiment."

"Korin, I said I need to confirm that my process works first. You're not listening to me, or worse, you're listening, and, as usual, you're ignoring what I said and going off to do what you want."

"Herbert, we're partners in this. I need to feel I'm contributing and controlling some of it. Besides, I know you'll make the experiment work. I'm the one who inspired you to think of the right answer. I can talk to Oscar without saying more than I need to. You let me know when you get the gumballs back."

"Okay. That'll work. I could pretend an enormous amount of work is involved. But in reality, I'm just going to set the controls so that the gumball disappears out of our dimensional space, and then bring it back a nanosecond later. The time frame will be so short that it will look as though it never left," said Herbert.

"So how will you know it really did leave and come back?"

"You worry about keeping the professor in the dark. I'll worry about how to track the gumball. Deal?"

"Deal."

As Korin dropped Herbert off, she picked up her cell phone and dialed Oscar. She was more excited about the possibilities of Herbert's discoveries than she had ever been about anything. Korin now had a better idea of what Herbert was thinking. Somehow she needed to figure out how to get him to move forward with the patent filing in order to protect her investment.

CHAPTER 8

*I have recently been examining all the known
superstitions of the world, and do not find
in our particular superstition (Christianity)
one redeeming feature. They are all alike founded
on fables and mythology.*

—Thomas Jefferson (1743–1826)

"Hello, this is Oscar Cantor. How can I help you?"

"Well, first off, you can drop that professional tone," said Korin.

"Korin. It's been awhile. I thought I'd hear from you after you got back from Europe. What happened?" He strained to keep from showing he was delighted she'd called or implying that he'd thought about her.

"Girls aren't supposed to call boys. Didn't your mother tell you?" she replied.

"Somehow I'm guessing you missed that lesson, Korin. I'm also guessing that you're calling now because you have something very interesting going on."

Oscar Cantor was a tall, good-looking African-American with a distinct self-important air that Korin poked fun at from time to time. He was fifty-two, a professor at Stanford. He'd published twelve books, his first at the age of twenty-nine. The books were far from bestsellers, but each was a bit more popular than the last, and, over time, this had made him modestly wealthy and well known—at least within a certain culture of those interested in history, religion, and mythology and how science shaped them all. He was the Joseph Campbell of his day. He had nowhere near the financial resources Korin had. Although it was untrue, he felt intellectually inferior to her, but he would give up his tenured position at Stanford before admitting it.

"You remember last time we talked, you told me I needed more excitement in my life? You told me I needed to do something bad, something really bad," Korin said.

"I don't remember saying that. What I remember is that last time we were together, we were doing something bad that was ever so good," Oscar replied.

"I remember that as well, and I'm looking forward to more of that. But you're not going to tell me you don't remember our long, philosophical conversation."

"Hey, I'm a Stanford professor. I talk a lot. That's what I do. I need to fit in with all these rich white guys. You can't expect me to remember everything I say to all the attractive women in my life."

"I like the 'attractive woman' part, but give me a break. You know what you said about me. You said I was too conventional for my own good and that sleeping with you was probably the only 'bad' thing I'd ever done. I thought about that. I thought about it a lot, and I also thought that being a bad girl made me happy."

"Happy is good. What's your point, Korin? You're bringing this up for a reason."

"I need to talk to you face to face. Can I come over to your office? It's important."

"Where are you now?"

"I'm in my car."

"Okay. Where's your car?" asked Oscar.

"Well, I knew you'd say yes, so I've been driving toward your office while we talked. I'm at Stanford now, and if I could just find a parking place, I could come up to your office. Will that work for you, or should I just go find someone else to tell and make them rich and famous?" asked Korin.

"Okay. But only if it doesn't take too long and doesn't make me too rich or famous."

"Spoken like a true academic."

Oscar hung up the phone and leaned forward in his chair to check his email and wait for Korin to arrive. He wouldn't go down to meet her, in part because he always made efficient use of his time, but mostly because he wanted, as much as possible, to avoid being seen with her. Oscar alone drew attention, but when he and Korin were together, everyone noticed. He was in a long-term marriage and was currently struggling with where his future lay.

While waiting, he gave a passing thought to straightening up his office. It was always in a state of disarray, with piles of papers covering his desk and floor. The most striking objects were the masks hanging on all four walls. Whenever an important visitor toured the building, his escort stopped at Professor Cantor's office to ask if Oscar would spend a few minutes telling the visitor about the masks. He almost always obliged, and although his descriptions were generally accurate, he often added a fact or two for dramatic effect. Although the basic masks were wooden, they were decorated with rough and polished stones, sea shells, feathers, bone, horns, and teeth from animals and humans.

Korin often asked for information about a mask, and he was more careful to be accurate with her—not because she would have known truth from fiction, but because the truth was easy to remember, and Korin might ask about the same mask more than once. As he contemplated the idea of wearing one of the masks to amuse Korin, a knock came at the door. He let her in without a word, and she placed her purse on a pile of papers stacked on a small, round table near the front of his office. She turned toward him as he closed the door, and they embraced. They held each other close and moved their hands across each other's body until Korin ended the embrace gently but firmly and sat down.

Neither Oscar nor Korin had had an extramarital affair before beginning this one, which had now lasted for almost a year. Oscar loved his wife and Korin her husband, but there was such passion between them that they put their marriages at risk to continue their affair. They often talked about their foolhardiness. In the first few months, they'd mentioned the possibility leaving their spouses and being together openly. For now, however, the affair continued, and they put aside thoughts of ending either the affair or their marriages.

"I could tell from your voice you wanted to talk about something important," said Oscar. "Whatever it is, it has your interest in a way nothing has since I've known you."

"I'll need to watch that. I didn't think I was that transparent. Before I start, I need you to understand that this is only between us at this point."

"Understood."

"I'm working on a project that has enormous potential. It could change my life."

"You've just come from one of those Tony Robbins self-help seminars, haven't you?" Oscar joked.

"This isn't funny. I'm very serious about this. I need your knowledge and expertise about some historical events."

"I'm not a historian," said Oscar. "I teach religion and mythology. What I know is more focused. If you want to know about the signing of the Declaration of Independence, I'm not your guy. If you need information about the religious thinking and activities surrounding the writing of the Declaration, I can help you."

Korin already had a good idea of what he did. She'd taken a general class he'd taught three years earlier, which was where they met. He wasn't sure what Korin had in mind. Even though he was distracted by his own problems, he sensed this was worthy of his attention.

"You often talk about how different things might be if we had a clear understanding of what really happened at some pivotal historic event," Korin said. "One time in our class, you asked if we thought Christianity would exist if there had been a film crew at Christ's crucifixion. I thought about that quite a lot. I'm going to ask you a different but related question. Would Christianity continue if that film of Christ's crucifixion surfaced today?"

"I suppose it would, because religion is based on belief, not facts. No one, particularly not Christians, would believe the film was real."

"Put the issue of film verification aside for now. Could you provide the details on the scene, the people, their clothes, and their language? Could you paint the picture well enough so that no one could seriously doubt that he was seeing the actual crucifixion of Christ?"

"I know as much as anyone in the world about it," said Oscar. "But a great deal isn't known. I could fill in details. Sure, other scholars in the field might disagree with some of them, but yes, I could give you a reasonable and well-informed description of how such a scene may have appeared."

"If you can recreate details of the crucifixion, it could be very useful to me. There could be a lot of money in it."

"Who are you working with? Is there going to be a movie?"

"I just know someone who may be willing to pay you a great deal of money for your expertise," Korin said.

Oscar walked around his office. He looked away from Korin and tried to hide his interest in making lots of money. He lifted a fertility mask off its hook on the wall and held it over his face. "I'm not interested in money. I'm interested in sex."

"So am I," said Korin.

"Did you think I meant with you?"

Korin stood up and removed Oscar's mask. "I know you."

"Yes, and I know you, but what's the point of all this?" he asked.

"I'll tell you more later. Just keep all of this to yourself and think about what those details would be. Research it if you need to so the details are all very fresh in your mind. Write out a description of everything. The clothes, the landscape, the wood of the cross, the metal for the nails, everything you can think of. I have to go now, but I'll call you tomorrow and give you more on where this is heading." Korin hugged Oscar and left before he had a chance to say anything.

Oscar paced around his office, thinking about how differently she had acted today. She would never ask him to do something without a purpose. He'd always felt his connection to Korin would provide many interesting possibilities, and this just might be the most interesting ever. The thought lifted his spirits at a time in his life when they needed lifting. He reflected back on the conversation in which he'd told her to do something bad and wondered how much influence, if any, he had on her. He thought about telling her about his current situation but was concerned that sharing it would change their relationship. For now he would keep it to himself.

CHAPTER 9

He who knows best knows how little he knows.

—Thomas Jefferson
(died July 4, 1826, fifty years to the day after
the signing of the Declaration of Independence)

The work in Herbert's lab had taken him much longer than Korin expected. His communications with her were sporadic. At first, he told her that the gumball would be returned only if he retrieved it almost instantaneously. He explained that he directed a laser at the gumball, with a detector positioned on the opposite side. He activated the machine, and the detector momentarily sensed the laser beam, which confirmed that the gumball had, in fact, disappeared and reappeared. Herbert said this was the basic proof that the gumball left our dimensional space for some other dimension. However, when Herbert tried to leave the gumball in another dimensional space for longer than a fraction of a second, it could not be retrieved.

Korin detected an increasing level of frustration in Herbert's voice. He described to her a tedious process of increasing the time frame in incremental amounts measured in only nanoseconds. This yielded some interesting results. Most of the gumball was retrieved, but a portion was lost. Herbert explained this was the data he needed to calculate the relative motion of our dimensional space with respect to the dimensional space into which the gumball had disappeared.

After weeks of additional experiments, he finally adjusted the parameters of the nanotron field to get the results he wanted. The next day, Herbert told Korin what he'd accomplished, and as she'd expected, he was giddy with excitement. Now that the experiment worked, he needed additional power before applying it to objects other than gumballs. Herbert had spent much of his own money on large electrical generators, and he used Korin's investment to purchase and install additional generators, which he connected as his efforts moved forward.

Korin had visited Herbert more than once. She noted increasing levels of frustration followed by irrational levels of excitement. When he finally succeeded, he was so intoxicated with his results that Korin was unable to tell him about the plan she was developing. She waited for his euphoria to subside before asking him to meet her, Alan, and Oscar. She suggested they get together at one of Herbert's favorite hangouts, a place she didn't much care for.

This meeting wasn't easy to arrange, but it was the sort of thing she was good at. She'd been the vice president of business development in several Silicon Valley start-up companies. Although she'd never been CEO, those in the know credited her with successfully moving the companies forward, because the best that could be said about the products of some of the companies was that they didn't hurt anyone. Someone really good at business development was more unusual in the Valley than a good CEO or computer genius. Korin easily made the connections, got the deals done, merchandized the products, and then eventually sold the companies at an enormous profit to herself and other early investors. She intuitively knew that by assuming a less intimidating role as VP of business development as opposed to CEO, she could make deals work.

The present situation was similar in one respect to all others—she wanted a return on her investment. It was different from every other project because she understood that to make money, Herbert's unusual requests would have to be satisfied.

Korin had first met Herbert and Alan in a corporate acquisition she structured. Both of them were what she called "scary smart," meaning that they knew so much about the science and technology of their respective fields that she was completely overwhelmed and, in some ways, frightened. They both recognized, however, that although she would never understand the technicalities of their work, neither of them would ever have her interpersonal skills.

As for Oscar, from the beginning, he had admired the way she connected concepts effortlessly and made people like her—even those negotiating against her. For her part, she'd quickly determined that Oscar had no business skills and that his common-sense knowledge had been driven out of him by the academic world.

The four of them met in a drafty bar in Redwood City called City Pub. The place wasn't sleepy—or lively—just very mediocre. Its ordinary nature made Korin confident they wouldn't be noticed. A few tables stood on an expanded area of the sidewalk outside the bar most of the year, and a sign on a large arch at the end of the street read, "Redwood City, Climate is Best by Government Test." It was seldom too cool or hot to be outside, but they chose to sit at a dimly lit table inside, where it seemed more private.

In many ways, the four of them could not have been more different. Korin was beginning to appreciate some of their individual motivations and wondered about others. Despite the many successes they'd all had in life, each remained dissatisfied. They were all hungry for something more.

Korin felt confident that what they were to talk about today would be the seed crystal that would put them on a track toward obtaining Herbert's goal and, more importantly provide her with an enormous financial return. She'd been unable to dissuade Herbert from moving forward with his hoax. In formulating her thoughts, she saw some interesting possibilities for the hoax as well as the patent filings she wanted. She was drawn toward the idea of doing something outrageous, and at the same time pulled back toward a sensible reality of something less risky.

Herbert and Alan were seated, drinking beer and talking, as Korin and Oscar arrived. She caught their attention for a moment and waved to them. They each nodded slightly and then continued their conversation. As they did, she thought that their hardly noticing her really bothered her. She was accustomed to men noticing her. Not getting recognition from an asexual man was understandable, but Alan had always noticed her outfits in the past. She had made a special effort today, but nothing. She wondered if she was just too old for her looks to turn heads. She found some relief from the reality of this disturbing possibility in the knowledge that their absorbing conversation might involve aspects of their project of which she wasn't yet aware.

"Thank you both for coming," said Korin, as she and Oscar sat. "Have you two been here long?"

She watched carefully as they responded. They both seemed nervous and looked away. She expected this. They must be hiding something.

"No, not really," said Alan.

"It doesn't matter," said Korin. "I've told you both a little about why I asked Oscar to come along."

Once they were seated and talking, Korin was pleased that Herbert and Oscar seemed to relate to each other well. She watched as the three men interacted, ignoring her.

"Herbert, wouldn't you like to tell Alan and Oscar what you've been working on?"

Herbert took another drink from his beer, put it down, and looked up as though he were about to speak. Instead, he picked up a pen and wrote a series of symbols on his napkin, symbols recognizable only by physicists.

The three others looked at each other and then back at Herbert.

"Give us a break, Herb. You know we can't read that crap. What's it supposed to mean?" asked Alan. "Have you come up with something important?"

"Oh, it's important all right," said Herbert. "About as important as anything could be. It means my beer mug is empty," he said with a laugh, signaling for the waitress to bring another beer.

Herbert loved to joke. He loved drawing others into believing something was really important and then letting them know they'd been misled by their own scientific ignorance. He'd never been the popular guy in school. Far from it. His pranks were a way of getting back at those who had made him the butt of their jokes. It got him noticed and served as the impetuous for him to form the Hackers group at MIT. The stunts generally resulted in amusing only Herbert. Others merely looked on with curiosity about what this odd physicist might have thought was funny.

Once Herbert had had his little joke, he pulled his phone from his coat pocket, turned it on, pulled up a video, and slowly turned the screen toward them. It showed a large bulldozer on a wooded area of Herbert's Woodside estate. Herbert pushed the "play" button, and the others watched the bulldozer levitate off the ground thirty meters or so and then return to its original position.

His friends all had the same basic thought: Herbert had created a fake video. "That's nothing. I can make a video of a bulldozer doing a hell of a lot more than that," Alan said.

Herbert turned his phone off, put it back in his pocket, and looked down at the table top. In a soft voice he said, "It's not just a video. It's not some kind of trick. It's real."

"Is that what you're going to show us? Are you going to take us to your place and show us the real thing?" asked Korin.

"Yes. That's what I'm saying. I think it's ready for others to see. But we have to wait until I finish my meal."

Herbert ate the burger he loved with an order of really big fries—the kind that still tasted and looked like the potato they came from. They talked, but the conversation was disjointed, and Korin noticed Herbert kept his mouth filled with food or drink to avoid saying more than he wanted about the demonstration he was about to give.

She reflected that their conversation had similarities to those before some life-changing event—just before a graduation, the birth of a child, or a marriage. Something very big was clearly about to happen, something that was outside of the scope of their current level of understanding. They talked more about other things—recent movies and books—even something as boring as the weather. The time passed strangely, and Korin could feel the anticipation of the others as the meal finally came to an end.

Oscar had been unusually quiet in the bar and later in the car as they drove together toward Herbert's place. She didn't question him but felt a sense of uncertainty.

Herbert had bought his home ten years earlier, largely because it was secluded. The house itself wasn't extraordinary, but there was, for the San Francisco Bay Area, a great deal of land. He left the surrounding trees in place for privacy but used part of the land for the construction of two buildings.

Building #1 was filled with computers, tables, white boards, modeling components, and every kind of communication device. From there, he video-conferenced with others locally and around the world. This is where Herbert did his thinking. On one wall was a framed photo of Robert Oppenheimer smoking a pipe. The photo was positioned over a handwritten note card signed by Oppenheimer saying, "Man's most difficult task is thinking." The computers allowed for sophisticated calculation, but Herbert often reminded Korin that everything in the room was nothing more than a diversion from his "most difficult task." One evening when she had gone to visit him, she thought he wasn't in. He had turned off everything except a small light over the chair where he sat with a white pad of paper and a pencil. When she finally saw him, he looked up and started to explain what he was doing, but he couldn't. Without much said, she left him with his pencil in Building #1, where everything originated for Herbert.

Building #2 was by far the largest building on the property. It was an elaborate structure with complex expensive equipment on which much of Korin's investment had been spent in order to move the technology forward to the next level. Herbert cared little for the conventional luxuries of life and spent most of his money on the contents of Building #2.

Building #2 was often occupied by two of Herbert's closest friends. In different capacities these engineers designed experiments at the nearby Stanford Linear Accelerator. Peter Ford was Herbert's age. They had attended MIT together, and although he was overweight, Pete bounced about with the energy and unpredictability of a three-year-old. He had an unusually mischievous nature that Herbert took to decades ago. Pete could build anything and especially delighted in constructing equipment designed by Dan Richtman. Dan, also an MIT classmate, served as the interface between Herbert and Pete. Although Pete and Dan were compensated well, Korin knew they would have paid Herbert for the opportunity to play with all the toys of Building #2.

Herbert arrived first at his estate, opened the gate, and waited for the others before closing it behind them and leading them off the paved driveway onto a gravel road toward a wooded area. He stopped, exited his car, and signaled his friends to do the same.

Herbert wore khaki pants, a white button-down shirt, and an older, suede sport coat. It was rare to see him wearing anything else. This outfit was as much his "dress up" as it was his "dress down" clothes. Many other things he did reflected his inability to dress for the right effect. Still, although his clothes were awkward and uninspired, the substance of his work was consistently remarkable.

80

"That's one big bulldozer," said Korin, as they all approached Herbert. In fact, none of them had ever seen a bulldozer up close.

"No use wasting time." Herbert removed a rather crude-looking remote-control device from a small case he carried. After he pushed a number of buttons and apparently set some parameters on the remote, the bulldozer began to rise. It did so without a sound and continued to lift just as it had in the video back at the bar. Herbert lowered it back to its original place, and they all approached the huge machine in amazement. Oscar and Korin were so stunned they lagged a bit behind, but Alan ran up to the bulldozer and put his hand on one of the giant treads. "I knew it!" he said. "It's a God-damn balloon!" He looked back to see Herbert smile. Alan even laughed a little, with a goofy inhalation, an air-gulping laugh reserved for particularly nerdy folks.

"I can't believe you got us out here to pull a silly trick. Okay, I admit it, you really got me. But I'm going to go now, and I won't be fooled again." Korin was outraged, felt she'd been cheated by Herbert, and contemplated ways to get her ten million dollars back.

Herbert's three friends rolled their eyes and together started back toward their cars.

"Oh, just one thing," said Herbert. "Before you go, you might want to take a look over your heads."

They looked up and saw what appeared to be another bulldozer overhead. Having already been fooled, Oscar said, "Fool me once, shame on you; fool me twice, shame on me." He kept walking with the others toward their cars.

Herbert continued working buttons on his remote control. As his friends quickened their pace toward their cars, he moved the bulldozer over their heads to a point only a few feet in front of them, and then he lowered it. He dropped it slowly enough to prevent damage but fast enough to shake the ground when he put it down. The other three stopped and turned to Herbert. The little smile they all knew had returned to Herbert's face.

"What the fuck is going on, Herbert?" said Alan with a look of confused anger and astonishment.

"I've used a field of nanotrons I created to move the bull-dozer," Herbert said. "When I got it to where I could fly it around, you understand, I couldn't resist playing with it. But I figured that my neighbors might see it aloft, and they did. So we made the balloon to provide an easy explanation. I figured I could just show them the balloon, and they would go away without suspecting what's really going on."

"Of course, a simple and easily understandable explanation," said Oscar. "The fact that it's false is unimportant to them. Don't people even question why you might have a balloon in the shape of a bulldozer?"

Herbert thought for a moment and said, "No. I'm an odd enough guy that no one much questions anything I do or have."

Korin saw that Oscar was obviously excited—and at the same time humbled, even a bit humiliated—by what he had seen. Herbert had done something that could change the world, while Oscar taught mythology to pseudo-intellectual eighteen-year-olds. While she speculated about this, she also recognized that something was different in how Oscar was acting. She dismissed her speculations as based on her insecurities about their relationship. Still, if everything between her and Oscar was unchanged, he had something on his mind that Herbert would never be thinking—getting laid. Sex was important to Oscar.

"I suppose you want to tell us how you did this," Oscar said with an air of arrogance only he could put on words. He then added sarcasm by saying in the most disingenuous way possible, "We're just dying to hear the details of your flying bulldozer."

Korin stepped up. "What Oscar really means, Herbert, is that we're all impressed. But we're not physicists, and can't understand the details—or maybe even the big concepts. You'll have to dumb it down for us—particularly for Oscar." Korin was still hurt about the balloon deception, but now she saw even bigger possibilities for the technology than before. She felt bad for having thought Herbert was cheating her. She liked him; all of them did. He was a strangely likeable guy.

"Well, I'll see what I can do. Why don't we go inside?" Herbert began walking toward Building #1.

They walked over loosely packed gravel that crunched under their feet. Herbert reached down and picked up a handful of the smooth pebbles and poured them from one hand to the other. He smiled as he made eye contact with Korin, and she wondered what he was thinking. He winked at her and threw the last of the pebbles over his shoulder.

CHAPTER 10

*The ability to convert ideas to things
is the secret to outward success.*

—Henry Ward Beecher (1813–1887)

Alan and Korin had had other business relationships with Herbert and had been to Building #1 before. Oscar had not. As the four of them walked along the gravel road on a cool March afternoon, Oscar reflected on how he might see the world differently after leaving the building later that day. Maybe a world he had thought of as flat would be explained for the sphere that it really was. He felt how early explorers must have—a little afraid, excited, and full of expectations of what was to come.

After tossing the pebbles backward, Herbert punched numbers into a panel on the door, and it opened. They walked in and looked back at the door as it closed and the lights inside came on. Herbert led them all to a small room with a screen mounted on the wall facing the door.

"I'm embarrassed to do this, but I'm doing what you asked. I'm dumbing this down," Herbert said as his three guests took chairs facing the screen. Sitting behind them, he turned on some of the equipment. The screen showed a title, "The History of Energy."

"All of us use energy every day. Mankind's first source of energy was fire. For hundreds of thousands of years, man used it for heating, cooking, and light." Herbert showed images of cave dwellers and people of ancient civilizations using fire to cook and light a path.

"I could really help you out with your 'show and tell' presentation," said Alan. "My new programs will make those cavemen look as real as any movie you've ever seen. But I'm sorry for interrupting you, Herbert, please go ahead."

"Initially, fire came from burning wood. Over time, wood became scarce, and a shift was made to coal. Okay guys? Is this boring enough for you?" Herbert's voice contained a hint of exasperation.

"It's working for me so far," said Korin. "Keep going."

"The use of wood, coal, oil, or gasoline is all based on chemical reactions. Some reactions are a little more or less efficient than others. But regardless of the efficiency of the conversion of that energy to *work*, vast amounts of potential energy remain in the resulting molecules.

"This started to change with the discovery of atomic energy. An atomic reaction extracts about a hundred-thousand times as much energy from the fuel as compared to a chemical reaction, but even here, only a very small portion of the matter itself is converted to energy.

"By changing the level of energy generation from molecules to atoms, the energy yield goes up a hundred-thousand-fold. What you just saw with the bulldozer was the result of a new energy source that doesn't rely on chemical or atomic energy. It's something very different. By creating a field around an object, it's possible to change the dimensional space where the object is positioned. Using the nanotron allows the object to slip between different dimensional spaces. More on that later.

"When the chemical energy of gasoline is burned in your car engine, some of that energy is put to work. The exploding gas moves the pistons. The pistons move a crank shaft, which, through a series of gears, turns the wheels, and the car moves—*work,* as that word is used in the physics world—is done.

"A nuclear-power plant splits atoms and creates heat energy. The heat turns water to steam. The steam turns the blades of a turbine, and the turbine, through a series of gears, turns a generator. A generator is nothing more than an electric motor in reverse. As the generator turns, it generates electricity—enough to power an entire city from a piece of material the size of a baseball. Okay. You guys are following me so far, right?"

"Sure. If physics were really that easy, I could have taken it in college," Oscar answered.

"Well, if Mr.-Couldn't-Convert-Centigrade-to-Fahrenheit is getting it, you can assume the rest of us are fine. Continue," said Korin, hoping for more of a reaction from Oscar.

"The chemical energy of wood, coal, or gas could be used to make the same steam the nuclear reaction creates. It would just take a lot more material or fuel to generate the same amount of energy. In a nuclear reaction, less fuel can be used to generate the same amount of energy, because much more of the energy in the fuel is extracted.

"If you've followed what I've said so far, you understand that our ability to generate more energy isn't about using greater amounts of fuel or more efficiently converting the energy to *work.* It's about extracting more energy from the fuel you have."

"Herbert, so far you've only talked about other technologies," Alan interjected. "You haven't told us a thing about how you got these results. What makes it work? How are you able to generate so much more energy?"

"You're right, Alan. I'm getting there. I've just learned to get everyone's attention by describing some things people are familiar with first. Korin and folks just like her have finally beaten that into me," said Herbert in a humble way.

"To create this new particle field, which changes how mass moves, I merged classical physics with quantum physics. Physicists who deal with the movement of mass that we can actually see describe the universe with equations originating with Newton and then Einstein. This doesn't mean that Newton or even Einstein developed all of classical physics. Many others have done and continue to do important work in that field," explained Herbert.

"Why is it called 'classical physics'?" asked Oscar.

"In a way, that's a good question," Herbert answered. "I say 'in a way,' because it doesn't really matter what it's called. It could be called 'regular physics' or 'standard physics' or 'large particle physics' or anything else. What's important is that from the beginning of history until the early 1900s, it was the only kind of physics there was. At that point, around 1920, physicists such as Niels Bohr developed quantum mechanics. None of the rules of physics up to that time could be used to describe how subatomic particles moved in this newly discovered world of quantum mechanics — the subatomic world. It was clear to physicists that there was now a new kind of physics. Although the existing equations worked to describe objects large enough to see, they were useless in describing the movements of subatomic particles.

Of course, it was also true that while the equations of quantum mechanics worked to describe the movement of subatomic particles, those equations were useless in describing the movement of large particles. Physicists started to refer to physics developed up until that time as 'classical physics' and the new physics as 'quantum mechanics.'

"Physicists next looked for equations that would work for both large objects *and* subatomic particles. Leonard Susskind made some progress in this area with 'string theory,' but the two worlds of physics have never been merged. I decided to try to merge the actual engineering used in the two different types of physics. Until now, no one ever thought to study quantum mechanics by using the same type of devices used in studying classical physics.

"The idea of merging the engineering technologies of the two worlds came to me after I read a paper by a Spanish physicist Ganan-Calvo on fluid dynamics."

"Herbert, when you start using terms such as quantum mechanics and fluid dynamics, you start to lose us," Korin said.

"Not to worry," said Herbert. "I've got some graphics on all this that will show you what I'm talking about. You've all seen water flow out of the end of a hose. It starts out in a column the shape of the hose. As it moves away from the end of the hose, it starts to break up. What physicists have known for some time is that it breaks up into particles that have a diameter equal to twice the diameter of the stream of water when it comes out of the hose. Here's a graphic showing what I'm talking about."

Herbert then went through a set of slides he'd shown Korin and included in the agreement with her.

"The electron stream is focused to make a stream of much smaller particles, and by directing this focused stream, it's possible to create a *field* of particles—which I call nanotrons—around an object. That field allows any object within it to slip between different dimensional spaces," Herbert explained.

"I used the field generator to create a nanotron field around the bulldozer and move it into and out of our dimensional space. The bulldozer can be raised to any height and left there for nearly any length of time, and I'm sure you noticed the process made no sound. That's why the lie about it being a balloon worked so well." Herbert looked at his friends to see if they understood. They nodded that they did.

"But I still don't understand how you make a real bulldozer float in the air. How does it work?" asked Alan.

"Think of our dimension as a stream flowing along. If you're in the stream, you're flowing along as well. But if you can get out of the stream and onto the shore, you've stopped, though the stream continues," said Herbert.

"Okay, I follow you so far," Alan said.

"Now, imagine the stream can flow in any direction, even straight up. If you were in a stream moving straight up and then got out of the stream, you'd start to fall. If you got immediately back into the stream, you'd start going up again. To make the bulldozer hover, I'm moving it in and out of the stream, or in and out of our dimensional space, which is moving," said Herbert.

"Fascinating," said Alan. "Totally and completely fascinating."

"Who else has seen your flying bulldozer? Who else have you explained this to?" Korin asked.

"Dan and Pete, the guys who helped me design and build the enlarged particle generator that makes a nanotron field big enough to surround the bulldozer. That's all," Herbert answered.

"How comfortable are you that Dan and Pete haven't told anyone?" she asked.

"I know them both from MIT; that's forty years ago. I've always been able to count on them. Well, almost always," Herbert joked. "I'm just kidding. They're fine. Now, can I rely on the three of you to not say anything to anybody?"

"Sure," "Absolutely," "No question," said his three friends in order as they followed Herbert out of the room and then out of Building #1.

Oscar could tell Korin and Alan were more than a little stunned by what they'd just heard. He wondered what possibilities they might be contemplating. He'd been told something new and wonderful about how the world worked, and his newfound knowledge was about to provide many possibilities. It was scary and exciting at the same time. He thought about his current health situation and wondered if somehow Herbert's process could change his prognosis.

Despite being overwhelmed by what he'd just seen, Oscar tried to piece together some of Herbert's presentation with what Korin had asked of him. He wondered why she wanted him to be part of this meeting. And what did Christ's crucifixion have to do with anything? Oscar was starting to feel as he often did at Stanford faculty meetings—invited but not truly part of what was going on. At one such meeting, they'd discussed the qualifications and papers published by a professor at another school. The man had been someone Oscar knew, yet no one had asked him for an opinion, and, as it turned out, the administration had extended an offer to him without even mentioning it to Oscar. He was hurt, but he had decided to react positively. He would do the same now.

"I'm impressed by what I've seen," Oscar said. "I don't have the words to describe how I feel. I doubt that anyone would. Although I'm glad to be here, I don't understand why I am."

"That was my idea," said Korin. "Herbert asked me to invest, and so far I'm delighted that I did. He also asked me to come up with an idea that would use this technology to do something different before we move on with making money. You're part of that idea."

"I assume I'm part of the idea as well?" asked Alan. "I've been working with the nanotrons to run computer software. Herbert never told me about this part. He also insisted we not file for patents. That concerns me. I don't see how we can make money if we have no patents. I may buy into some plan, but the money is of great importance to me. Frankly, Korin, I never thought of you as being interested in anything besides the financial return. You'll need to explain."

"I agree that the money is important, and we need the patents. We have to file for patents," Korin insisted.

"It's all based on my work. I'm not going to file if it requires telling others," said Herbert.

"I understand," said Korin. "I've been researching the issue. I believe there's a way for everyone to get what they want. Everything is tied to the nanotrons. If we own the nanotrons and the process for generating them, we own everything."

"How are you going to own the nanotrons?" Alan asked. "You can't patent electricity, so you can't patent nanotrons. They exist in nature. No one can own them."

"You're correct that no one can own electricity, but nano-trons *don't* exist in nature. They need to be made. I did some serious research on this point, and even basic chemical elements have been patented. They're patentable because they're artificially produced. They don't exist in nature. I looked it up. Here's a patent on one of the elements in the periodic table." Korin opened a black leather folder she had carried with her and handed Alan a copy of U.S. Patent 3,156,523.

"So you're getting a patent on the nanotrons?" Oscar asked.

"That's the first part of the plan. It's the part that's most interesting in terms of making money. But there are other possibilities here," Korin said.

"I'm not following you. What are you talking about?" Alan asked.

"Indulge me for a moment," Korin said. "We're in a unique position. Even though we're not world leaders, we have the ability to alter history. I know that whatever we do, Herbert's work will change the course of human events. The question is whether we grab control of the wheel and determine how that change takes shape, or we let others shape the future."

"Let me interject something here," said Herbert. "The basic nanotrons are mine. I invented them. I asked Korin to figure out a two-part plan. The first part is how best to make a lot of money with this. The second part is something for me. I want to have a little fun with the nanotrons before everyone knows what they can do."

"When Herbert first asked me to come up with something that would change the world with a plan surrounding how this invention unfolded, I was reluctant," Korin said. "As I thought it over, I thought it was possible. Other people think they have the right to change the world. So I wondered why I'd let Hillary Clinton have all the fun. We can work together on this project to bring about all kinds of changes. We have a unique opportunity."

Oscar started to see the possibilities. Korin had explained Alan's videos and he knew Alan could make people watching his videos believe almost anything, particularly if the videos could be combined with the real effects of Herbert's flying bulldozer. Oscar was the only one of the four with knowledge of what people believed and why they believed it. He had started out wondering if he fit into this plan in some insignificant role, but now he thought he just might be able to control the plan and its ultimate results. He didn't understand Herbert's process or Alan's programs, but he knew much more than they did about people's thoughts and the history of their beliefs. He took satisfaction in knowing that the others thought most Europeans believed the world was flat until Columbus sailed in 1492. To the contrary, nearly every educated European for two thousand years before Columbus had read Aristotle's *On the Heavens,* which clearly explained, with supporting evidence, why the world must be a sphere. Although some of this information was generally available, it wasn't distilled and understood the way Oscar understood it. To be successful, the others would need him to provide a real appreciation of the details.

"So, what's the plan?" asked Alan.

"For now, I need to do some additional work. I've figured out the basic concepts, but I need to perfect a lot of the details," Korin answered.

"The one thing we all need to agree on is complete secrecy. If any of this gets out, it will limit what we'll be able to do," Herbert said.

"I agree. I won't tell a soul," Oscar agreed.

"Okay, but just agreeing to secrecy won't work if someone else finds out or if someone else discovers the same invention. Are you going to file patent applications on this, Herbert?" Alan asked pointedly.

"I'll agree to filing on the nanotrons, but not on the use of them to move things. If I did that, I'd have to tell others. I'd have to tell a patent attorney. The attorney would need to interact with others to get the patent application written and filed. Then people in the Patent Office would see it, and it would become public. It's just too much exposure and way too risky."

"I don't like leaving out anything from the patent. However, we can file on the nanotrons and show them as useful in improving computer speed. If we can claim the nanotrons it should work. I understand your emphasis on secrecy," said Alan. "I still don't know what the plan is, though."

"We intend to pull off a hoax," Korin said, "something bigger than anyone has ever done. It will break all the rules, even cardinal rules, so Herbert has been calling it the cardinal hoax. I don't have a detailed plan, and I didn't think we'd be talking about this yet. Let me just say that the hoax will center around religion. That's why Oscar is here."

"Religion! I can't believe what I'm hearing. Why would you waste this on religion? That makes no sense," Alan said.

Korin had introduced Oscar to Alan years ago when Oscar needed help with an unusual software program. Oscar knew Alan held religion in great contempt. But for now, Oscar wanted to see the plan move forward—or at least to understand his role in it better. "I know how you feel, Alan," he said. "Religion has far too much influence on many things in our lives. Religion is probably the biggest opponent to gay marriage. Maybe we could change that."

"Let's not focus on any particular thing right now," said Korin. "I suggest we not get into a debate at this time. Let's go home and think about the possibilities."

They all agreed.

Oscar was hoping to be on his way before Korin could speak to him, but she called to him as they walked toward their cars. "Oscar, wait."

"What's up?"

"I thought we could meet. Let's go to our usual motel."

"Ahh, Korin, I really can't. I just can't," he said, looking at Korin's obviously stunned and saddened face. "We'll talk later."

As he got in his car and drove off, Oscar wondered what he should say to Korin. He lamented that even though Herbert's invention might be the greatest scientific advancement of all time, it wasn't going to change his current situation. Nothing, he thought, could change that.

CHAPTER 11

The glow of one warm thought is to me worth more than money.

—Thomas Jefferson (1743–1826)

The next morning, after Jim left for work, Korin took the children to school and then sat on the back deck of her home. As she looked out at the trees, an acorn fell in her lap. She picked it up by the stem and twirled it back and forth between her thumb and index finger. She thought of Oscar, and some guilty feelings returned. The guilt seemed secondary now, as Jim hadn't paid her much attention lately. She wondered why Jim had been distant. Perhaps she should call Oscar. Intellectually, she understood that what Herbert had shown them dwarfed the significance of any personal issues. However, emotionally, she focused partially on Jim's lack of affection, but primarily on Oscar and why he had rebuffed her advances. She wondered if her feelings toward Oscar were far stronger than his feelings toward her. When they were together, she felt such passion and lust that wasn't there with Jim. She feared that her feelings toward Oscar might be altogether misplaced. She had to know, and she had to know now. She picked up the phone and called Oscar's office. "Hi. It's me. Can you talk?"

"I'm just about to head off to a class. What if we hike the loop around the dish this afternoon? I can change after class and meet you."

"Okay. The Alpine Road entrance at four o'clock."

"Great," said Oscar. "See you there. I gotta go. Bye."

Oscar had seemed uncomfortable. His voice sounded different, and she knew his class didn't start for another half-hour or so. She took some comfort in knowing he was at least a bit emotionally shaken by her call. But that wasn't enough, because she also imagined there could be many different reasons for his emotional state. She paced across her deck, picking up acorns, throwing them out into the woods, and not liking many of the thoughts that came into her head. Maybe Oscar didn't want to be involved with her anymore. Maybe she had just been his play toy. Doubts arose until she twisted the cap off yet another acorn, threw both pieces far out into the yard below the deck, and decided to work in her garden. Pulling weeds and watering generally took her mind off of whatever was disturbing her, and today was no exception.

Korin intentionally arrived about five minutes late at the small, unpaved parking lot off Alpine Road that served as an entrance to a hiking area she often used. She wanted Oscar to be concerned and start to worry, as she was always on time.

"I thought maybe you changed your mind." Oscar embraced Korin.

"I was gardening. I guess I just lost track of time. Are you ready to go?"

"I brought an extra water. I thought a good hike might help take the edge off whatever is on your mind," he said.

"Do you think something is on my mind?" asked Korin.

"I knew you were upset yesterday. I should have told you earlier that I was just too tired to get together after seeing Herbert."

"Oscar, it's not just about yesterday. It's about how you feel about our relationship. I need to know how you feel. To be able to continue this, I need to know I can trust you completely."

"You have to know how I feel about you," Oscar said. "And as far as trust goes, I'm the one who can't trust you. You came and asked me questions about the crucifixion without telling me why, when you already knew what Herbert was doing."

Just being with Oscar made Korin feel better. She didn't answer right away and picked up their walking pace as they went by several cows grazing nearby.

"I had promised Herbert not to say anything until his work was further along. I got you involved as soon as I could." She noticed that Oscar had trouble keeping up with her.

"I've told you before that I have some real insecurities about our relationship," said Oscar. "When I found out you knew so much more about what Herbert was doing and didn't tell me, it hurt. It made me question our relationship, and I felt like the token black guy on the outside. You couldn't understand."

"Maybe not. But I'm often the only woman, and I've been in a lot of situations where I knew more than a little about how it feels to be the only different one in a group."

"We've had some version of this conversation before. Although we don't agree, there's at least some understanding of how the other feels. I don't want to debate it again. I told you I was tired yesterday. Let's drop it." Oscar reached to hold her arm and tried to slow her pace as they walked up an incline.

"I'll drop it if I can get your help on what I want to do with Herbert's new invention," Korin said.

"Wait a minute. That's a much bigger deal. I don't even understand what you want to do," Oscar protested.

This was not turning out as Korin expected. She had thought Oscar would be completely on her side. She had involved him based on the expectation that he would help her even if she didn't tell him anything. She slowed her pace, put her hand on his shoulder, and looked him in the eye. "I need to know you're with me on this. It's so important to me, very important."

"Thanks for slowing down. As for my help, tell me what you need. Tell me the details of your plan. Once I understand what you're planning, I can get on board."

Korin took a deep breath. "I've told you about Alan's videos and you've seen Herbert's bulldozer. You know there's a lot of potential there. In a nutshell, I want to convince everyone that we're showing them the actual crucifixion of Christ. I want to present a video showing that he didn't die on the cross and that, therefore, he never rose from the dead."

"Oh. Is that all? What are you, fucking nuts?"

"Calm down. Let me explain. I believe it can happen."

"You've told me Alan's videos look real," Oscar said. "I'll assume he could make one of me having gay sex, and if I saw it, I might believe it happened. But people who believe Christ rose from the dead will always believe that, regardless of any proof to the contrary."

"Some will, yes. But many have doubts, and for them, it's all a matter of setting it up the right way. We can use Herbert's and Alan's inventions to show people some very believable events that they'll want to accept as true. Once they believe that we're showing things as they really happened, we show the crucifixion."

"This sounds completely insane to me. Even if I helped you, we could get caught. That would be extremely unfortunate for all of us."

One part of Korin wasn't concerned with getting caught. She wanted to control the power, and enjoy the excitement of it. At the same time she had increasing doubts about going forward with something so risky. The more real it seemed the more uncertain she was that any of it was rational. Although it seemed absurd she wanted the option of moving forward. To keep the option open it was her job to convince him of everything she could to move the project forward. She searched for something to say. "Oh, so then you're afraid? Maybe I figured you all wrong." That sort of taunting seldom worked on women, but it often did with men. It was simple and obvious, yet still effective.

"I'm not afraid. But I'm not nuts, either," said Oscar. "What would be in it for me if I went along with this? I'm not saying I will..."

"What do you want?" Korin leaned into Oscar and pushed one of her breasts against his arm as they continued to walk.

"Oh, come on." He pulled away. "Let's keep sex out of this. I'm talking about a percentage ownership in the whole enterprise."

"I was just testing you," Korin said. "Sure. We can talk about that. I made a capital investment in the company in return for a percentage. Herbert put a pre-money valuation on the company of a hundred million dollars."

"Korin, I'm a history professor, not a financier. What does that mean?"

"When companies are first formed, they need money," Korin explained. "So someone picks a value for the company. Let's say the value is a hundred dollars. If an investor agrees it's worth one hundred dollars and wants to be an equal-share owner with the company founder, he invests a hundred dollars of his own, and the founder and the investor each own half the company, which is then valued at two hundred dollars."

"So if you agree that Herbert's new company is worth one hundred million dollars, you'll need to invest one hundred million in order to own half of the company?"

"That's correct," said Korin. "However, in this case, I only put in ten million to buy out ten percent of Herbert's original shares."

"You know I don't have that kind of money."

"I understand. You can *earn* your shares. It's called 'sweat equity.' Your services are valued, and you get shares based on what you do," said Korin.

"I see enormous risk here. If I'm going to do this, the payoff has to be commensurate with my risk."

At this point, she saw that Oscar's mindset had changed from wondering whether to participate, to contemplating how much money he would make. This is where Korin had wanted and expected him to be. "Assuming the money is there," she said. "Can you do it? Can you get me details on how the actual crucifixion of Christ would have looked?"

"No one knows for sure how crucifixions were carried out. I know as much as anyone, though. I know the different theories."

"Why isn't more known?" asked Korin.

"Many reasons. First, written records were either not kept or not preserved. Second, there's little archeological evidence because people who were crucified weren't always buried. Often they were left on the cross as examples to others. They rotted on the cross or were eaten by animals."

"That's awful!"

"Punishment for crimes was often very brutal," said Oscar. "Most people would be quite surprised to know what crucifixion was really like around the time of Jesus. Others have made movies—Mel Gibson's is fairly well known. But those movies were meant to sell tickets and support the basic premise of Christianity. No one knows for sure what happened back then."

"Interesting. Well, if no one knows for sure, and you know what's known, we should be able to put something together," Korin concluded.

"Sure. I can describe something that's believable."

"I'll get back to you on the financial issues. I'm sure I can figure out something that will make you rich."

"Rich would be good, very rich would be better," said Oscar. "What might even be better is if you'd slow down. I'm totally out of breath."

CHAPTER 12

One need not be a chamber to be haunted;
One need not be a house;
The brain has corridors surpassing
Material place.

—Emily Dickinson (1830–1886)

Herbert had enjoyed the absurdity of a flying bulldozer, but it had a serious purpose. It was part scientific and part psychological. He had shown that he could instantaneously switch matter between two different dimensional spaces and make a big, heavy object look as though it was hovering in mid-air. Now he wanted something more. He wanted to know if he could project the field over great distances and if he could do it with people. Herbert had arranged to meet Dan Richtman for breakfast at Buck's, a small restaurant in Woodside near his home where he most enjoyed having breakfast.

"Good morning, Dan. Thanks for coming over." Herbert approached the table where Dan was already seated with a cup of coffee.

"Good morning. No problem. It's always great coming here, if only for the interesting décor." Dan looked around at one bizarre fixture after another on the walls. There was a model of a 1955 Chevy next to a sailfish that seemed to be jumping over a flying saucer.

"Let's order." Herbert signaled the waitress. He requested his standard breakfast. "I'll have a raspberry jelly doughnut, a side of bacon, and a black coffee."

"I'll have a western omelet, toast, hash browns, and an orange juice," said Dan. "And more coffee when you get the time."

"I've been thinking about the field," Herbert began after the waitress had gone. "What it is and why it's able to do what it does. I don't understand it yet, but I think I'm getting closer. At first, I thought I could use equations—the same way physicists try to figure everything out. But I don't even understand how to start the equations. The nanotron stream doesn't produce enough energy to move one of the ball bearings in that bulldozer, let alone the whole machine. When I accepted that, I knew the bulldozer never moved."

"Okay, Herbert. If it never moved, how does it get from one place to another? What you're saying doesn't make any sense."

"What I mean is that it doesn't experience motion through time and space the same way we do when we walk across a room or drive a car along a road. The field makes it possible for anything inside the field to slip out of one dimensional space and into a different dimensional space, and back again. If I adjust the field so that something inside it is in our dimensional space now, then slips to another dimensional space, and then comes back to a new position in our dimensional space, it appears to move or undergo what we understand to be motion. Right now it's all a bit clumsy. For this to work, I need to be able to go between places in very short periods of time."

"How is it not motion if it starts in one place and ends up in a different place?" Dan looked confused.

"It appears to move because of the way I've adjusted the field, and I do that based on my own prejudice about how things work in the universe. I think of objects as being in one place at a time. A moving object starts at one point at a given time, and then as time moves forward, the object moves to another place. But I realized that I should think about time and space differently and consider adjusting the field differently. What if the field were adjusted to be around an object in two places at the same time? The object wouldn't move; it would just be or exist in both places at the same time."

"So why don't we see two bulldozers when it moves from one place to another? —or should I say when it exits in one place and then exists in another?" asked Dan.

"It's because I never understood what was happening before. I thought of motion in a very classical way. I tried to make things move by adjusting the field around the bulldozer at one place and then adjusting it around the bulldozer at another place at some time a fraction of a second later. I never even thought to try and put it in two places at the same time."

The waitress arrived with their food. Overhearing the last part of their conversation, she said, "Well, if you guys think you need to be in two places at once to do your jobs, just try waiting on ten tables in this place at breakfast." With that, she placed the food on the table and walked away.

"There you go, Herb. All you had to do was come here and ask the waitress."

"She would have come to the problem without any prejudice. That's what I really needed," said Herbert. "It's all the things we think we know already that keep us from learning."

"So can you put the bulldozer in two places at the same time?" asked Dan.

"I think so. But let me eat before I explain." Herbert cut the raspberry doughnut into quarters and positioned the pieces in the order in which he wanted to eat them. Taking a sip of his coffee, he ate one of the quarters, enjoying the contrast of the bitter coffee against the doughnut's sweet jam and powdered sugar. He repeated the process with the remaining pieces, taking the time to savor the coffee and then the doughnut. He wondered about his fascination with the meal and why he had no such fascination with the attractive waitress walking by their table. By the time he was done, Dan had practically inhaled his omelet, hash browns, and toast. He drank his juice and waited for Herbert to speak.

"It never ceases to amaze me. You are one fast eater," said Herbert. "Have some of my bacon while I tell you what we'll need to do in order to put one thing in two places at the same time.

"The bulldozer has a very irregular shape. This may affect the way it's held in the field. It also makes it more difficult to set coordinates for the field holding the bulldozer in a different space. To make it work, I need to put the field around a large sphere of space surrounding the bulldozer. The gumballs are easier, but they're still a little irregular. I need a perfect sphere. A perfect sphere would be easy to coordinate because its outer surface is equal distance from a single point—that point being the center of the sphere. By putting the center of the sphere and the center of the field at two different points, the sphere and everything inside it should come to exist at two different places at the same time."

"So you want me to design some kind of sphere? Is that it?" asked Dan.

"Not just any sphere. It has to be a perfect sphere big enough to hold at least four people. Something that can hold food, water, and oxygen for them for a few days—and it needs to be airtight."

"So something similar to the space shuttle in the shape of a sphere?"

"It doesn't need any heat shields," Herbert replied, "but otherwise, yes. What do you think?"

"Let me work on some drawings and run them by you."

"Dan, I want it built at my place. Tell the people constructing it that I'll use it to project star images on the ceiling. Tell them it's a planetarium. I think that will work to keep it secret."

"Just one question, Herb, before I go. If you get this to work, is the world really ready for two of you?"

Herbert smiled. He had always told Dan everything about the science, but he didn't share much else. This had always worked between them because they were both passionate about the science. Herbert had a great deal he considered sharing, but he thought it best to leave well enough alone. Some things, he thought, are best kept to oneself. "I think one of me is plenty."

"Speaking of *one* of you, why is it you're always alone? I know you interact with others, but you never seem to have a partner. Hell, you never even date, as far as I can tell," Dan said.

"I'm just too busy. I have no time for dates."

"Well, if you don't want to talk about it, I'm okay with that."

"Let's save that conversation for another time. For now, let's just say I'm working on the issue." Herbert looked at a group of musical instruments hanging on a wall painted with musical notes. He read the notes and hummed the tune to "Somewhere Over the Rainbow" as he walked out of Buck's with a smile on his face.

CHAPTER **13**

We are what we think. All that we are arises with our thoughts. With our thoughts, we make the world.

—Gautama Buddha (c. 563–483 B.C.)

"Hello, Alan. Thanks for coming down here. Please have a seat," Oscar said. "As I told you, I appreciate you having had me over to your place to see your new program in action. It's impressive. I'm hoping I can get your help with my next presentation."

"Well, thanks for the compliment, Oscar. Putting it to use in your presentation could be a good test of how well it works on a large group." Alan stood up and walked over to a group of masks on the Oscar's office wall. "Why do people wear masks?"

"To hide who they really are," said Oscar.

"I'd like to try one."

"Be my guest."

Alan unhooked a dark-brown wooden mask with deep orange coloring on the forehead. He held it in front of his face and looked out through the eye slits. The mask was long and narrow, and its chin reached down to the top of Alan's abdomen.

"Interesting that you picked that one," said Oscar.

"Why's that?"

"It's fairly unusual. It was made to represent the face of an alien race that the tribe believes visited their early ancestors," said Oscar. "I've never had anyone in my office focus on that mask."

"It must remind me of something." Alan placed the mask back in its place on the wall. It did, in fact, remind Alan of something. It also made him think about how we all hide behind layers of desperation or diversion. He had hidden things about himself, and although he'd made strides to improve this, he continued to keep things—very important things—about himself from others. He wanted that to end.

Oscar walked toward a whiteboard in his office. "What I'm trying to do is offer a credible explanation about how and why people changed their thinking from one religion to another over time. If I just offer an academic explanation, people may see the logic of what I'm saying, but they won't visualize it and believe it. I need a way to get my audience to see what I'm talking about while I'm lecturing."

"Tell me a little more about what you're trying to do. Who's your audience?" asked Alan.

"In a word, 'academics.' Other people not unlike me. But don't be misled into thinking all academics are alike. These will be men and women, black and white, young and old, and, perhaps most importantly, 'believers' and 'nonbelievers' in organized religion and the existence of God."

"So we'll need to do something that makes your points while not directly challenging their core beliefs," Alan suggested.

"I want to show people how transitions could be made from one basic core belief held for centuries to another very different core belief." Oscar wrote out a flow diagram on the whiteboard.

"As amazing as my program is," Alan said, "it doesn't show what people think or how they think or any mental process."

"I understand," said Oscar. "But the thought process had to begin with concrete images before abstract concepts of God were ever conceived. We need to start with those concrete ideas and show how they evolved. There's no written history of the beginning of religion. Some people believe that such a history exists, and a good example is the Bible's book of Genesis and the story of Adam and Eve. Belief in those stories as actual histories of the beginning of the universe—or the evolution of humans—requires disregarding scientific facts. Originally, people worshiped things that seemed all-powerful to them. Objects such as the sun, the moon, and the stars are the focus of many early religions. Because the sun has the most influence on the lives of people, it's no surprise that it had the most influence on the formation of early religion. It isn't difficult to imagine why people worshipped the sun because of the influence it has on all living things."

"The sun still has an all-powerful influence on our lives. Why don't people still worship the sun?" asked Alan.

"That's the core question I want to address. The leaders of every current religion will tell you that their religion shows people the 'true way' or the 'true God,' and that, therefore, they gave up the old ways. For example, Christians will tell you that Jesus was the only Son of God and that this provided a compelling reason to follow the teachings of Jesus Christ as their Lord and Savior. There's some truth in what they say."

"Does that mean you believe Jesus was the Son of God?" asked Alan.

"That's a much more complex question than you might realize."

"How do you mean? It seems straightforward to me. Either you think Jesus is the Son of God, or you don't," Alan said. He saw things in black and white. Oscar's approach was filled with shades of gray, and Alan knew he could learn something from him. He appreciated that they were both minorities, very accomplished, and quite passionate about the positions they advocated. Alan was, in fact, a member of a minority even smaller than the gay community, but he wasn't willing to share that with Oscar.

"In the first place," Oscar responded, "when you ask the question, you assume I believe there's a God. More importantly, you assume that I know what your understanding of God is and you know what mine is. Those are big assumptions."

"Okay. I understand what you're saying. Let me break my question down a bit. Do you believe there's a God?" Alan asked.

"Regardless of how I answer the question, you won't have the answer you think you have. If I say yes, you would assume that I subscribe to the same ideas as you regarding the existence of some supernatural all-powerful being. If I say no, you'll assume I don't believe in the existence of what you believe God is."

"Oscar, you know that I don't know much about religion. I'm good at asking questions of computers. I know how to do that, and I realize that I don't have enough expertise in religion or God to ask you meaningful questions."

"Great. Then I've taught you more in a few minutes than I can teach most students in a semester. You've realized that we don't have a well-defined and commonly agreed-to vocabulary with which to discuss topics such Jesus and God. Most people will incorrectly assume that when they say a word such as 'God,' we know what they mean and that others accept the same meaning we assign to it. This is almost never the case."

"It's the same in the computer world, 'garbage in, garbage out.' Everything needs to be well defined, or neither the user nor the computer knows what's going on. Is all this going somewhere in terms of your presentation?" asked Alan.

"Absolutely. You need to have a better understanding of my thinking to help me convey my thoughts to others."

"Do you believe that Jesus is the Son of God or not?" Alan laughed in understanding of why it was a meaningless question.

"I know that people believed that the sun in the sky was God and that it deserved their worship. Over time, people made a transition from worshipping objects such as the sun to worshipping concepts such as Jesus being the Son of God."

"I'm sure you know that's going to require a lot of explaining."

"Absolutely. People want to believe in something greater than themselves. It's easy to believe there's a 'Great and Powerful Wizard of Oz.' The sun served that purpose for centuries in many civilizations. Take the Aztecs. They believed they needed to cut out a human heart every day as a sacrifice to the sun God to make sure the sun would rise the next day. It's difficult to imagine people being more fearful of a God. However, as fearful as they were and as 'great and powerful' as the sun might have been to them, the sun became predictable and definable. It's so predictable that another civilization arranged massive stones at Stonehenge to show precisely where the sun would rise at the beginning of spring. Let me show you."

Oscar brought up an image of Stonehenge on the computer screen at his desk. He pointed to the space between two stones where the sunlight shone directly through on the first day of spring.

"If you look at how the stones are arranged, there's no doubt that the people who built Stonehenge knew a lot more about the sun than the simple fact that it rose in the morning and set in the evening. They understood how the sun moved along the horizon and exactly when and where it rose and set every day."

"So now you're going to tell me why Stonehenge is in such disrepair and why people no longer go there to worship the sun," said Alan.

"The answer is in the precision they used to define God. They originally saw the sun as all-powerful and mysterious. If you think about how life was lived thousands of years ago, it's easy to understand how a bright ball in the sky might be feared and worshipped."

"Makes sense to me," Alan interrupted. "I've always been totally captivated by things I see in the sky."

"Over time, people developed the ability to define precisely what the sun did, or to say it differently, they figured out what God—or in their case, the sun—was going to do and when God was going to do it. This not only removed the mystery, but it allowed people to understand that the sun did not have free will. The sun always did the same thing in precisely the same way. After Stonehenge was built, this knowledge was not limited to just a few people. Anyone could go to Stonehenge and see where and when 'God' was going to be at a given point in time. The mystery was gone, and when that mystery disappeared, there was no longer a 'God' to worship. People had used reasoning to pull back the curtain on the Wizard of Oz and show that the man standing behind it had no powers beyond what they themselves already had."

"Well, that's easy enough to see with something as well understood as the sun rising and setting. But today people believe in God as the creator of man. It's much more complex."

"Yes, Alan, it's more complex but still explainable. Today many people who believe in God think that everything was created by 'intelligent design.' People support that theory by asking a group of questions: 'Do you know a bridge built without a bridge builder? Do you know a ship built without a shipbuilder?' These analogies are intended to lead us to the conclusion that some intelligent entity such as God was necessary to create everything. At one point in history, such as before Charles Darwin, this may have seemed logical. However, now that natural selection is understood, 'intelligent design' is clearly nothing more than a fairy tale, and these questions answer nothing."

"Hold on. I'm not saying I agree with the 'intelligent design' position, but the questions make a point, don't you agree?"

"I don't agree that they make a logical point," said Oscar. "Biologists could give a better explanation of how natural selection works, but basically, genetics simply makes a very large number of variations. Most of those variations don't survive. Over time, the environment selects the best, or most adaptive, variation."

"Why is that explanation better than the one offered by the creationists?"

"If God did create everything, it still leaves us wondering where God came from. Natural selection may not explain everything, but it does explain much of where living things originated. It fits much better, as compared to the 'intelligent design' idea, which is only a belief and doesn't even rise to the level of a theory, because a true theory must have some supporting factual basis. Evolution and natural selection explain why there's a definite genetic relationship between living things. It explains why ninety-nine percent of the life that ever existed on the planet is now extinct. It explains how and why many living things have superfluous components. If God created all living things, and God is perfect, why would most of what He created be extinct now? And why would so many living things have superfluous parts? Would God do this to confuse us? As science progresses, fewer and fewer people will need a God to explain things. They'll no longer need a Wizard of Oz."

"That's interesting. I see where you're going with this. You want to show your audience the thinking of people at different points in time. Specifically, what their thinking was when they pulled back the curtain on their religion." Alan walked over to Oscar's computer, which was showing the different images of Stonehenge. "Can you send me all these pictures?"

"Sure," said Oscar, "I'll send you these and a lot more. But understand that I don't want this to come off as though I'm trying to persuade anyone about anything. I want it to look as though I'm just presenting the facts."

"Do you want these people speaking in their native tongues or modern-day English?" Alan asked.

"I've given that some thought. If they speak in their native tongues, I'll need subtitles, but if they speak in perfect English, it will seem too staged. So I want them to speak in the international language of science."

"What's that?"

"It's broken English. I've been to science conferences all over the world. The researchers are from everywhere, and English is not the native language for most of them. But English is the only language of which they all have at least a limited understanding—so they end up speaking English. Their English is 'broken.'"

"I think I get it. You figure it will sound more real if they all speak the way nonnative-English-speaking scientists sound," said Alan.

"I got the idea back at your place when you talked about merging different people. I'd like to merge people and their speaking patterns. If I send you some dialogue and some basic ideas on what they'd be wearing, can you make me a video?"

"The dialogue you send will be key to making this work. I can create the characters to speak the words, but what they say will need to ring true."

"I get it," said Oscar.

Alan had heard Oscar talk about many topics and felt that he had a natural persuasive ability. The two of them talked on for some time and bounced ideas off each other. When Alan left, they had some specific dialogue written down and an outline of ideas that Oscar agreed to develop further.

Before leaving, Alan took the same mask off the wall and put it on. He turned his phone to camera mode and asked Oscar to take a photo of him wearing the mask. He contemplated telling Oscar why it fascinated him, but he wasn't ready.

CHAPTER 14

We don't receive wisdom; we must discover it for ourselves after a journey that no one can take for us or spare us.

—Marcel Proust (1871–1922)

"Can I have the table toward the back over by the fireplace? I'm waiting for some friends," Herbert said, arriving back at the City Pub.

"Sure thing. Can I get you something while you're waiting?" asked a young waitress with chestnut-brown hair.

"Certainly. I really love the hand-crafted draft beer here, but I'm not a big fan of drinking dark beer with a burger. Nothing as dark as your hair. Something in between that and a platinum blonde," said Herbert.

"I've got something in mind, Devil's Canyon Blonde Ale. I know the brewer there. He's really good." The waitress walked toward the bar, passing Alan on the way in.

"Hello, Herbert. How are you?" Alan approached Herbert with his hand outstretched. They shook hands, and Alan sat down next to Herbert, facing out toward the front door.

"Well, I'll be much better when my beer gets here. How have you been, Alan?"

"Fine. I want to say a few things before the others get here. You know what I wanted to use my videos for. Am I going to get what I need out of this?" he asked.

"Absolutely. No one besides me knows what you're looking for. I'll keep it that way. When the rest of this plan comes out, you'll see that you'll be getting more than you asked for—much more."

"I want to show you something." Alan pulled out his phone and pulled up the photo Oscar had taken of him wearing the mask.

"What is it?"

"It's me wearing a tribal mask intended to represent aliens that visited the tribe long ago. I *knew* others had seen them."

"Maybe you're right. But just keep it to yourself for now. If you can hold on a bit longer, I'll get you what you're looking for."

"I'll be patient for now."

"Have you been fooling anyone with your videos?" asked Herbert.

"I met with Oscar, and we're working on a video together. He's doing a big presentation to a group of academic types on how and why people change their thinking on religion over time."

Herbert did not show his surprise. He wondered if Korin had told the others about his childhood experience at the hands of the priest. It wasn't something he wanted shared. For now, Herbert wasn't overly concerned. He would first make a gentle inquiry.

"Really, Alan? I had no idea you had any interest in religion."

"You're right. I don't—at least as far as organized religion goes—but I've always wondered why people think the way they do about religion."

This response was fairly innocuous, but Herbert wondered if it was leading to questions about how his childhood experience had turned him against religion. He led the conversation in a direction he wanted. "That's easy, Alan. Most folks believe they have no choice. They believe they have to think that way. Most people think as they're told. Almost every member of any organized religion is following the same religion as his parents and grandparents. If people weren't such sheep and realized they had the opportunity to think about what they were buying into, very few would be members. But they still believe the same things they were taught from the time they were small children. They believe that if they're not members of their parents' denomination, they'll burn in hell."

"I don't disagree with you," said Alan. "But that doesn't explain why so many people believe in God or why people believed in other Gods at one time and then changed. Oscar's got some interesting ideas on that, and I see this as a chance to test my software in front of a large group."

"Speaking of Oscar, that's him, and Korin's coming in now." Herbert partially stood and waved to his friends.

Korin and Oscar approached the table at the same time the waitress brought Herbert's beer. Korin embraced Herbert and then Alan and turned to the waitress. "I'll have what he's having," she said, pointing to Herbert's beer. "Do you guys want the same thing?"

"Sure," said Oscar. Alan nodded in agreement, and the waitress went off for three more beers.

"Herbert, I'm guessing that you won't have anything quite as amazing to tell us as you did last time we met," said Korin.

"Well, you'd be surprised at what some clear thinking and a lot of money can do. I'm still working on the same basic concept, but I had a new idea on how it might be developed. I've got people working around the clock on the development part." Herbert raised his beer for a long drink.

"What's the new idea?" Alan asked.

Herbert had many things going on inside his head. Some of them were as important to him as his work on the current science project. However, as in his conversation with Dan, he wasn't comfortable talking about those other matters. This was making him feel increasingly guilty, and a bit lonely.

"I tried for a long time to use equations to figure out how the field I created could move something as massive as a bulldozer. It just can't be done. Once I understood that it couldn't be done, I knew why. The answer is that the field can't move anything within space/time as we know it. It allows entry into a separate dimension that isn't part of the three-dimensional space we experience."

"So what's important about that?" asked Alan. "How does providing entry to another dimension allow you to move a big bulldozer?"

"It doesn't move it. What happens is that it allows it to leave our dimensional space and slip into another dimensional space—one that we can't see. I'll call it a second dimensional space. It then comes back from the second dimensional space to wherever I refocus the field in our dimensional space. Once I understood this, I had the idea of focusing the field at two different places at the same time."

"But isn't that what you were already doing?" asked Korin. "Isn't that how you quickly moved the bulldozer from one dimensional space to another?"

"No. I was thinking in more conventional terms, so I focused the field around the bulldozer initially, and then in a fraction of a second later, I focused it in a place where I wanted it to reappear. I just never thought to focus the field in two different places at the same time," said Herbert.

"I would think that if you focus the field in two different places at the same time, it would stay where it is," said Alan.

"Well, you'd be right," said Herbert. "But it will also exist in the second dimensional space."

"So does the field make two bulldozers?" asked Korin.

"I don't think there are two bulldozers. That would require the creation of matter," said Herbert. "I'm not sure what happens at this point. It could be that all the matter of the bulldozer flips back and forth between our dimensional space and the second dimensional space so rapidly that it seems that there are two bulldozers. I found that it's possible to make one object appear to be in two different places at the same time. But I don't think there are really two of them. Physicists have known for some time that one particle can be in two places at the same time."

"Herbert, I don't think of myself as an uninformed person, but I've never heard of something being in two places at once," Korin said. "I never leave one of these meetings with you guys without learning something new."

"Well, I never leave one of these meetings without getting a great burger and a couple of beers," said Herbert. "But back to the two-places-at-once story. I'm having a sphere built that'll be big enough to hold four people. When it's done, I'll see if I can put the field around it and put it in two places at once."

"Maybe this *is* more amazing than last month. Are you saying we could get in the sphere and be in two places at the same time?" Korin asked.

"There are many possibilities. One is that two objects are actually present at the same time, but in different dimensional spaces. But it seems more likely that one object essentially vibrates at the speed atoms vibrate, and that a single object moves from one dimensional space to another at that vibrational speed. There are other possibilities, as well.

"If it works, the really interesting part might just be one person realizing two different consciousnesses at the same time," said Oscar. "Would it be two separate people with two separate consciousnesses or two people with a single consciousness? This is physics that becomes spiritual, and it's the type of event that could change the way people view religion."

"Oscar, I understand what you're saying about it possibly changing religion," said Alan. "As you said in your presentation, science influences religion by allowing people to understand a mystery. Once they understand it, it's no longer a religion; it's science."

Herbert didn't visibly react to this. He didn't want the others to see him as a person out to bring down the Catholic Church as revenge. However, he took great joy in hearing that if things worked as he hoped, religion could soon be very different. He reflected back on his childhood experiences. As he did, he had reservations about what he was planning. This was a far bigger event than shooting a cardinal with a BB gun, and if it went wrong, the consequences were sure to make the final years of his life quite dismal. Regardless, he had to try it. He owed it to himself.

"I thought being pregnant was an incredibly interesting experience," Korin said, "but this could be spectacular. If there were really two of me, or, as you say, Herbert, one of me in two places at once, that would change the way we all think about ourselves and about each other."

"I hadn't thought about the social aspects. But I did think maybe I'd be able to enjoy the same beer twice." Herbert raised his glass and signaled for a toast with his friends. He was acting. He wanted them to see him as someone who now contemplated the social aspects of his work. Although it was becoming increasingly difficult, he even wanted to think of himself in that way. His thoughts had carried him far beyond the pure science of the project, and he believed he had to keep those thoughts to himself in order to get the end results he wanted.

"When we're done eating, could we go over to your place, Herbert, and see what you're building?" asked Korin.

"Sure. I've got a crew there, but they think they're building a planetarium. So don't say anything that blows my cover on that."

With a plan in place, the four reverted to conversation about everyday matters. Alan asked Korin about her kids, and she asked him about Jeremy's acting. They discussed the French fries, the beer, and even Korin's new haircut. Despite the small talk, Herbert knew that all of them were thinking about the extraordinary events they had been experiencing. He knew they would be wondering where it was all going and what they could do to steer it in the best possible direction. They each had enough life experience to know that opportunities were wonderful things to have. The possibilities before them now were all-consuming, and, at this point, Herbert believed he was alone in knowing where it might lead.

CHAPTER 15

*Courage is the price that life exacts for granting peace.
The soul that knows it not, knows no release from little
things; knows not the livid loneliness of fear.*

—Amelia Earhart (1897–1937)

Herbert arrived first to open the gate. Alan drove in, and Korin followed with Oscar.

"You can park over there." Herbert pointed to open spaces beside two pickup trucks. Alan pulled in, followed by Korin.

"You seem to have a lot going on here," Korin said as she approached Herbert.

Herbert led them to an area between Buildings #1 and #2, where a sphere twenty feet in diameter sat. Its outer surface had a smooth, mirror-like quality with a single, small opening into which some makeshift stairs led. Half of the sphere was below ground level, so the buildings shielded it from the view of neighbors. The exposed, upper surface was an unusual color of muted pink.

"What's with the pink color?" asked Alan. "Is it some kind of gay statement?"

"If you want it to be a gay statement, so be it," Herbert answered. "It's called 'Mountbatten Pink.' It was developed during World War II and named after the general. It's the best color to camouflage something in the dark—it's very difficult to see in low light. Turns out the military didn't want to paint their ships and tanks pink because it seemed too feminine. Because I do eventually plan to use this as a planetarium, I thought it would be interesting to color it to blend into the darkness. Besides, I liked the whole World War II story with General Mountbatten. I'll tell it to you another time if you're interested."

"The weird things you know never cease to amaze me," Korin said. Herbert's reference to a historical event got her thinking about the hoax he wanted to pull off. Regardless of what he'd told her, she believed he was dramatically affected by what he had experienced as a child. Although she had a clear financial motivation regarding why *she* wanted to perpetrate the hoax, she needed to tap into the motivations of the others to get their complete cooperation. "Can we go inside the sphere?" she asked.

"Sure," Herbert said, "It's not finished, but it will give you an idea of what I'm doing."

He led them into the sphere, where the floor was about four feet below its center-line. Portions of the floor were transparent, revealing electronic equipment below. Large, flat screens rose above the floor-line all along the inner circumference. There were four windows in the form of small, horizontal slits equally spaced around the sphere. It was a work in progress. To Korin, the project could be described as a precisely arranged group of high-end electronics put in place with detailed craftsmanship.

"It will contain everything four people need to live for a week," said Herbert. "The communications equipment is all state-of-the-art, and although the windows are very small and can be sealed completely from the inside, cameras positioned around the sphere will show everything outside on the screens."

"It's very impressive, Herbert," said Korin. "Assuming the field works as planned, what do you plan to do with the sphere?"

"I'm the science guy," said Herbert. "I'll make it work. I'm hoping for some ideas from you on what we'll do with it."

"Let's go somewhere where we can all talk privately away from the workers," said Korin. "I have a plan that will require a lot of work and considerable risk."

Korin reflected back on the hovering bulldozer and imagined that if the sphere hovered in the same way, without a sound, those seeing it would imagine the sphere to be a spaceship with aliens inside. She saw the possibility of Herbert accomplishing a hoax that matched the magnitude of his invention. In her mind's eye, she saw the four of them moving in the sphere and pretending to be aliens. Herbert's unstated motivation of revenge on the Catholic Church could be realized if he could tell the world there was no Santa Claus, Easter Bunny, or Jesus rising from the dead. He could revel in telling everyone there was no talking serpent in a tree and no Moses parting the Red Sea. There were so many aspects of religion that were based on nothing more than fairy tales, and religious wars had caused—and continued to cause—so much bloodshed. Would such a plan, she wondered, let Herbert go behind the curtain as Dorothy had in the *Wizard of Oz* and show the world that religion was all based on smoke and light?

They left the sphere, and after a short walk, they were back in the room of Building #1 where they'd first met to hear Herbert talk about his work.

"I've known the three of you long enough to understand something about your basic personalities," Korin began.

"You're smart, creative people, but you're all rebels. You don't conform to the way society in general thinks about things. You all enjoy a good joke and revel in fooling others from time to time. All of you realize what an enormous opportunity we have here."

"Making this sphere doesn't seem directed toward making money for anyone. What kind of opportunity are you seeing?" asked Oscar.

"The money will come from the patents covering the nanotrons. In a few years, every computer in the world will run off nanotrons, and royalties on that alone will make billions. However, I'm not just talking about making money as the opportunity. The opportunity is in using this technology in a way that changes to the way people think," said Korin.

"I understand your wanting to change society. But that won't make us money. What will we be selling to make money? The patent only covers the nanotrons, and you can't even see them," Oscar protested.

"You can't see electricity either," Korin noted, "but you buy it. Trust me, the money will be there. But if we work this right, we have a chance to change the world in a positive way. With all that in mind, here's my plan: We position the sphere where it will be noticed immediately. Although we're careful not to say so, everyone will assume it's an alien ship, a UFO. Because of the way the sphere moves, we won't have to say we're extraterrestrials, but we won't deny it. Once communications are established, we'll have a lot of power. The world will be listening. They'll ask questions, and we'll offer answers.

"Alan's video technology can provide answers. The video answers will draw on Oscar's knowledge of religions. We'll use the videos to show that religions are not based on reality. We'll show the world that Jesus rising from the dead is as make-believe as the Easter bunny bringing eggs."

When Korin stopped talking, she realized she'd said more than she intended. She'd contemplated sending up one small trial balloon after another until she felt comfortable with saying more. However, now that she'd put a bold plan out in front of the group, she felt more unsure of the idea than ever and desperately wanted to know what they thought. There was nothing but silence, which to her seemed to last forever. She couldn't interpret the looks on their faces.

Finally, Oscar broke the silence. "Korin, are you feeling all right? This isn't the sort of thing you would say."

"I'm fine. I know it's very unusual. But this is an unusual situation."

"Let's put aside how risky it is and focus on the religion part first," Oscar continued. "Even if we could pull off looking like an alien spaceship, why would people believe aliens' answers about their religions?"

"This is where your knowledge of religion and Alan's new video technology come in." Korin responded. "You know more about the details of historically unexplained religious events than anyone. With your knowledge and Alan's videos, the evidence will be compelling. Not everyone who sees what we present will change their beliefs, but many will, and it will create enormous doubt in the minds of many others. Oscar, you've always said that if you take the mystery out of religion, people will no longer believe. If it's presented in a way that appears factually accurate and treats all religions the same, it will work." Korin moved her hands as though she were holding the idea in front of her and forming it for the others to accept.

"I, for one, love it." Herbert slapped his hands against the top of his thighs.

"I'm more than a little skeptical that this has any real possibility of working," Alan said. "I'm not so sure someone wouldn't just decide we're hostile and start shooting at us— especially if we say things that upset their religion."

"It's true that more blood has been spilled over religion than anything else," agreed Oscar.

"I'm not saying there's no risk," said Korin. "But Herbert is for it, and it's his invention providing the opportunity. Would you guys be willing at least to work on a plan for doing it? If, after we've planned it, it seems doomed for failure or some-one has a better idea, we change our plan."

"I could live with that," said Alan.

"I must admit your plans have been very successful thus far in life," added Oscar.

"I'll be going forward with work on the sphere regardless of the plan," said Herbert. "I can think of some modifica-tions that would help. I'm not interested in getting shot at or blown up, but I may be able to add some features that will deal with that contingency."

"Herbert, when do you think you'll finish the sphere?" Korin asked.

"Maybe another month. If you've ever had any construc-tion work done, you know it always goes slower and costs more than you expected."

"We've got a lot of planning to do between now and then," said Korin. "Oscar, what if you work with Alan on videos that answer questions people might ask about religion?"

"We were doing that already," Oscar answered, "for a pre-sentation I'm giving."

"No, don't show the video you're working on to anyone. If you do, someone may make a connection," said Korin.

"I understand," Alan said. "Also, if I'm going to do this, I want to include something in the answer about Jesus having gay sex."

"I've got no issues with gay sex, Alan," said Korin. "But if we try to push too far away from what people believe and want to believe, we may accomplish nothing. The best chance for success will be with a story that fits with the current version but leaves out any supernatural powers."

"I agree," said Oscar, "but most people are smarter than you think. No one understands what happens when we die, and, therefore, no one knows what rules to follow while alive in order to determine where, if anywhere, he goes after death. The accepted Christian idea is that Jesus is a loving and forgiving being. Having Him make positive comments about gays would not be a stretch."

"Understood," said Korin. "I think we've got our work cut out for us. We should not email each other on this, other than to set up a meeting. Any communications should be face to face. Let's act as though this is the 'quiet period' before an initial public offering. Take the usual advice of litigation counsel that anything written down can, and probably will, be discovered by the other side. And with this project, everyone beyond the four of us is 'the other side.'"

"That works for me," said Herbert. "I've been in a 'quiet period' for a long time. Continuing that won't be a problem."

"Sure," said Alan. "I did tell Jeremy about my video work. But not telling him about this plan is probably a very good idea. He would worry about me way too much."

"Why are you all looking at me?" Oscar said. "It makes me nervous when a bunch of white folks start staring at me."

"Very funny, Oscar," said Korin. "Let's go. We'll be in touch."

Korin wanted to end the meeting before too many questions arose. She had an initial go-ahead from all of them. The further along the plan went, the less likely anyone would pull out. She felt more alive and hopeful than she ever had. Making money was important, but she realized there was an energy and sense of adventure about the project that was changing her view of the world.

Korin walked out with Oscar, leaving Herbert and Alan behind. As she left her fears about the risks as well as the total absurdity of the hoax returned.

CHAPTER 16

Better than a thousand hollow words,
is one word that brings peace.

—Gautama Buddha (c. 563–483 B.C.)

"So, Oscar," said Korin. "Let's use this ride back to come up with ideas on what an alien might say about religion on earth."

Oscar looked at Korin but said nothing. He was concerned about her idea. He wasn't sure he would get all the money he wanted. More importantly, he didn't know if he would get it as quickly as he needed it.

"Before we talk about what aliens might say about religion, let's talk about the business part of this. I want to put something in place that gives me a better idea of how and when I'm going to be compensated, even though we're only patenting the nanotrons."

"I understand," said Korin. "I told you that Herbert put a hundred-million-dollar pre-money valuation on the company. That's a ridiculously low valuation, even though we're patenting only the nanotrons. He could just as easily have said a hundred billion dollars. My point is that Herbert knows this will generate more money than he needs and, for the right person and reason, he'll be generous with it."

"Herb has made donations to Stanford that indirectly funded some of my work, so I know he's a generous guy. But those were charitable deductions for him. Here, I'm asking for something just for me. How can I be sure I'll get a meaningful financial remuneration?" asked Oscar.

"I'll write up an equity agreement tonight. I'll talk to Herbert about it, and ask him to give you one percent. If the company is worth a hundred billion dollars, your share would be worth one billion dollars. Will that work for you?"

"Sure. I had thought this would be a difficult issue. If you can make the one percent happen, it will certainly be enough, though I do want to make sure the agreement gets written up. But is that it? You're making money based only on the value of the company?" Oscar asked.

"You'll own stock in the company after we make all this public. The value of the stock will be determined in the marketplace, and you can sell your stock."

"But that will take a long time, won't it?"

"That depends on how all this unfolds."

"Is there some way I could get some of the money sooner?" Oscar asked.

"Interesting question. I was thinking of hedging my bet on this. We could make a lot of money by buying commodities," Korin responded.

"Explain."

"I'm not sure about doing this, but we could buy gold, wheat, cattle, or just about anything. If people think aliens are coming, the value of all of them will skyrocket."

"So why not do it?" asked Oscar.

"I don't want it traced back to me. I may be able to prevent that possibility. I'm just not sure. Let me get back to you on it. For now, keep it to yourself."

"Do you want to talk about what aliens might say now?" Oscar asked.

"You must have some ideas on what aspects of religion an alien might focus on."

"All religions have some form of prayer. An alien might be curious about prayer," said Oscar.

"Why is that?"

"First, prayers are just another word for wishing—and everyone knows wishing doesn't make it so. Calling a wish a prayer doesn't change that, and every religion is based on prayer," said Oscar. "For example, I could say I wish I could get into your panties today, or I pray to God I get into your panties today. To an alien or anyone looking at it logically, both are the same because you—and not some supernatural entity—control the result."

"I get the message. Religion is prayer- or wish-based. What else?"

"Second, all religions have some idea about how the earth, the stars, and mankind were created. None of them comes close to proposing anything that could be real. Science doesn't know everything about how the universe was created, but the Big Bang and natural selection are not theories. They're facts. It's just that the whole thing is so complex that not all the details are known."

"What else?"

"I was saving the best for last. All religions are the primary cause of sexual repression. If you haven't guessed, that's the real reason I favor your plan."

Oscar was and always had been a very sexual person. He was attracted to Korin in many ways. She understood this about him, and he knew he could use this to divert Korin from focusing on why he was agreeing to the plan.

"Sometimes I can't tell if you're joking or serious," Korin said.

"Oh, I'm serious about all three. I'm praying for the Big Bang and know if it doesn't happen right away, religious sexual repression is the reason." Oscar leaned over and kissed Korin on the neck. She smiled and, at the same time, pushed him back in his seat.

"Korin, I've got a serious question. Why do you think people will stop believing in their religion just because they think aliens from another world tell them a new story line? Religious people are incredibly prejudiced about their beliefs."

"It's because we're going to *show* them, not just tell them. You'll agree there was a great deal of prejudice going on during the O.J. Simpson trial, right?"

"Sure. On both sides."

"One of the reasons O.J. got off was that the jury believed there was a lot of police prejudice. But what really clinched the acquittal was when O.J. got up and tried on the bloody glove, and it wouldn't fit. Do you remember?"

"Sure. It was the whole 'If it doesn't fit, you must acquit' defense."

"What if I could show the jury *why* it didn't fit? What if I showed them a video of O.J. talking to a doctor about his arthritis? What if the doctor told O.J. his hands would swell up if he failed to take his medication? What if I later showed O.J. flushing the medication down the toilet?"

"The 'If it doesn't fit, you must acquit' defense goes out the window."

"Right. I know some people will still ignore the evidence. But if we poke enough holes in the case, some will be convinced."

"So why not just show the jury a video of O.J. killing Nicole? Wouldn't that be more convincing?"

"They would think the video was faked. There needs to be a diversion. You have to show them just enough so they draw their own conclusions. If we show them too much, they'll think up reasons why it's not so. Remember, whatever we send out, they'll believe it's coming from aliens. They won't know if the aliens should be trusted. So we need to show them bits and pieces that they put together themselves to reach the conclusions we want them to reach."

"So you see it as similar to making an argument to a jury when there's only circumstantial evidence?" asked Oscar.

"Many things in life require that same kind of skill. I've made many successful presentations to venture capitalists. They won't invest if you show them everything. You need to strategically feed them just the right pieces, and let them come to their own conclusion. It makes them feel smart. They believe they figured it out and didn't have the answer shoved down their throats."

Oscar understood the importance of what Korin was saying. She was serious, and she relied on him to give her answers. At the same time, he was enjoying the moment and wanted her to do the same. "What I wouldn't give to be shoving something down your throat right now!"

"Are you even listening to anything I'm saying?" Korin reached over and slapped Oscar's thigh hard, but playfully.

"I'm listening. I'm just thinking of something different. You can't blame me for that," he said.

"I know. But you need to understand I want this to be successful. I want it more than I've ever wanted anything. To make it work, I need you to put your heart and soul in it as well."

"In order to make this work, I'll need to be prepared to answer any question from anyone in the world. I'll need to know everything about every possible question the world might ask. I'm a smart guy, but that's a tall order."

"We'll cheat," Korin said matter-of-factly. "It'll be easy. They'll never be able to decide who should be in charge of asking the questions, let alone what they should ask. Can you imagine the world agreeing to do something in a focused way? We can use their bickering to our advantage. I'm guessing Alan can put together a program that will receive and sort questions on the internet. Then we just present a list of the most frequently asked questions. We'll limit the number of questions to whatever we decide on. We can figure that out ahead of time. If you know the questions, you should be able to come up with good answers."

Oscar felt uneasy with the idea of "cheating." He believed cheating was something he should never participate in himself and should discourage in others. But he trusted Korin, and rationalized that she meant something different from the meaning he gave the word. Overall, he wanted to go forward with the plan and saw her idea as a way of getting some things he wanted. "Whatever we do will be artificial to a degree," he said. "I know a lot more about religion than most people. Why don't I write the questions?"

"Now the professor in you is coming out. Don't treat this as an academic exercise where everything has to fit a certain form. If you just listen to what people ask, you'll know what their concerns are. You'll identify their doubts and can take advantage of them."

"All right. All right. I get it. Give me a break, Korin. I'm not used to business deals, let alone a hoax. You're going to have to lead me through this—and, I think, you'll be bringing Herbert and Alan along as well."

"I can do that, and more. I can and will make this plan successful. If you guys trust me and listen to me, we can do something different, exciting, and potentially very worthwhile."

"Korin, I have to tell you, I never thought you'd come up with a plan that connected Herbert's work with Alan's, let alone figure out how to meaningfully work me in. It's all very clever."

"Thank you for saying so. But save the flattery until we make this work. I'll expect a lot of compliments then."

"Tell me this, Korin... What caused you put this particular group together? There's no way you could have known there'd be a plan all three of us could work on. What did you see in the three of us?"

"I'm good at figuring people out. When I meet someone, I try not to prejudice my thinking about him in either a negative or positive way. Then, as I get to know him, I usually see aspects that make me like him less. There are very few exceptions; the three of you are among them. The more I know about each of you, the more I like you. That was unusual enough for me to want to get us all together."

"Why three men? Why not another woman?"

"Oscar, I'm not sure how to answer that. Maybe I like being the center of attention—another woman might steal some of it. I'm joking, or at least I think I am. It's Herbert's project, and he had already involved Alan somewhat. I picked you because you're the best person for what we're going to do. I intuitively knew that if I got the three of you together, something great would come of it. Does that make sense?"

"I can buy that. Let me ask you something else. Where do you want the alien spaceship to land?"

"My first thought was the National Mall in Washington, D.C., near or over the Washington Monument. There's a lot of open space there, and I like the image of the sphere above the monument. If Herbert can do *two* spheres up there, one on either side of the column, it would be too funny not to do it."

Oscar laughed and hit his thighs with both hands. He leaned back in his seat and watched Korin drive down Interstate 280 toward Stanford. "I like that image, as well. But I think we might be taken more seriously if we didn't look like the world's biggest penis. What about places outside the U.S.? The Emperor's Palace in Tokyo has even more open space, and it's surrounded by more people than you'd have as your immediate audience in D.C."

"That could work," Korin agreed. "A side benefit is that not many Japanese people have guns, so it's less likely someone will shoot at us. Where else do you think it would work?"

"I've always liked Amsterdam. The people are very tolerant of everyone from everywhere. I can't say that about many Americans and certainly not about the Japanese."

"That's an interesting idea," said Korin. "We could use their tolerance as a reason why we, as aliens, chose to go there. It could help make an important point. We can all get behind pulling this off in a way that promotes tolerance and condemns intolerance. The four of us could be unknown heroes for not only reducing sexism and racism, but also discrimination against gays and nerds. Alan and Herbert would have to be enthusiastic about that plan."

"Something directed to sexism or racism isn't focused on the original antireligion plan."

"First, I never thought of doing something against religion *per se,*"Korin said. "In every field, when people discover that the basis of their thinking isn't correct, they change. I want to show the world that at least some of what certain religions believe is incorrect. But some of the basic ideas such as 'doing unto others what you would have them do unto you' are valuable. I don't want to change that.

"Second, religion is the basis for much of the world's intolerance. Therefore, promoting greater tolerance and explaining that many specific, unique features of individual religions are false are two very compatible ideas. If people can see that the important parts of different religions are all the same, they just could become more tolerant of each other. So I don't see my wanting to promote tolerance as a lack of focus on the original idea of debunking certain aspects of religion. I see it as the underlying concept of what I want to achieve."

"I'm following you. So far we're considering the Mall in Washington, D.C., the Emperor's Palace grounds in Tokyo, and Amsterdam. How about Mecca, Saudi Arabia? We could put it right above the Ka'aba."

"What's the Ka'aba?"

"It's a cube-shaped building. All Muslims who are able, and can afford to, are supposed to make at least one pilgrimage to Mecca in their lifetime. This pilgrimage is one of the Five Pillars of Islam. The Ka'aba was originally built by Abraham and his son Ishmael, and all prayer is made in the direction of this place."

"That would certainly get the attention of the Muslim world. For the same reason, perhaps the Vatican in Rome would work, or Jerusalem in Israel."

"There are many possible religious centers," Oscar said, "and then there are national capitals, population centers, and educational institutes. There are so many possibilities. We need to think about what we're trying to achieve and the potential impact of being in one place and not another. Certainly being over the United Nations building in New York would be a possibility. Whatever you think about the UN, it does have representatives from around the world."

"You're right, Oscar. There are simply too many possibilities and too many unknown factors that could make picking one place better than another. Assuming Herbert can put us in more than one place at the same time, I had thought of being in multiple places at once. But that may just multiply the number of things that can go wrong. I like the idea of the UN building. If we were from outer space and knew anything about earth, it would be a logical choice. Let's not spend too much time on this now. Let's go with the UN and have other places in mind—places we might 'visit' while on earth to create a certain effect."

"Let's think about it further," Oscar agreed. "For now, we'll say it's the UN building. If we think of something better, we'll change the plan. We could start at the UN and then give our answers at different times from different places on earth. If we're answering a question about Islam, we do it from over the Ka'aba. If it's a question about Christianity, we do it from over Saint Peter's Square at the Vatican or from a religious site in Jerusalem. It will create the impression that the aliens go to the correct place to relate the factual information they provide in their answers."

"Oscar, I like that idea. I like it a lot. We'll need to put some thought into where we would answer a question about the 'Big Bang,' but we'll figure that out."

"How about Hiroshima?"

"I'm not sure if you're trying to be amusing with that, Oscar, but I doubt many people, at least in Japan, would think it's funny."

The drive passed by quickly for Oscar. When he drove the route by himself, he enjoyed the view of the grass- and tree-covered hills. The scenery looked too rural for a route through a major population center. At one point, he glanced at the smooth surface of the local reservoir and imagined what it might be like to spend an afternoon there with Korin. But he thought it would never happen. "Well, I think this has been a productive drive back. There's my car over there, Korin."

"Okay, I see it. Here we are." Korin pulled off 280 and into the parking lot of a building complex at the Sand Hill Road exit. "I'll send you an email about getting together."

Before he got out of her car, Korin unbuckled her seat belt so she could lean over and kiss Oscar passionately. They held the kiss and continued to hold it. Oscar longed for the same kind of passion in his own marriage. Neither of them wanted to say goodbye, and in their kiss, as always, each said something to the other.

"That wasn't your usual kiss. Your mind is somewhere else. I think I know where," said Oscar softly in Korin's ear as he pulled away.

"Sure, it's on the project."

"Korin, it's not the project. It's your doubt about doing it at all. You're a rational person and this plan is something you have grave reservation about."

"You're right, but I can't tell Herbert. I know he wants something like this, and without his support there won't be any company," said Korin and she leaned back in her seat and covered her face with both hands.

"I understand, but don't do it if it makes no sense to you. Give it some thought. There's no need to decide right now. If you want to talk about it I'll be there for you," said Oscar as he opened the car door and left.

CHAPTER 17

Work out your own salvation. Do not depend on others.

—Gautama Buddha (c. 563–483 B.C.)

Korin arrived at home to find Evan and Camille sitting on the floor playing a video game. They sat near a floor-to-ceiling window that extended the entire length of the living room. Large oak trees outside filled the window frame, and the southern part of the San Francisco Bay appeared a few miles in the distance.

"Hi, Mom," said Camille.

"Hi, guys." Korin bent down to kiss each on the side of the face. She loved being with them and seeing them interact. "Who's winning?"

"Who do you think?" Camille answered. "He's always the winner." There was no resentment in her voice. If anything, there was pride mixed with a sense of well-being. Camille felt very special just knowing that her brother excelled at video games. She herself didn't care much for any of them, but she did love her brother.

"You're such a sweetheart." Korin leaned over to embrace and kiss her daughter again.

There was no answer from Camille. Korin often wondered if she appreciated her mother's compliments or just assumed that was what Mom did.

In that small exchange, Korin understood what might be the biggest challenge of her plan. Camille played video games with her brother solely because she loved him and it was the right thing to do. She didn't think she'd go to hell if she didn't play with him or to heaven if she did. However, Korin understood the biggest lie of all behind religion: people only acted positively, generously, and kindly toward others if they believed there was a reward in the afterlife for doing so—and a punishment for not. Could aliens with no semblance of religion, and no belief in God, convince earthlings that intelligent beings elsewhere in the universe were good to each other just because it was the right thing to do? Maybe, just maybe, others could be shown that it wasn't God, Jesus, or any other religious figure that made them kind; it was something that was a part of all of us.

Sitting between her two children, Korin felt more content than ever. She wished the feeling could last forever. She had her family and a lover. Although the affair with Oscar sometimes created great mental conflict for her, she had pushed that aside. She was more passionate about the current project than she'd ever been about anything. This feeling of contentment was an unfamiliar feeling. Despite all her accomplishments, she'd always felt discontent.

The project brought her closer to Oscar. She loved him, and had accepted their very limited time together because she also loved Jim and the children. Time had led her to a better understanding of why being in both relationships at the same time could work. Love wasn't something that got smaller, she rationalized, when it was divided among different people. She hadn't loved Camille any less when Evan was born. In the same way, she didn't love Jim any less because of Oscar. If she could love more than one child, why couldn't she love more than one man? One love at a time was only a rule society had imposed on itself. In some ways it was as nonsensical as religion. People should be good to each other because it was the right thing to do, and they should love each other for the same reason. For now, she needed to figure out if she was doing the right thing. To move forward with the hoax seemed dramatically more irrational than any extramarital affair. Yet at this time she believed she needed to continue going forward with both. Giving either one up seemed impossible.

CHAPTER 18

Without health life is not life; it is only a state of languor and suffering—an image of death.

—Gautama Buddha (c. 563–483 B.C.)

Korin had given considerable thought to the project but hadn't met with any of the others for several days, and to Korin it seemed like an eternity. She decided to go see Oscar unannounced, and talk it through with him.

Korin remembered details, even meaningless ones, and knew his class schedule. She drove to the Stanford campus, and after being frustrated with the lack of parking decided to park in a faculty space near his building and risk the ticket. She reflected on this seemingly minor infraction later, and realized that if she hadn't broken the rules and taken this space, her life and that of many others may have been quite different. The seemingly trivial act of illegally parking got her to Oscar's office door at precisely the right moment to overhear a conversation that would change her motivation in a way that made her determined to see the hoax through.

On reaching his office door she hesitated momentarily to adjust Oscar's name plate, which had slid partly out of its support.

Without intending to eavesdrop, she heard one side of the conversation Oscar was having on the phone. She heard the terms "pancreatic cancer" and "terminal prognosis" and as she did it was as though someone had reached inside her and ripped her insides out. She was unable to move, and unable to block the voice that continued to not only talk about the disease, but became increasingly irritated as he repeated his position about refusing treatment.

She heard him clearly say, "If I'm dying in a few months anyway, I'm not going to let the medical establishment use me as a guinea pig during that time. That's final!" A few months! She heard his words over and over as she managed to walk away.

It all fit somehow. He would never had considered going forward with the hoax unless he felt he was going to die. It wasn't like him to want the money so badly, but now it made sense. She went home, could hardly sleep and the next morning she rose early and opened an email from Herbert. The subject line read, "Meeting?" and the text read, "Today at my place at 10 A.M.—bring doughnuts."

She loved Oscar deeply, and knowing that he might be gone soon wasn't something she could accept. Risks related to the hoax now seemed less important. Somehow the hoax just might help. Korin pulled herself together, and resolved to figure out a way to save Oscar.

She made calls to Alan and Oscar to confirm that they were coming, and she would bring the doughnuts. She knew a family-run bakery not far from the house, and Herbert liked their doughnuts better than anyone else's. But it wasn't just where she got them; Herbert appreciated her picking them up. Her recognition that he had no one special bringing him a treat was part of what made her so good with people.

On hanging up, Korin went to the living room and opened her laptop. She wanted to get her thoughts together on how to move the basic project forward and, at the same time, make her personal plan work. For now, she decided to facilitate the latter by talking to Herbert alone. After the others arrived, she would focus on four issues:

First, the initial landing site and the other locations where the sphere might go. Second, the questions that would be asked at each location, while limiting the communications to texting, rather than speech. Third, the answers to the questions, and, lastly, how long they would be on earth as aliens.

She thought of these issues as the "where, what, and when" of the project, and although they had consumed her over the last several days she now redirected her focus toward saving Oscar.

She had no plan for Oscar at the moment, and needed to distract herself, to burn off energy. She put on her workout clothes and went to her in-house gym. She warmed up on the treadmill, switched to the stair-stepper, and ended up on the rowing machine. The exercise was working. She focused better. With time to cool down, shower, dress, and, of course, get the doughnuts, she would still arrive at Herbert's early, and be able to talk to him alone.

Herbert had given her the code to his gate, so she went in without contacting him on the intercom. She was surprised by what she saw. Herbert sat on a small, wooden stool near the entrance to Building #1. The top of the stool was maybe one foot high, making it level with the top of a circular tub filled with water and soap suds. Quark stood in the middle, all soaped up. He barked as she approached.

"Hi, boy. You look like you're having fun." She petted Quark with one hand while passing the doughnut box to Herbert with the other.

"Thank you so much. I'm starved. Do you mind if I eat one?"

"That's why I brought them. Eat up."

Herbert wiped one hand on a towel draped over his leg, opened the box, pulled out a powdered jelly doughnut, and began eating it. A look of contentment came over his face as he closed his eyes and chewed. Powdered sugar dropped on his shirt. "These are really great, Korin. Aren't you going to have any?"

"No thanks. I'm trying to keep my girlish figure. I came early so I could talk to you alone."

"Sure, go ahead," said Herbert.

"I want your agreement not to tell the others about what I'm about to say."

"Interesting. It wasn't that long ago that I told you the biggest secret of my life. By the way, I'm glad I did. Just being able to tell the story made me understand it better. So, Korin, of course, I'll keep your secret."

"It has to do with Oscar. I know why he's going along with this project, and the basic reasons tie into why I'm now totally committed to this as well," said Korin.

"I thought both you and Oscar were doing this for the money. That's a strong motivator. But there's more?"

"Yes, there's more. Sure, I want the money, as does Oscar. But it's *why* he wants the money that's important."

"Don't tell me. It's to support his habit—his vintage Porsche habit. I know he's addicted," said Herbert.

"No, that's not it. It's— Damn it. I hear a car. Look, it's Oscar. We'll need to continue this later."

Herbert finished rinsing the suds off Quark and did his best to dry himself as he and Korin walked toward the two arriving cars.

"Good to see you." Oscar shook hands with Herbert and gave Korin a short embrace.

"Hello, Korin." Alan hugged Korin and kissed her on the cheek. "How's my old friend?" He embraced Herbert.

"The sphere is done," said Herbert, while eating his second doughnut. "I've used the field to move it, and it works. I'm excited about showing you. It's quite amazing."

"Well, you're an amazing guy, Herbert. I'd expect no less," Korin said.

"Let's go over to the sphere. I want you all to experience how it feels to be in it." Herbert led them to it. "I've done a number of things that you'll want to see. The inside has a bathroom, as well as food and water. The outside is fitted with several different antennae, which are only for use while it's in place here."

"So when it moves somewhere else, you take the antennae off?" asked Korin.

"Well, the antennae stay here, but they're not taken off. Let me explain. The sphere is built in layers, or shells. The antennae are all connected to the outer layer. I can focus the field around an inner layer and put that inner layer and everything inside it somewhere else. The outer layer and antennae stay here. That way, anyone standing here and looking right at it can't tell whether the sphere is here or gone."

"You're sneakier than I thought," Oscar said. "That way, if anyone who worked on the sphere suspects something, he can come here and see it in place as it should be."

"Yes, and there's more," said Herbert. "The outer layer of the sphere is a screen onto which we can project Alan's video or anything else to show to those on the outside."

"Trashy fake movies projected on a big ball for the world to see. Are we selling tickets?" Alan said. Oscar laughed, and Herbert gave a look of confusion, and wondered if anything was funny.

"How far are you from having it ready for a test flight?" Korin asked.

Herbert took time explaining the tests he had run. First, he'd put plants and insects inside and found they were unaffected. He then caught some mice in a nearby field, using homemade traps he'd built years before, and they were also unaffected. He performed the initial trials on his own land in an effort to avoid visual or radar detection. Working at night to hide the sphere from view as it silently hovered over different areas of his property, he took the extra precaution of taking Quark to an elite dog resort. He couldn't quiet the dog while the field was on.

"It's ready," said Herbert. "I'm eager to go, and I have an idea on where to try it."

"You're really full of surprises today," said Korin. "Where were you thinking? Wait, don't tell me. It's got to be the nerdiest place on earth. I'm going to guess Cambridge, Massachusetts, at MIT. Isn't that where you went to school?"

The Hackers got their start there, and their hoaxes had inspired Herbert to want to pull off the biggest hoax ever.

"Yes, I went to school there, but that's not where I was thinking," Herbert answered.

"I'm guessing she had the right idea—just the wrong place," said Oscar. "You want to go to Groom Lake. Is that right?"

"I'm impressed," Herbert said. "One, that you would guess the right place, but also that you knew 'Area 51' is sometimes called 'Groom Lake.'"

"I've heard of Area 51," said Korin. "It's where they test all the secret military aircraft. Is that right? But where exactly is it?"

"It's about ninety miles north of Las Vegas. It's a rectangular block of land about six-by-ten miles with a large military base in the center. It was first selected in the 1950s for testing the U-2 spy plane. There's a dry lake bed there that can be used for landing—that's Groom Lake." Herbert showed them a map on his computer screen.

"Wouldn't it be illegal and even dangerous to go to a secret military base? I'm not interested in going to jail or getting shot at," Alan said.

"Nor am I," said Herbert. "This area has been known for many UFO stories. The tourists or 'true believers' who go there to see UFOs can't go into Area 51, so they go out Nevada Highway 375. There's nothing out there except for mile markers. A local rancher has a mail box known as the 'Black Mailbox,' though it was white when I saw it. It's the only landmark on this highway. Many of the true believers say they've seen flying saucers there, and it's become a gathering point. That's where I want to go."

"Do you think that no one will believe anyone who sees it there? Is that it?" asked Korin.

"That's part of it," said Herbert. "Area 51 is part of Nellis Air Force Base. The Nellis Range Complex includes Groom Lake, or Area 51, and the Tonopah Test Range, and they're both used for testing all kinds of advanced technology—not only planes such as the SR-71 Blackbird and the F-117a Stealth Fighter—but the world's most advanced tracking equipment. I need to find out if they can track the sphere. If they can't track it, no one can."

"What if they can track it?" Korin asked.

"If they can track it, the whole plan is off. There's no way we can pull off a hoax if they can track us," Herbert answered.

"So what if we go to the Black Mailbox, and there's no one there to see us?" asked Alan.

"I don't really care that much whether the true believers are there," Herbert answered. "But if we stay there long enough, someone will come. The 'Cammo Dudes' always show up."

"Who or what are the Cammo Dudes?" asked Korin.

"It's a nickname for an anonymous private-security force. They wear camouflage fatigues with no insignia and drive around the area in Jeeps with federal government plates. They're more of a tourist attraction than the base itself, because the true believers never get to see the base—it's off limits."

"So you're betting the Cammo Dudes will see us and report what they saw, is that it?" asked Alan.

"I'm counting on it," Herbert said.

"The story is that the military knows about UFOs, but they never tell the public. If that's true, how will you know if they can track you? They might track you and then deny there was anything to track," said Alan.

"We'll know, definitely and soon. The Cammo Dudes will report what they see. The base will electronically confirm the sphere is there. Once they do that, we leave. I'm not sure the military does hide information about real UFOs. But even if I'm wrong, I know for sure they'll try to track the sphere once they detect it. If they can, it doesn't matter what they say publicly. They'll be here in Woodside in no time if they track us back here. If they don't show up here, then they can't track it. I'm betting they can't."

"Makes sense to me," said Korin. "When are we going?"

"No time like the present," Herbert said. "If you guys are up for it, we'll give it a try."

"Well, I don't want to be the party pooper. I'll go," Oscar said.

"What? Are you all nuts?" Alan shouted. "How do we know people can survive this? What if Herbert turns on the field, and we all disappear forever? What if we all end up at Area 51 dead? This doesn't seem well thought out to me. I think I'll stay behind and see if you come back."

"He does have a point, Herbert," Korin said. "No person or large animal has ever been in the sphere when the nano-tron field was applied."

"I've told you about my tests. It works. It's safe. I haven't done it with a person inside. Not because I don't believe it's safe, but because I wanted to share the experience. This is a historic event. If we do this, we'll be the first people to undergo interdimensional transport. There's no guarantee, and I know it's untested on humans, so it's a guess, but I can't see why it wouldn't work."

"Your guess is better than anyone else's guarantee," said Korin. "I'm in." She knew Alan was right. This was very risky. But she felt the risk was worth taking. For now, she would keep that reason to herself.

"I'm looking forward to the looks on the faces of the folks at Area 51," said Oscar. "So I'm in as well."

Korin had figured Oscar would go if she did, and she also imagined that their decisions would not affect Alan.

"I guess my place in history will be as an observer," said Alan. "Let me know how it feels when you get back. I'm not even comfortable flying on an airliner. I'm out. Maybe we can talk by radio while you're out there?"

"That won't work," said Herbert. "Even if the radio worked, there's too much chance that the radio signal will be tracked back here. We'll video what we see and do."

"Okay then, it's settled," Korin said. "The three of us will go, and Alan will wait here."

"I need to put Quark in the house before we go. He's cleaned up, and sometimes he'll take a nap after a bath. I'll put him where he feels safe. He doesn't seem to like the field. He barks every time I turn it on." Herbert called Quark, and Alan walked along with him toward the house. "Thanks for setting this up," Alan said when they were out of the others' earshot.

"I told you we could make it happen. Did you set things up from your side?" asked Herbert.

"I just made sure there would be people out there. They don't know anything else," said Alan.

"Once we're gone, send your friends a text message. See if you get an answer."

"That should be very interesting indeed," said Alan.

The two of them shook hands, leaving Quark inside and walking back to the sphere.

CHAPTER 19

*A man travels the world over in search of what he needs
and returns home to find it.*

—George Moore (1852–1933)

It was still mid-morning, and the temperature in Woodside was typically perfect, not hot and not cool. Large oak trees surrounded the area. The sound of a nearby blue jay startled a small black squirrel and sent him running over the grass. Herbert's sphere was dramatically juxtapositioned against these natural surroundings. The most technically advanced object on the planet sat silent and motionless in this natural setting until Herbert pushed a button on a remote control, causing a ramp to extrude from the side of the sphere. Just above the ramp, a door slid open, and the blue jay went silent.

"I recognize that," said Oscar. "Isn't it the same design they used in the movie *The Day the Earth Stood Still?*"

"Cool, isn't it?" A gleeful smile came over Herbert's face. "We won't use the door until we get back here, so others won't see it. I wanted a sphere that was smooth on its surface. With this door, there are no rough edges."

"Why is that important, Herbert?" asked Korin.

"It makes programming the field around the sphere much easier. The field takes an object outside of our dimensional space. It allows the object to slip into another dimension, or, I should say, it surrounds the object with nanotrons so that it can slip out of our three-dimensional space and into another one. I programmed the field so that it will bring the object back into our three-dimensional space at another place. When the object is a sphere, the field is set at equal distances around its center point. Shall we go on board?" Herbert gestured at them to begin walking up the ramp and into the interior of the sphere. He gave a final nod to Alan.

Four large chairs sat on hemispheres extending from the deck. They were pink, more specifically Mountbatten pink, and appeared not only reclinable, but rotatable.

"Sit where you like, but let me have that one in front of the main controls," said Herbert. "This will be a lot easier and faster than you might think. I'll close the door. I entered the coordinates over the Black Mailbox earlier. These buttons have numbers to match the numbers on the screens around us. Go ahead and turn them on."

The screens lit up, showing Alan and the surrounding area of Herbert's estate.

"Do you want to say anything to Alan before we go?" asked Herbert. "Just flip this switch on, and you can talk to him over a speaker system."

Korin flipped the switch. "Are you sure you don't want to join us?"

"Quite sure." Alan smiled contently and waved.

Korin was ready. Many thoughts went through her mind. She wondered what her family would think if she didn't return. Although the purpose of the project was to undermine organized religion, she had no fear that God would interfere and cut it short. She appreciated that it was irrational to move forward so quickly. As a good scientist, Herbert had no doubt understood that he should have conducted additional tests before subjecting himself and his friends to the nanotron field. But he was impatient and had great confidence in this working out well. In addition, right now there was a different clock running for Korin, and it took precedence and compelled her to move the project forward as quickly as possible.

Oscar clearly understood that this was his chance to participate in the biggest historical event of all time. He couldn't resist. The excitement showed in his eyes, which pleased Korin.

"If you're ready, we'll go," said Herbert. "Alan, we won't communicate with you while we're gone, and we should be back inside of one hour."

"Understood." Alan backed away from the sphere as if he expected some sort of "blast off."

Herbert clicked an icon on the computer screen, and they were gone. The only sound Alan heard was Quark barking inside Herbert's house. The only sounds inside the sphere were their voices. No engine hum, no air rushing by, just quiet.

"We're here," said Herbert. "See that white mail box? It's the famous Black Mailbox, and some true believers are here, as well."

"I didn't feel anything," Korin said. "But you're right. We're here, and I see people below us on screen eight. But it doesn't seem as though they see us. There's no reaction."

"We're about a hundred meters above the ground," Herbert replied. "We're above their normal field of view. They'll see us soon. Just wait. I'll zoom in on them with the camera for screen eight."

"That looks to be an old VW van," said Oscar. "I had one of those in college. I loved that van. "You're right, Herbert. The young woman near the front of the van must have just spotted us. She's pointing right at us with a look of complete wonderment."

"She must have told the guy she's with. He's looking at us now too," Korin added. "This has got to be as exciting for them as it is for us, and probably scarier."

"They're not the only ones who see us," Oscar said. "Look at those three guys on motorcycles on screen nine. One of them has a camera. I can't tell if it's video or not, but he's taking pictures."

"Someone else just saw us," said Herbert. "Radar from the base has scanned us. They'll notify the Cammo Dudes, and we should see them in the next few minutes."

"I'm surprised the people out there aren't completely hysterical," Korin said. "Seeing an alien spaceship has to be shocking."

"They don't really know what they're seeing," Oscar said. "At this point, they may think it's a test aircraft from the base. We haven't fired any 'death rays' at them. They have no reason to feel threatened, and, after all, this is why they came out to the Black Mailbox. They wanted to see aliens."

Korin didn't hear the excitement she had expected in Oscar's voice. He kept looking around at each screen and at every part of the sphere. "Look at screen seven," she said. "There's a family with two children about the ages of my kids. They're looking at us but don't seem frightened. But you make a good point, Oscar. If they saw this somewhere other than here, they might be reacting very differently."

Oscar made no reply and rose partially out of his seat before sitting back down.

"The radar is still tracking us," Herbert said. "This is about to get very interesting. I'm going to zoom way in on screen one. You see that small, moving dot? I'm betting that's the Cammo Dudes coming. That Jeep has got to be going a hundred miles per hour, maybe faster. I'm guessing the base told them to come out here and take a look."

"Should we leave before they get here?" asked Korin.

"What, and miss all the fun? If we leave now, they'll have seen us on radar, but have no visual confirmation except from these true-believer types here. Let's wait," said Herbert.

"Do these Cammo Dudes carry guns?" asked Oscar calmly, while looking intently at Herbert's face.

"They have handguns. They may carry rifles or some type of automatic weapons in the Jeep, but I've never seen anything beyond their handguns," Herbert answered. "But they're coming to see us, not take shots at us. Once they get here, we'll wait long enough for them to confirm our presence back to the base."

"Then we're going right back to Woodside, right?" Oscar asked. "Maybe the true believers find us interesting, but these Cammo Dudes with guns will know we're not some test aircraft built by the government."

Herbert was far more excited than Oscar. Korin couldn't tell what Oscar was thinking, but whatever it was didn't match with the situation they were in. His suggestion to Herbert that they return to Woodside wasn't said out of fear. The test had been run and it seemed prudent to him that they return.

"You guys are worrying way too much." Herbert smiled at Korin and Oscar in a way that showed he was delighted with himself. "It will be fine. But we may not want to go straight back to Woodside. We need some real excitement. We need to make sure they have every opportunity to track us."

Now that Herbert had the sphere working, Korin could tell he didn't want the feeling of excitement and satisfaction to end. That was Herbert's equivalent to having great sex. He was having too much fun to stop.

"They're a lot closer now," said Oscar. "One of the Cammo Dudes is looking out of the back seat window with binoculars. He must see us."

"If he sees us, they've called the base to confirm visual contact. The base will scramble F-16 jets," said Herbert.

"Jets? What the fuck, Herbert? I don't want to be here when jets get here." Korin's tone conveyed her uncomfortable emotions. "Herbert, aren't you more than a bit concerned? When the Air Force sends jets, they send them to blow things up!"

"I'm concerned," said Herbert. "But more than that, I'm fascinated by what's happening. Look, the Cammo guys are at the Black Mailbox and out of their Jeep. But they don't have their guns out. One of them is on a radio, one is using a video camera, and the other is talking to the true believers.

"They must have scrambled the jets right away," he continued. "Maybe even before the true believers saw us. The jets are headed toward us. Get ready for some vibrations when they go over."

The sphere remained in place a hundred meters above the desert floor, making no sound at all. Then the screens showed two jets approaching. As they came within a thousand yards of the sphere, Oscar rose from his chair and calmly walked over to a panel covering a window, touched a button until it slid the panel partially open. He saw the jets, not on the screen in some abstract two-dimensional way, but as voracious three-dimensional war machines headed directly at him. The jet passed, and vibrations shook the sphere hard enough that Oscar lost his balance and fell as he reached to close the panel. "Jesus Christ, that was close," he breathed. "They flew right over us. Herbert, I'm sure I heard my mother calling. We've got to get the hell out of here before someone does something that ruins our whole day—like firing a missile at us."

Oscar's voice was completely different than it had been seconds before and now Korin knew why. Until he opened the window panel, he had believed Herbert was making everything up. Now he knew it was real.

"Calm down, Oscar," said Herbert. "How long did it take us to get here? Don't answer that. I'll tell you. It took no time at all. Zero time. We can be back home in zero time. Just relax and enjoy the show."

"Look, the true believers are watching the jets now. They don't even think we're interesting," said Korin. "That's fascinating. They must think we're some kind of balloon or hovercraft. Because the jets make all the noise and spit fire out their asses, they get all the attention—such is life."

"Here come the jets again," Herbert said. "When they get here, we'll leave. We just need to make a quick detour." Just as the jets were about to reach them, Herbert clicked another icon on his computer screen, and the sphere was no longer over Area 51.

"Where are we?" Oscar asked, this time with genuine curiosity and wonderment in his voice. He looked from one screen to the next and buckled his seat belt.

"You said you wanted to get out of there," said Herbert. "I got us out of there."

"This is our detour?" asked Korin.

"Yes. That tower on screen one is the tower at Beale Air Force Base."

"Just where is that?" Oscar asked.

"It's about forty miles north of Sacramento, practically on our way home. It's an Air Force base named after an early California explorer—a guy named Edward Fitzgerald Beale, who came to California in the 1800s."

"Why are we here?" asked Oscar. "And let's get out of here before they send more jets."

"We're here to make sure they can't track us," Herbert said. "The folks at Area 51 will be looked on with suspicion. They'll even question themselves about whether they really saw something. If Beale tracks us and confirms visual contact, then together they'll know there was a real sphere—and they'll probably assume there were two spheres because we moved too fast. We'll just wait here a minute or so. Keep watching the screens."

"What are we waiting for?" asked Korin.

"Look to see if anyone down there or in the tower is watching us."

"It's hard to see inside the tower," Oscar said. "But there are some people on screen five coming out of that building walking toward a parking lot. I'll zoom in on them."

"Okay, look at screen three. That guy is pointing at us and looks excited. That's the kind of reaction I expected," said Korin.

"The other guys must have heard him," said Oscar. "They see us now. One of them ran back into the building. Look, others are coming out now. They definitely see us."

"Okay, the radar scanned us, and they've seen us, so we're outta here. I'm wondering how we appear on radar," he added thoughtfully. "The sphere oscillates between our dimensional space and another. If the beam crosses us when we're not here, there's nothing to reflect the beam back. But some of the signal will bounce back."

Herbert moved the mouse, and a click on another icon took the sphere back to Woodside.

"That was an enormously exciting and very strange experience," said Korin. "There was no feeling of movement. It seemed as though we changed the channel on a TV, and there we were some place hundreds of miles away. There was no real excitement in the travel, but seeing the people react to us was incredibly exciting."

"You felt no movement because we didn't move," Herbert explained. "We were at a first place at a given time, and then, at the same time, we appeared at another place. We experience no movement through our three-dimensional space. Assuming I'm right, no one will track us here. Still, we should get out of the sphere, go inside, and wait a few hours. If no one comes looking for us, then we know they couldn't track us. I'll open the sphere door."

"So, did you do anything yet?" Alan asked, seeing his friends leaving the sphere. "What happened?"

Before exiting, Oscar slid back the window panel he had opened just before the jets flew by. On confirming that the calm, quiet greenery of Herbert's estate was there, he walked out the door and down the ramp toward Alan.

"We caused quite a stir," said Oscar, "It's all on video, if you want to watch it, although it might be similar to watching someone else's wedding videos. It's a big deal to them but no one else gives a damn. We can just give you the five-minute recap."

"Let's all go over to Building Number One," said Herbert, "We'll be more comfortable there."

"Great," said Korin. "I can run some of my ideas by you, and we can come up with a solid plan for going forward."

CHAPTER 20

Man's mind, once stretched by a new idea,
never regains its original dimensions.

—Oliver Wendell Holmes (1809–1894)

Herbert watched as Oscar walked over to a small button positioned below a window. Oscar stared out of the window, pushed the button and opened the window panel. He understood what Oscar was doing. The experience seemed unbelievable to him as well. As Korin walked down the ramp, he noticed something—the shape of her body. It was a curious feeling for him, and he wondered if perhaps it was caused by the rush of adrenalin from their unforgettable experience. They had done something no one else had ever done, and they had only weak reference points by which to describe it. Herbert wanted to write down some thoughts. Would the others write or do something else to mark the occasion? He speculated about what reports Alan might have heard already and about what Korin had wanted to tell him earlier. But for now, he joined his friends in walking toward Building #1 and talking about what had happened.

"Did you really go to Area 51?" asked Alan.

"We went there and to Beale Air Force Base." Herbert looked at Korin and saw, for the first time, how attractive she was.

"Really," said Alan. "How did it feel?"

Herbert momentarily felt very uncomfortable, thinking the question was directed at his new-found feeling.

"It was certainly exciting and surreal," said Korin. "No feeling of movement, and all I could see was what was on the screens. It seemed as though we were the people on TV, and we could see the people in the audience watching us!"

"You're right," said Oscar, as they entered Building #1. "That's a good description. I had to be sure it was real, so I looked out a window when the jets flew over. I thought maybe they were going to blow us out of the sky. They caused a vibration in the sphere that was different from what I expected. That's why I fell. Did either of you notice that?"

"That's very perceptive of you, Oscar," said Herbert, "The vibration was different for a reason. I set the field to oscillate, and as it did so, the sphere was in the space we know at one moment and in another dimension the next. We were flickering or oscillating between dimensions while we were there, but it didn't appear that way until the jets flew over. The vibration felt different because we were only there, in our time and space, half the time to feel the shock waves. Because the oscillations were so rapid, they weren't noticeable at all until the vibrations from the jets were added. Similarly, you don't notice a light bulb going on and off sixty times a second. We never see the other dimension, and you never see the light bulb off. Your eyes send information to your brain. However, your brain only understands and interprets signals based on the dimension we're familiar with. Any other dimension is dark or invisible to us."

"Why did you make the field oscillate?" asked Alan.

"I wanted the sphere to be positioned up in the air. If I had just put it in the air in our dimension, it would have fallen from the sky in the same way any object falls. The sphere has no propulsion system to keep it from falling. When I oscillated the field, the sphere rapidly slipped back and forth between the two dimensions, and it would never fall."

"Herbert, I don't understand the idea of going to another dimension. I never saw another dimension. I didn't feel anything different. Can you explain what you're talking about?" Korin asked.

"In a word, no," said Herbert. "Your brain isn't capable of understanding it."

"Is that your way of telling me I'm not smart enough? — that I'm not as smart as you?"

"Not at all," said Herbert. "Let me explain. Humans are different from other animals in many ways, and one important difference is their brains. Specifically, their frontal lobes. In the middle of the 1800s, doctors noticed that many people with severely damaged frontal lobes appeared to be mentally unaffected. They could walk, talk, and do most everything people with normal brains could do. This led to thinking that the frontal lobe doesn't do much, and that view continued for over a century. In 1949, a Portuguese doctor named Egas Moniz won the Nobel Prize in Medicine and Physiology for developing the surgical procedure called the frontal lobotomy. Thousands were performed."

"Herbert, come on, I may not be as smart as you, but I haven't had a lobotomy," said Korin.

"I'm aware of that. Let me finish," said Herbert. "What doctors began to find out was that when the frontal lobe was damaged, the person appeared normal, but some of them had no ability to plan for the future. When people with frontal-lobe damage were asked what they planned to do tomorrow or next year, they said they didn't know. What's more interesting is the answer they gave when asked about their thinking process when asked about their future plans. They said it was similar to being asleep or being in a space with nothing there, nothing to touch, nothing to hold onto or to hold them up in any way."

"I'm following you, but I don't get what this has to do with why I didn't see another dimension."

"Well, Korin, if you keep interrupting him, he can't tell you," said Alan.

"Okay. I'll be quiet."

Herbert continued. "Only *Homo sapiens* developed a large frontal lobe. Therefore, conventional wisdom holds that only people, but not other animals, can plan for the future. A great deal of evidence supports this—evidence put together by people who study brain function. What I'm trying to tell you is that, similarly, *Homo sapiens* with normal brains simply cannot perceive another dimension. If asked about it, they have nothing to reference, nothing to grab onto."

"So *you* can't see the other dimension either?" asked Korin.

"I cannot," he said. "I believe we may be able to learn how to perceive it. But that may require the development of a new area of the brain, and so it could take a long time. It took two million years or more for *Homo habilis* to develop the bigger brain of *Homo sapiens*. We'll need to see if we can learn to see or perceive of other dimensions with our current brains. If we can, perhaps we can learn to perceive of other concepts, such as infinity."

"So our brains only perceive three-dimensional space," Alan asked.

"That's right."

"I had thought of a string or wire as one-dimensional and a sheet of paper as two-dimensional." Alan mused. "But when you explained about the lobotomized brain having no reference point to think about the future, I realized that I can only think of a string as it exists in three dimensional space. I can think of a two-dimensional piece of paper, but only as it exists in three-dimensional space."

"That's interesting," said Oscar. "No doubt there are many things we're not capable of perceiving."

"Do you guys hear something?" Korin asked, suddenly alert. "I thought I heard a car driving up."

"I'll go check," said Oscar.

Herbert immediately assumed it was the authorities sent over from the tracking stations at Area 51 and Beale. He wondered how they could have tracked the sphere. It just didn't seem possible, but he never had unexpected guests. Who else could it be? Should he go outside with Oscar? He wasn't sure. He watched as Oscar confidently walked out to encounter something Herbert assumed would put an end to his plan to avenge what the church had done to him. For a moment, he felt defeated.

CHAPTER 21

*A timid person is frightened before a danger, a coward
during the time, and a courageous person afterward.*

—Jean Paul Richter (1763–1825)

Oscar had heard the car coming before Korin said
anything. He was fascinated by the brain's inability
to perceive anything other than three-dimensional space,
but now he refocused on their current situation. He left
Building #1, and, as he opened the door to the outside, he
saw flashing lights atop a car in the driveway. One of the
two men in the car appeared to be on the radio. Having had
less-than-pleasant experiences with law enforcement in
the past, Oscar didn't approach the car. He waited patiently
in front of the doorway with the door closed, and he kept
both his hands visible and at his side.

Both men exited the car. They wore law enforcement
uniforms and sidearms, and they approached Oscar casually,
watching him closely as they approached. One man walked
behind and to the right of the other.

"Hello. I'm Officer Green, and this is Officer Mills. I guess
you know why we're here."

Oscar did not react. It was possible they were just the first
of many who would come about the sphere. The advanced
systems at Groom Lake and Beale must have tracked them

to this location. It was the only reason they'd be here, he thought. Other agencies would have asked them to get there quickly to look for the sphere. But something didn't fit. The officers weren't looking around as though they wanted to find a spaceship. They didn't appear overly curious or nervous in any way. Experience told him that staying calm and thinking was the best course. Maybe, Oscar thought, just maybe their arrival was purely coincidental. Maybe it was connected to something else.

"How can I help you?" asked Oscar.

"Our department tried to phone you. We weren't able to get through on your home number, so we used our emergency fire key to open your gate and came in to make sure you're aware of the fire. It's still a few miles away from here, but we're asking folks to evacuate. It's for your own safety."

"Well, I appreciate your letting me know." Oscar silently breathed a sigh of relief. "How much time before the fire gets here?"

"It may not get here. But to be on the safe side, we're asking everyone in the area to be out by five o'clock."

"That's only a few hours away. But if you're telling me I should go, I'll go," Oscar said.

"Okay, then. We'll be on our way."

Oscar reflected on what had just happened. He was quite pleased with how he had handled the matter. If any of the others had come out, it wouldn't have gone well. He patiently waited as the police walked away, got in their car, and drove off. Once they were gone, Oscar went back inside.

"Well, it's all over. They're onto us. They tracked the sphere, so we'll never be able to pull this off," Oscar said in a deadpan voice.

"Amazing," said Herbert. "I would have bet incredible odds that they could never track us. I can't understand how they did."

"I'm surprised," said Alan. "No one ever believes a UFO story. Even if they tracked the sphere, I wouldn't have thought they would follow up by sending police out immediately to investigate."

"This is enormously disappointing," said Korin. "But it just means we have to come up with a completely different idea."

"Gotcha!" Oscar shouted. "I was joking. They didn't track us! They were only here to warn Herbert about a fire that may be headed this way. They say they want everyone in this area to evacuate by five o'clock."

"Don't do that to me, Oscar," said Korin sternly. "You had me quite upset."

"Calm down," said Oscar. "I just couldn't resist. I had to fool you. Alan fooled you guys and then me with his video. Herbert fooled us with his bulldozer balloon—and you, Korin, your plan is to fool the whole planet. I figured I was entitled. But I also did it to see how you all would react. That was interesting."

"What do you mean?" asked Korin.

"When we pull this off, unexpected things will happen. We can't plan for everything. I wanted to have some idea how each of you might react to an unexpected event."

"Speaking of unexpected events, what about the fire?" Alan asked nervously.

"I can deal with that," said Herbert. "If the fire comes here, I can use the field to put water on it. The field is set now to go around a sphere twenty feet in diameter. I can project the field around a twenty-foot-diameter sphere of water in the Pacific Ocean and put that water on the fire."

"Great," said Korin. "I love working with you, Herbert. No problem is too big. With that in mind, let's focus that big brain of yours on what we as aliens might say to people on earth."

"Thank you for the compliment, Korin. I get so few from attractive women. But I think Alan and I should focus on the science part and defer to you and Oscar on what gets communicated."

This response seemed odd to Oscar. First, he'd never heard Herbert refer to Korin as attractive. Perhaps he wanted to distract her, but he was also looking at her differently. More importantly, Herbert always wanted to play a major role in plans. Why was he deferring to others on part of his biggest project ever, and why was Alan agreeing with him? There was another piece to this puzzle.

"Fair enough," said Korin. "But I'd appreciate getting some thoughts from each of you. Oscar and I discussed this, and we thought we would first appear over the United Nations building in New York."

"Really? The UN building?" Herbert sounded surprised. "No one puts much importance on the UN these days. I was thinking the Vatican."

"We thought of that but decided against it for two reasons. First, aliens wouldn't necessarily think the UN is meaningless—it's the only place where all nations meet. Second, hovering over the Vatican would add to the perception of the Church's importance—something I think you want to avoid," said Korin.

"Makes sense to me," said Herbert.

"Great," she said. "I've learned from business deals that the first thing said often dictates how you're perceived. Also, saying less is almost always better. Our words will be dissected. We need to make an initial statement that will lead to the conclusions we want. We'll communicate only by texting, not by talking. We want to appear peaceful, so I suggest the first thing we say is, 'We have come here from another dimension. We mean you no harm. We will wait here one hour. At the end of that hour, you can ask us to stay or leave, and we will comply.'"

"If they ask us to leave, is the whole project over?" Alan asked.

"It could be," said Korin. "But that simply won't happen. They'll be far too curious. They won't ask us to leave. If I'm wrong, we can end the project and come back here. It would still be an incredible hoax if that's all that happened. But if we never say we're going back to another dimension, we could just appear in another city or country and try again. We have several backup locations in mind. We'll need to react in real time to whatever happens. What do you think might happen, Oscar?"

"There's not much information to predict how it will go. There are some records indicating that the Native Americans were unable to understand or appreciate in any way what the large sailing ships from Europe were as they approached. At first, they were unable to see the ships in their true form, and some individuals could not see them at all. Maybe it's not much different from us being unable to see the other dimensions when we're in the sphere. There's also the Orson Welles *War of the Worlds* radio event. Simply by hearing things on the radio, many panicked. Then, of course, there are the thousands of UFO events we hear about. Even though those events may all be imagined, the people reporting them truly believe they saw a spaceship from another world."

"Oscar, you don't know what people have seen. You don't know if people really saw UFOs. Regardless, aren't you forgetting something?" Alan asked.

"Of course," said Oscar. "When something is staring you right in the face, it's difficult to see. We saw the reactions of quite a number of people less than an hour ago. We may see more of that in the coming days. But it will be very different when we're over the United Nations building. The true believers at Groom Lake expected to see an alien spaceship. They weren't sure whether they saw a UFO or a new experimental aircraft being tested by the Air Force. We didn't see the reactions of the people who tracked us at Groom Lake or Beale. But they may well be questioning their equipment in the same way they questioned the people who claimed to have had visual contact. Right now, I'm guessing no one knows who or what to believe."

"I think you'll see more reaction over the next few days," Alan suggested. "There'll be videos, not to mention reports from the people. Your test flight is going to create quite a stir. Mark my words. Some of the effects could be very negative. Have all of you thought about how this could impact the lives of others?"

"Sure," Korin responded. "But it won't be all bad effects. I'm convinced there will be more positive effects than negative. There are no guarantees about anything in life. The bigger the actions, the bigger the risk, and this has got to be up there as the Mother of all actions ever taken. You, Alan, and many others criticized President Bush for invading Iraq and President Obama for adding even more troops. The invasion may have been the wrong thing to do, but at least Bush had the testicular determination to do what he believed was right. He knew lives would be lost, but believed in the long run the world would be a better place with Saddam gone and Iraq free."

"Yes, but they're elected officials. We're not. This is anarchy," said Oscar.

"Call it whatever you want," Korin said. "The way I see it, those elected officials got where they are because of circumstances. George W. Bush could never have become president if his father hadn't been president, and if one Supreme Court justice had voted the other way, Al Gore would have been president.

"Korin does have a point," said Herbert. "Right now, we're being presented with a set of circumstances that gives us considerable power. If we don't use it, someone else will. The technology won't remain secret forever. Eventually others will figure this out."

"Throughout history, leaders have always made decisions knowing that lives would be lost," Oscar said. "Sometimes they act for selfish, personal reasons, and sometimes they hope that the world will be a better place in the end. I'm not sure George W. Bush is better able to make such a decision than we are."

"I see your point. Nevertheless, I want to see the reaction to today's test flight before I agree to anything further," Alan said.

"Let's assume we go ahead," suggested Oscar "Let's also assume that after we offer to stay or leave, they ask us to stay. What's next?"

"I've given this a lot of thought," said Korin. "I originally wanted to focus on how illogical religion is, but that may create too much push-back from religious leaders. There are four of us, so I came up with three more topics for the aliens to explain how they do things differently. This will require more work to prepare, but it will be worthwhile. First, explain how the aliens are confused by the racism that pits one race against another. Second, comment on nationalism, which pits one nation against another. Third, question our educational system, which teaches memorization in place of independent thinking. What do you think?"

"While I appreciate your enthusiasm, Korin, it's far too much," Herbert said. "I have no problem with us mentioning that the aliens have evolved differently in their culture. People will expect differences. But we need to have a focus. If we go after everything, we'll end up accomplishing nothing. Of the four areas, religion is the most vulnerable. I want to keep the focus there."

Oscar found this response quite interesting. A few moments earlier, Herbert had given him and Korin control over the focus. But when Korin moved off the religion topic, he objected. Oscar wanted to know why.

"I agree with Herbert," said Alan. "You always tell me to keep my focus when we pitch to a venture-capitalist group. Similarly, we must keep our pitch here focused on one issue. It's a big issue. If we have impact there, it will bring about major changes and, hopefully, most of them will be for the good."

Oscar also found Alan's comment odd. Why would Alan support Herbert so enthusiastically?

"Okay, maybe you're right," Korin agreed. "Maybe it's too much. Keeping it focused is the way to go. Even within the field of religion, we may want to concentrate on Christianity. But if we do, we have to make sure we aren't saying Christianity is the only false religion."

"All religious leaders rely on the same basic mentality," said Oscar. "In order to keep followers believing in their religion, there must be unsolved mystery. A God or set of gods has always been at the center of the mystery. Religion teaches its followers—no, requires them—to be satisfied with the religious explanation without understanding how the universe really works. There's some overlap in this thinking with the way nationalism works. People must believe that the laws and culture of their nation are superior to those of others, without any real desire to understand and appreciate the others. And yes, Korin, the same is true of racism. But we need to let others connect the dots. If they do, they'll conclude that seeking a true understanding is a better way than relying on unfounded beliefs about gods, countries, sexual orientations, or races."

"Let me interrupt," Herbert interjected. "So I can plan my part, when do you feel we'll be ready to go forward with the real thing?"

"Well, do you need a certain period of time to get ready?" asked Korin.

"I want to check and recheck all the equipment after the test. Then I want to teach at least one of you how all the important things work in case something happens to me. I wouldn't want to leave the three of you stuck in another dimension or on top of the UN building. I'll also have to get all the supplies we'll need and put backup equipment in the sphere. I'd say one month would cover it."

"What about you two?" Korin asked, looking at Oscar and Alan.

"It depends on what you want done," Alan answered. "I can't give you a video on the history of Christianity in one month. If you want two or three short scenes and tell me exactly what you want, I can do that. But I need a script from Oscar first."

"I have some ideas," Oscar said. "I can get you some information to start working on within a few days, but I can't say when I'll be finished. It'll require creativity. I can't just snap my fingers and make everything happen."

"Okay, I understand, but it can't drag on forever," said Korin. "Let's plan on going September first. That gives us two months. We'll go at six-thirty in the morning our time. That's nine-thirty in New York."

"We could see where things are in one month," Oscar suggested. "Then we'll adjust if needed."

"Sure, but let's assume the first of September is a hard date that we must make. Otherwise, the schedule will slip," said Korin. "I'll work with Herbert at first to make sure I understand how the controls work. Once I've got that down, I'll work with Oscar and Alan on the videos."

"For now, I think we should turn on the TV," Alan said. "Let's see if there's any news on the fire, and more importantly, let's see if there's anything on the sphere."

Oscar was curious about how quickly the three of them were able to agree. He had a reason for taking on such a risky endeavor, but he wasn't sure about the others. He listened closely and watched each one as they surfed the TV channels. As often happened in the Bay Area, the weather changed. The winds died down, and the fog rolled in. The fire was under controlled.

Oscar wasn't at all surprised that the national news made no mention of the sphere. It was too early for reports to come in from officials at Groom Lake or Beale Air Force Base. After an hour, they all became bored with the so-called news repeated on CNN. But then Oscar walked behind Alan, who was searching for stories on his laptop. He watched the sphere hovering on Alan's screen as two military jets flew by so fast they were not identifiable.

"What did you find, Alan?" asked Oscar.

"There are web pages dedicated to information on UFOs. If someone sees something interesting, they can put up a picture or video. It looks as though one of the true believers filmed your test flight and put it on the internet."

CHAPTER 22

Manifest plainness,
Embrace simplicity,
Reduce selfishness,
Have few desires.

—Lao-tzu (604–531 B.C.)

They all left Herbert's and went home. The lack of news coverage frustrated Alan. The single video on the internet appeared to have been taken with a cell phone and immediately uploaded to the blog where he found it. The video was less than thirty seconds long, and the quality was poor. It began with a ground-level shot and then panned up to the hovering sphere. The video jerked about, apparently in the hands of an inexperienced user. At first the only sounds were that of the person holding the camera. Then came off-camera statements such as, "What is that?" The roar of the two jets flying by the sphere drowned out that voice and others. The camera followed the jets, and the video ended with them disappearing in the distance.

Alan had called home as he left Herbert's, and Jeremy anxiously awaited his arrival. It was a typical, cool, San Francisco summer evening. Jeremy had placed an unopened bottle of champagne in an ice bucket. The bucket, partially wrapped in a pink napkin, stood on a small table in front of a half-opened, sliding-glass door. The Bay and lights of the Golden Gate Bridge were visible in the distance.

"Let me help you with that, love." As Alan walked in, Jeremy lifted the laptop from his lover's shoulder, placed it on the table, and removed it from its case.

"Thanks, Jer." Alan embraced Jeremy. "The champagne's a nice touch, but I'm disappointed in the video."

"I'm sure you're being overly critical. Let me see. You bring it up on the screen while I open the champagne."

They watched the video time and time again, commenting, laughing a bit, and a criticizing a great deal.

"Well, at least the champagne is good." Alan took another sip.

"What's your next step?"

"I could wait around to see if this video goes viral," Alan said with a smile.

"Not going to happen," said Jeremy.

"I could wait to see if another video surfaces. But I'm guessing that if there were another one, it would already be posted. Maybe the jet pilots will go public, but you know there's no chance of that happening," said Alan.

"Not in our lifetimes."

"I've got to go forward with the plan. I know it's risky, but it's the only way we can make people understand we're not crazy," Alan said.

"Well, I *am* crazy, but I did see those UFOs, so I understand."

"I'm set to meet with Oscar tomorrow morning to work out some details of what I'll put in the video."

The next morning Alan drove down to Stanford to meet Oscar in his office. After greeting Oscar, he walked over to examine the same mask he had worn not so long ago. "We need to come up with the opening video," he said. "It should be something that's not so old that it can't be verified, but old enough that there's some reasonably clear written evidence that whatever we show actually took place."

"Well, let's see. There's no such evidence of anything two thousand years old. If it's in the Bible, it can't be verified. No one knows its real authors or how long it was between an event's occurrence and when its description was reduced to writing. Then there are issues with incorrect copying, as well as poor translations. But we don't need to show an actual religious event. We could just show something related to religion. Maybe we show someone much more recent making a statement about religion?" asked Oscar.

"Do you have something in mind?"

"If you can make a video based on a painting, I do."

"Sure, I can get the basic facial features from the painting. The rest can be generated by the program," said Alan.

"I think we need to open with something that supports religion," Oscar said. "This will draw them in. A French mathematician named Blaise Pascal lived in the 1600s and is known for many great mathematical developments. He invented a mechanical calculator that was a forerunner of mechanical engineering. He's also known for 'Pascal's Wager,' which is a quasi-mathematical argument for the existence of God, or at least Pascal's reasoning for why we should all believe in God."

"I've heard of Pascal, but I didn't know he had strong opinions on religion," said Alan.

"He reasoned that no one could know the probability that God does or does not exist. However, he presented an argument that regardless of the probability, believing in God was prudent because there are only four possibilities:

(1) you believe in God, and you're wrong;

(2) you believe in God, and you're correct;

(3) you don't believe in God, and you're wrong; and

(4) you don't believe in God, and you're correct."

"Of those four possibilities," Oscar continued, "Pascal believed you're a big winner if (2) is true because there is a God, and you believed in Him. Conversely, you would be a big loser if (3) turns out to be correct because there is a God, and you did not believe. According to Pascal, possibilities (1) and (4) provide a neutral result. If there is no God, there would be no good or bad result because of what you did or did not believe. Religious leaders have advocated this as a valid reason to believe in God."

"You want to make the opening video of Pascal explaining this argument?" asked Alan. "I'm not sure I like the idea. He's French, so I assume he would speak French."

"He spoke English, but French was his native language, so I think he should be speaking French," said Oscar.

"If he could speak English, I'd rather do it in English. I did put other languages in the video I showed you guys, but I knew you wouldn't know if there was a mistake. It would be easier if it were in English. But why would this make a good opening?" asked Alan.

"We'll show the video and then, as aliens, ask questions about the logic of Pascal's thinking. That way, we won't appear to be critical of religion."

Alan didn't care for the idea. He doubted many people would have heard of Pascal, and he didn't want to make a video of someone speaking French. His main focus was showing the presence of a UFO over the UN. Including anything about religion was something he had reluctantly agreed to in order to get what he wanted. "Of course, we aliens would be curious about earthlings. But why would aliens want to know about Pascal's Wager? What would they ask?"

"I agree that aliens would have no particular interest in Pascal," said Oscar, "but they would conclude that the concept of God is important to people on earth. They might want to know why earthlings assumed God rewarded those who blindly believed in Him, as opposed to those who used the minds He gave them to question His very existence. They could ask why it wouldn't be just as logical to believe that God would reward those who questioned the existence of God."

"Okay, what else?" asked Alan.

"I think the aliens would ask if someone can simply believe because they're supposed to believe. If they do, are they faking it? Aren't they going to church without really believing? We, as aliens, will ask why any god would approve of faking it," Oscar suggested.

Alan didn't agree with Oscar, but he did not, at this time, believe it mattered. He just wanted to get the plan in action. "So we begin by showing them something from the past that they can verify as historically accurate," he said. "That makes sense to me. After we've drawn them in, we can show videos of past events that are less verifiable. That may work. It also shows that the aliens want to take a logical approach to the question of God's existence. Can you get me a script on exactly what you want Pascal to say?"

"Sure," said Oscar. "Pascal wrote quite a bit on this topic. I'll get you a writing that summarizes Pascal's Wager, and we can simplify the whole process by having Pascal read his own writing."

"What about the background? Would it be acceptable for him to speak outside, so trees or bushes are behind him?" said Alan.

"That works," said Oscar. "It also keeps us from having to fabricate the interior of a room in the 1600s. We could make one mistake there and blow the whole thing. The clothes will be easier, as we have portraits of Pascal wearing different outfits."

"Okay. You get me the portraits of Pascal and his writings on Pascal's Wager, and I'll get going on a video. What's next?"

"There are 2.2 billion Christians on earth, more than any other religion," Oscar said. "The basis of that religion is the resurrection of Jesus Christ. We show Jesus being nailed to the cross. Then we show the cross being taken down and Jesus removed from it for burial. Then we show him coming back to life."

Alan was Jewish, and though he wasn't what others would call a "practicing Jew," he didn't want to promote the idea that Christ rose from the dead. "Wait a minute," he protested. "I thought we planned to show that he *didn't* rise from the dead, that Christianity is based on something that never happened."

"Hold on," said Oscar. "We'll get to that. But this part has to be shown first. If we start with Pascal, we get them arguing logic. Once we win the logic argument, they'll say logic doesn't enter into the area of faith. Then we say that the faith in Christianity appears to be based on the resurrection. They'll be very hard-pressed to disagree with that. Then we show them your video, which confirms the crucifixion and the resurrection. There will be more to it, but we can gradually convince more and more people that the videos are alien recordings of what actually happened. We'll wait a while after we show each video to monitor the news channels for reactions from various religious leaders."

"One thing I'm sure of is that this event will be the only thing on any news channel. Wouldn't you think?"

"I'm sure you're right, Alan. Accept that the reporters will run out of things to say about a sphere hovering over the UN building. They'll be switching to others for comments all the time. Once we show the video of the resurrection, they'll get comments from every religious leader they can— and those religious leaders will all congratulate themselves for being right about the resurrection and Christianity in general. After we have that in place, we show the rest of the video."

"And what will that be, Oscar?"

"First, we show a conversation among the workers who take people off the crosses. Not all those crucified were buried, but some were. Remember, the workers are Jewish. They have to make sure their work is done before sundown on that Friday before the Saturday Sabbath. They assume all three of the crucified men are dead and take the crosses down. They remove the bodies and drag them toward graves, but they don't have time to bury them because it's already sundown. So they agree to return on Sunday to finish the burial. They leave all three bodies, and you focus in on Jesus's face. The close-up will show enough detail to reveal a beating pulse on his neck. It must be unmistakable that he's still alive."

Even though Alan had little confidence this plan would convince most Christians, he had no better one. His main interest was in devising a way to convince the world that UFOs were real. "I can do that," he told Oscar.

"Okay. While the video shows the beating pulse, we, as the aliens, make a simple statement: 'They only thought he was dead.' That should be all we need to say. We can rethink this and add to it later if we want. We could have a final scene where Jesus recovers and leaves the area."

"I like it. Technically, it works because no one needs to say much. The beating pulse says it all. I assume Jesus should look as he does in all the pictures?"

"Not quite," said Oscar. "The nails go in the wrists, not the hands, and he should be somewhat bigger, more muscular, and powerful-looking. In those times, you didn't make it too far in life if you weren't a robust and powerful individual. I can send you some images of the way others believe Jesus may have looked. Blend those with the traditional image of Jesus. People with more knowledge than most will buy into a more robust version of Jesus with nails in the wrist and a spear wound in the right side of his chest."

"Oscar, I can see how your plan works. We show that Jesus didn't die on the cross. But it's hardly definitive. They'll say he died immediately after the video ended and then rose from the dead."

"I know. I understand what it means. I have my reasons for doing it this way. So, to sum up, I'll get you some portraits of Pascal and a script of his Wager. I'll also provide a script on the workers speaking Aramaic and images of how Jesus might have looked. When you have something for me to look at, give me a call. Sound good?"

"Works for me, Oscar. So far, it doesn't appear all that difficult."

"Great. I'm a believer in KISS; you know, 'keep it simple, stupid.' I'm always preaching that to my students, so I try to follow it myself. I'll look forward to seeing what you've done."

Alan understood the plan and believed he could make the video Oscar specified. He often wrote videos programs for teenage boys and knew how to keep things visually simple. His skills would make this work. He also calculated that a fusion of his work with Oscar's ideas might eventually be accepted as real. Making it look real was more than a source of pride to Alan. If the videos were adjudged to be fake, the underlying purpose he had in mind would fail as well. At this point, he only had Herbert's promise that there would be something more to the plan than the others currently contemplated.

CHAPTER 23

It is better to travel well than to arrive.

—Gautama Buddha (c. 563–483 B.C.)

Oscar walked Alan out. As he strolled back to his office, he felt better about himself than he had in a very long time. He had enjoyed prior meetings with his three friends, but he had felt inferior to them. He was still in awe of what Herbert and Alan had done, but now he felt he was contributing to the project. He had gone from observer, to participant, to leader. This feeling had arisen as Alan asked him questions and looked to him to structure what they would present to the world. He had the power to influence the thinking of billions of people. He might even be the most powerful member of the group. Perhaps he would gain more control over the thinking of others than anyone ever had.

He'd had similar feelings before. When he first started teaching, he realized he influenced others' thinking. His books affected readers he never saw. But this was very different. Not only was it magnified many times over, but he felt both empowered and needed. He was center stage, and Shakespeare's quote that "all the world's a stage" became strangely real to him. As he looked around his office, he thought about the possibilities of doing something meaningful with his life.

He needed to share his thoughts with someone and called Korin. "Where are you now?" he asked her.

"I'm just leaving Herbert's place. Where are you?"

"I'm in my office. Alan just left a few minutes ago. I'm hungry. Are you free for lunch?"

"I'd love to see you for lunch. Where do you want to meet?" asked Korin.

"How about Lavanda in Palo Alto on the corner of University and Emerson? They have great wine, and I have some ideas to run by you."

"I'll see you there at twelve-thirty."

Oscar looked up from his table in the back of the restaurant when Korin walked in. He so enjoyed the way she walked, the way she held herself, and the smile that always spoke to him and him alone.

"What are you looking at?" asked Korin.

"Nothing."

"Don't give me that. You know you were watching me walk in. You just can't keep your eyes off me."

"I was trying to see if I could get the waiter's attention," Oscar said lightheartedly with the hint of a smile.

"Right. It's okay. I was thinking about you, too. But only because you were sitting behind a bottle of Château Latour. I was wondering what vintage you would have ordered."

"The 2000. I figured I'd get you to pay. After all, you're rich, and I'm the most powerful man in the world right now," said Oscar.

"Most powerful man, yes. But you're talking to the most powerful *person* in the world."

"Not any more. I think you turned over the power when you agreed to focus the hoax on religion."

"Pour me a glass of that Latour, and I'll let you know what I think about that after I've had some wine." Korin moved her glass toward Oscar.

"You have some of this, and you'll agree to anything." Oscar slowly poured the wine. "Let's toast to a successful hoax, a cardinal hoax."

"Very well. To a successful cardinal hoax. You said you wanted to talk. What about?"

"I was working with Alan on putting videos together. In one of them, we'll show Jesus on the cross. When they take him down, he'll appear to be dead. Then we'll zoom to his neck, where the viewer will see a beating pulse." Oscar paused. "What do you think?"

"Of course, I haven't seen the video, so it's not possible to judge. But won't that approach leave a lot of room for Christians to say he died later and then rose from the dead?"

"Yes, it will," Oscar replied. "It will allow people to speculate in many different ways. Which is what they do now. I'm not so sure that's a negative result. Even though I wasn't there to see it, I'm all but certain he didn't rise from the dead, but it would be reasonable to think that others believed he did. They had seen him nailed to a cross. Everyone else they'd ever seen crucified was dead. If Jesus did not die, if he recovered even for a short while, people might have thought he'd been resurrected. Such events could certainly form the basis for the myth upon which Christianity is based."

"Maybe I need more wine," said Korin dubiously. "I'd feel better if they saw him die, be taken down, and buried. Then show the grave weeks later with grass starting to grow on it. This is really good stuff. The wine, I mean."

"Making the video the way you suggest would raise even more doubts. Christians would say it wasn't Christ on the cross at all, but someone else. They would say the whole video had no relevance because it didn't show their Jesus. My way will create doubt in the minds of more people. The events will seem more real and will provide an explanation for the basis of the religion. No one wants to be told they are *completely* wrong. If you tell someone he's dead wrong, he reacts defensively. If you merely provide him with a reason for what appears to be a mistake, he'll be far more likely to reconsider his original position."

"Absolutely not, Oscar. You're dead wrong." Korin pounded a fist on the table, then looked up with a gentle smile. "Okay, I'm joking. I get your point. But I'll have to see the video."

"Sometimes it's not what's in the video, but what you leave out that's all important. Did you see Al Gore's film *An Inconvenient Truth?*"

"Sure. What's Al Gore got to do with this?"

"Well, he won an Oscar and a Nobel Prize, so people believed he had something to say. He told everyone we needed to stop putting greenhouse gases into the atmosphere, or the earth would get too hot. Right?"

"Right. What did he leave out?"

"The movie leaves you with the impression that greenhouse gases—mostly CO_2—are manmade," said Oscar.

"Sure, cars, factories, lawnmowers, all kinds of things. So?"

"All those things and many other manmade sources generate all kinds of pollution. It may be a meaningful amount. But it's only a tiny faction of the CO_2 generated."

"I'm not following you. Where does the CO_2 come from, if not from manmade sources?" asked Korin.

"Over ninety-five percent of the CO_2 generated on the planet comes from natural sources, such as respiration and microorganisms in the ocean. If we completely eliminated all manmade CO_2 sources—every car, truck, factory, lawn-mower, or what have you—the decrease would only be about five percent. I'm not saying that would or would not have positive results. The five percent could be very important and global warming disastrous. But if Al Gore had told the whole story, he would have been ignored, and he wouldn't have won an Oscar or a Nobel Prize."

"Interesting," said Korin thoughtfully. "So less is more. By not showing Jesus dead and in the grave, people will con-clude on their own that Jesus didn't die on the cross."

"Not everyone, but some will buy into the story and even suggest what may have happened next. For example, he may have recovered, seen people, and died thereafter of infections in his wounds."

"You're right about one thing, Oscar. The more wine I drink, the more powerful you seem to me and the better your story sounds. Seriously, I do get your point that regardless of what we show, others will explain it away or say that somehow it's not accurate. We may, in fact, have a better chance of convincing a greater number of people by showing there is a basis for Christianity, but that the basis is false."

"Korin, I had almost hoped you wouldn't agree."

"Why is that?"

"There's a lot of responsibility tied up in this. I wasn't jok-ing about possibly being the most powerful man in the world. We all understand that many famous actors and actresses aren't very bright people. However, their popularity gives them the opportunity to influence millions on all sorts of subjects. Being in control of what goes into these videos has the potential of influencing more people than any actor or world leader."

"Oscar, there are a lot of ways to look at this. You and I both know that what people believe changes over time. Some of that change is brought about by science. When people understood the sun better, they stopped believing it was a god. It's the same here: You're just allowing some of them to understand that Jesus was not God."

"It's based on deception, which bothers me." Oscar raised his glass for another sip of wine. "But Al Gore's video is based on deception, as well. There are a number of major errors in it, and they seem to be intentional errors. That doesn't mean it hasn't had a positive effect on reducing pollution—and I think nearly everyone wants less pollution. Perhaps I just need to accept that this is the way things are and move on... This *is* wonderful wine."

"Perhaps it's just the company you're drinking it with that makes it so special?"

"Perhaps. Let me close my eyes and try some." He did so. "No, it's just as good with my eyes closed—maybe better."

"You can't fool me, Oscar. I know how you feel about me."

Oscar didn't know what to say. He smiled at Korin, and she smiled back. They had discussed their feelings for one another so many times without coming to any conclusion about what to do with their situation. Each wanted to be with the other, but they were both in long-term marriages with children. At times, they had both wondered if their mutual attraction was based, at least in part, on the forbidden aspects of their relationship. Neither really knew the answer. Right now, they enjoyed being together, even if only to share some wine, talk, and have a good meal. Being with each other made them happy and alive—and that was good enough for now.

"I wanted to get your thoughts on the video ideas, but I also want to bring up another issue," Oscar said. "I have a feeling that Herbert and Alan may have something going on between them."

"No. I'm sure Alan is very committed to Jeremy, and Herbert's not interested in Alan," said Korin.

"I don't mean a sexual thing. I mean they have some other plan mapped out. They just seem all too agreeable about letting you and me run this forward."

Oscar had yet to tell Korin why he, himself, was so willing to participate in the plan. He felt his own motivation was the only legitimate one and believed the others must have their own reasons. He just couldn't understand what those motivations were.

"What do you mean? Can you give me an example of what you're talking about?"

"When you came up with a first statement for the aliens to make, Alan and Herbert readily agreed," said Oscar. "When you suggested that the sphere be over the UN building, they also agreed."

"Okay, but those were good ideas. They didn't have a better one, so they agreed to mine. Why is that strange?"

"You may be letting your ego blind you. If we forget about the details, I still find it odd they agreed to the overall hoax idea," said Oscar.

"Well, you agreed. Isn't that just as odd?"

This was an impossibly difficult question for him to answer. He didn't want to tell her the whole truth. He was sure it would change everything if she knew. The best he could do was a half-truth. "I'm doing it for the money." He said it convincingly and surprised himself how sincere it sounded. He watched her face and hoped for the best.

"Well, maybe in part. But you find it exciting as well. There's more to it than the money," said Korin.

"Anyway, I just want you to be aware of what I think about Alan and Herbert. Don't get me wrong. They're not bad people, but I'm all but certain they have their own agenda. There's something else driving them to be so agreeable."

"When you figure it out, let me know."

"For now, let's just savor the rest of this Latour. When we're done, I'll figure out where we can go so I can savor you," said Oscar.

Korin just smiled.

CHAPTER 24

There is no need for you to leave the house.
Stay at your table and listen. Don't even listen, just wait.
Don't even wait, be completely quiet and alone.
The world will offer itself to you to be unmasked,
it can't do otherwise; in raptures it will writhe before you.

—Franz Kafka (1883–1924)

"Hello, is that you, Herbert?" Korin noted Herbert's caller ID on the phone screen as she answered her phone.

"Yes. It's me. I know you were just here yesterday, but you should come back today. You wanted to tell me something before the others got here, and I've learned something about the field controls that I never knew before. I want you to see it. Can you come over now?" asked Herbert.

"Is everything okay with you and the project?"

"It's fine. I just need another person here to confirm something. When can you get here?"

"I could be there in an hour, but I can't stay long—maybe an hour, two at the most. Will that work for you?" asked Korin.

"It'll do. I think you'll find this very interesting and well worth your time. I'll explain when you get here."

"Okay. I'll be there within an hour. Bye."

Korin pushed the "end call" icon on her phone. She could tell he was far less interested in hearing what she'd wanted to tell him than in showing her his new discovery.

"Hello, Herbert," she said upon arriving at his place. "It's good you haven't blown yourself up or gotten lost in a different dimension. What's up?"

"Thanks for coming over. Last time you were here you were going to tell me something. What was it? You said it was something about Oscar."

"There's no easy way to say this. Oscar is dying. He's been diagnosed with pancreatic cancer. I just recently found out, and I also know he's refusing any treatment. He's got about a year left," said Korin.

"That's terrible. When did he tell you?"

"He hasn't told me, but I know it's true. How I found out isn't relevant. He really doesn't want anyone to know. I'm sure his doctor won't be able to change his mind about treatment," said Korin.

"Why not?"

"Since I'm not supposed to know he's ill, I haven't talked to him about it, but he's smart enough to know that he can't be cured, and doesn't want to be a pin cushion for some experimental clinic," said Korin.

"Is there anything we can do?"

"I believe there is. Give me a little time. When I have the answer, I'll need your help to make it work. For now, don't tell him you know. I'll let you in on the rest of my plan later. You should know he's participating in this hoax as way to get money for his family after he's gone," said Korin.

"What about you? Is it only about the money for you?"

"I'm not saying anything more for now. Let's move on. Show me what you wanted me to see."

"I'll get right to the point. Remember I told you we couldn't see things in another dimension and that I figured that was because our brains hadn't developed to that point?"

"Sure, I remember," said Korin.

"Well, I think I may have figured out the solution to seeing other dimensions."

"So now you're going to tell me I need to grow a second frontal lobe or something. Is that it?" Korin shifted from one foot to another in front of Herbert.

"You're joking, of course. But you do know something about the structure of the brain. I don't want to tell you things you already know. Did you know that there are different types of brain waves? The most common are alpha, beta, delta, and theta waves."

"I've heard of brain waves, but I don't know much about them." Korin sat down, crossed her legs, and leaned forward.

"Each type of brain wave operates at a different frequency—not unlike radio waves," Herbert explained. "If you close your eyes and relax, your brain generates a lot of alpha waves at a frequency of about ten hertz. It's not only brain waves—everything in the universe has a wave function. Every photon of light, every electron, every elementary particle we know of has a wave signature unique to the type of particle it is. We see different colors of light because of the different frequencies. We hear different sounds because of the different frequencies of the sound wave. The waves of sounds moving molecules through the air vibrate our eardrums. Likewise, the neurochemical reactions that create human consciousness and thought have distinct waves."

"Okay, Herbert. I get that waves are important. What does it have to do with your field generator and seeing other dimensions?" Korin displayed her normal impatience.

"Wave interaction is referred to as *resonance*. You've heard that something resonates, right?"

"Yes, but I never gave it much thought," said Korin.

"When two wave sources are in sync, each source emits the same wave signature. When I thought about this, I figured out we could see another dimension if we could get our brains in sync with that dimension."

"All right, but I can't change my brain wave frequency." Korin looked at him intently.

"Once I measure your brain wave frequency, I can put the field at the same frequency. I can change the field frequency until you resonate with another dimension, and I think you'll be able to see it. Would you be willing to try?" asked Herbert.

"What's the risk?" Korin stalled for time and wondered if somehow this could help Oscar.

"You ask the oddest questions at times."

"Why is it odd for me to ask what the risks might be?"

"Well, first of all, how the hell would anyone know the risks?" Herbert said in irritation. "No one has done anything remotely similar to this. It's all totally new. Second, in the sphere, you already shifted from our own dimension to another, and nothing negative happened. But mostly I find it odd that you're willing to play a hoax on everyone in the world, and yet you're worried about risks."

"I was just asking if you knew what might go wrong. That's what I meant by the question," said Korin.

"I don't know what the risks are, but I'd venture to guess they're substantially less than those we'll take in perpetrating this cardinal hoax. I'm no lawyer, but I would guess we'll be breaking all kinds of laws. If we're caught, the authorities will spend a great deal of time formulating a particularly awful and heretofore unheard-of punishment. There are lots of risks involved, but you're a risk taker. That's why I wanted you in on this." Herbert spoke with the passion he generally reserved for descriptions of science experiments.

"I never expected such an emotional response. A simple 'I don't know' would have sufficed. But I see your point. What do you want me to do?" asked Korin.

"Get in the sphere and sit in front of one of the windows. Look out and tell me what you see. Keep talking about what you see, and I'll gradually change the frequency of the field. If I'm right, when the field reaches a frequency that puts you out of resonance with our dimension, you'll see nothing out of the window. That part shouldn't be too difficult. I'll continue to change the frequency of the field gradually until you tell me you see something."

"Until I see what?" interrupted Korin.

"There you go again with the questions that have no answers. How the hell would I know? It could be anything. What would Columbus have seen if he'd sailed off the end of the world? I don't know. Just let me know when you can no longer see the surrounding area. Then let me know when you can see something."

"Okay, I can do that. This isn't another trick you're pulling on me, is it?" Korin looked directly into Herbert's eyes.

"Finally, a legitimate question. It would be a great opportunity to fool you. But no. I need your help on this. So get in the sphere, sit down, put on the headset, and tell me what you see."

"If I don't come back, tell everyone I just chose to stay in another dimension. This one is so last century."

"What are you talking about?" Herbert looked confused.

"It was a joke. At least it seemed funny to me at the time. I'll get in there and do as you asked." She walked up the stairs into the sphere, and the door closed. Although she'd been in the same place for the test flight with Herbert and Oscar, it seemed different without them—four empty chairs and a small window open in front of one of them. It was the same window from which Oscar had seen the jets fly by. The space had seemed like an amusement park ride for the test flight. Now it seemed like an execution chamber. She felt a bit relieved when she aligned herself so she could see Herbert. She walked over to the chair in front of the small window, sat down, put on the headset, and waived nervously to Herbert.

"Can you hear me?"

"I hear you just fine. No need to shout. I'm about to turn on the field. It'll be exactly as it was before, except that this time I'm not focusing the field on a new location. I'll just change the frequency. Just keep telling me what you see." Herbert began slowly changing the field frequency.

"Right now, I see you and your house in the distance. It all looks as I would expect it to look."

Thirty minutes passed, and Korin continued to repeat that she saw nothing different. Herbert changed the frequency of the field very slowly, not knowing what would happen. The experiment was similar to tuning a radio receiver to a radio station. Herbert moved through the frequencies slowly enough that if he did find the correct frequency, he could leave the field set there and not move past it.

"Herbert, something is happening," said Korin's excited voice. "Everything outside is getting dim, like when night falls, and it's getting dark."

"Great! How dark is it?"

"It seems to be about half as bright as it was."

"Okay, I'm going to start changing it again."

"It's black now, but more black than it is at night. It's completely black. I see nothing at all." Korin's voice reflected concern. Her discomfort with the situation grew, and she wondered if something had gone wrong. Was she going to spend the rest of her life in some other dimension? Minutes passed and still no contact from Herbert.

"Korin, you there?"

"Where the fuck were you? I thought I'd be trapped in here forever. What happened?" Korin saw the scenery outside the window reappear.

"It seems that when you're completely out of sync, I can no longer communicate with you. You can't see, hear, or in any way perceive signals from our dimensional space. Not unexpected," said Herbert calmly.

"Maybe not for you. But it was goddamn scary for me."

"I understand. Do you want to stop?"

"Well, to be honest, I do. But I'll put on my big-girl panties and keep going."

"That created quite an image for me. But enough of that. This isn't going to work exactly as I thought. When you're completely out of sync, we won't be able to communicate. I'll make some educated guesses about what the frequency should be. My thinking is that the frequency at complete blackout is halfway between two different dimensions. At the first one, you see our home dimension. At the other, you'll see some other dimension. I'm going to put the frequency back where it went black, and then very gradually move it a bit to either side and then back to zero. The whole thing will take less than five minutes. You good with that?"

"My panties and I are ready. Turn it on." Korin's confidence surprised her, in view of the level of anxiety she'd just experienced.

Herbert turned on the field and continued with the experiment. At first, it was as Korin expected. She saw nothing outside, nothing but black. Then the view changed, but it changed in an unexpected way. There were stars in every direction. This startled her, and she wondered if she'd passed out and awakened hours later, after nightfall. But the stars were different from usual—larger and brighter. An object that appeared to be a planet reflected light from a nearby star and floated still and seemingly motionless in space. As she continued to watch with fascination, the sky went black again, and then she could see Herbert's house in the distance. She stood up slowly, took off her headphone, and left the sphere. Words were hard to find, but she explained as best she could what she'd felt and seen.

"That's incredible," said Herbert. "It worked out just as I thought it would! Yes, you disappeared from view once you were out of sync with our dimensional space."

"So why was I seeing somewhere else?" asked Korin. "No, don't answer me. I'm starting to get it. I couldn't see our dimension because you put me out of sync with it, and I could see another dimension because you put me in sync or in resonance with it. Could you see me here?"

"I couldn't see you or the sphere part of the time," Herbert responded. "As you know, I couldn't hear you on the radio. When you're out of sync with our dimension, your molecules are out of sync, so you and the sphere don't appear to be here. The interesting part is that I could see you back here the instant your molecules were back in resonance with this dimension. This confirms what I thought. When I only change the frequency, the matter doesn't move from one dimension to another; it's just that by changing the wave signature of the matter, it's put in or out of sync with one dimension or another."

"So is there a lot of other matter around that we can't see or feel?" asked Korin.

"I believe that other matter is what scientists have been calling 'dark matter.' It has a gravitational effect, or, more correctly, it bends time/space, but otherwise we don't know it's there. We're out of sync with it."

"What do you mean by saying that dark matter has a gravitational effect?"

Herbert explained. "For decades, physicists have known that the stars in galaxies move in a way that can't be explained based on the matter we see. In order for galaxies to exist and move as they do, there needs to be a great deal more matter present. Current estimates are that we see about four percent of the universe. The other ninety-six percent is referred to as dark matter, and no one knows what it is."

"So I may be the first person to have seen dark matter—is that right?"

"Well, Korin, there's a lot I don't know about what you saw and what happened. But yes, you may be the first person, or at least the first person from this planet, to have seen the matter we now refer to as dark matter," Herbert said slowly. Everything was working out in a way that supported much of what he had speculated. There was more to this than Korin imagined. He now had evidence that there were other universes. Our universe is part of a multi-universe, he thought. The excitement left him intoxicated. He didn't want to share everything with Korin and thought it best not to say much more.

"This is a lot for me to absorb, Herbert," she said. "I'm feeling like Neil Armstrong when he first stepped on the surface of the moon. It's all overwhelming. If you're okay with calling it a day, I think I'll go home."

"We finished what I wanted to do." Herbert walked Korin toward the door. "We could try other frequencies later and see what happens. Why don't you talk to Oscar and Alan and see if we can all meet somewhere tomorrow?"

"I'll call them on the way home. We'll talk soon. Bye for now." Korin hugged Herbert goodbye. He held the embrace longer than usual, which seemed curious to her.

CHAPTER 25

*Do not spoil what you have by desiring
what you have not; remember that what you now have
was once among the things you only hoped for.*

—Epicurus (341–270 B.C.)

D riving home, Korin thought about how far she had come in life. She was born to a father who sold real estate in New Orleans and a mother who waited tables. They had always told her she could be anything she wanted to be. She'd imagined becoming rich and famous. But she never dreamed she would be the first to see something, maybe an entire universe, that no one had ever seen before.

She looked at the cars along the way and wondered about the lives of the people inside. A boy maybe ten years old appeared to notice she was driving an unusual car, a dark green Bentley convertible. She smiled, and he waved.

She was filled with a euphoria she'd never felt before. The more she knew about Herbert's work, the more she appreciated how much it would impact the world — although it wouldn't change Oscar's situation. Realizing this caused feelings of discontent to return.

"Hello, Korin?" said Oscar as he answered his cell phone.

"Yes, it's me. Where are you now?"

"I'm at Alan's. We're working on the videos. Where are you?"

"Well, I'm back in this dimension now. But an hour or so ago, I wasn't so sure I'd ever be here again." Korin waited to hear Oscar's response.

"So you were having wild and crazy sex?" Oscar asked jokingly.

Korin laughed. "I wondered what you might say, but hadn't considered that. I guess maybe I should have, knowing you. No. I wasn't having sex, and you should know by now that you're the only one who puts me into another dimension—at least in that way." She silently contemplated why that was.

"What are you talking about then? I'm not following you."

"I was with Herbert. We did a little experiment. I literally ended up in another place, a whole new universe or dimensional space. Herbert wants us all to meet tomorrow morning at nine-thirty, and I think his place would be best. We can explain it then. Ask Alan if he can make it. I'll be home in twenty minutes. Send me an email confirming for both of you after you talk to Alan." Korin changed lanes to pass slower-moving traffic along the rolling hills of Interstate 280 headed south.

"I'll send an email. Do you want to hear about the videos?"

"Of course I do. Can you ask Alan to bring them tomorrow?" She changed lanes again to pass others and checked her speedometer. She was going over eighty miles an hour, but it seemed so slow. "Are you working the language issue out?" she asked.

"I'm less concerned about it now," Oscar said. "Until a hundred years ago or so, of course, there were no audio recordings. Language is always changing. If the language seems different, no one will know why, and they'll just assume that's the way people spoke back then.

"Sounds like it's all going well."

"Yes. Alan is very creative. I tell him the basics, and he comes up with some amazing stuff. You're really going to like this."

"I don't know. I'm very hard to please." Korin intended her comment as a joke, at least in part.

"I'm well aware of that—perhaps more than anyone. But I haven't let you down yet, have I?"

"No, indeed, you have not. I look forward to seeing you, Alan, and the videos tomorrow. Bye for now." Korin tapped her earpiece to hang up the phone and continued driving home. She slowed down and went with the flow of the surrounding traffic. She was feeling a bit more content because she could tell Oscar was enjoying what he was doing. Contentment was an unfamiliar feeling, and she liked it. She liked it a lot. But the feeling was fleeting, as she needed a solution to Oscar's medical condition, and she could not be sure if the one she had in mind would work.

Korin often had access to information long before others did. Inventors and entrepreneurs presented business plans to her in hope of obtaining financial backing. Their plans often included groundbreaking technological developments. Her job was figuring out which plans to fund and which to pass on.

Just over two years ago, three doctors involved in cancer research had come to her venture-capital firm for funding. They had formed a small company and wanted to develop a drug. The data they presented was compelling. In human cell cultures, their compound selectively killed cancer cells.

One group of tests was on pancreatic cancer cells. Korin had been ready to invest until the intellectual property report came back. They had no patents and seemed unlikely to obtain any that would provide commercially meaningful coverage. The compound they were using was old. Others had taken it for years and some of the people had unknowingly treated themselves for cancer. There was nothing to patent. She and her firm decided not to invest, and she had been enormously disappointed. What seemed to be a promising drug would never be used. Investing hundreds of millions of dollars without solid patent protection was out of the question. But she remembered the people involved. She needed to get the drug for Oscar and, if possible, ask for their help in administering it. More importantly, she needed to change Oscar's mindset about not being treated. She wanted him not only to take the drug, but to truly believe the treatment would work. The thought of making money from her investment was secondary now. Doubts she had about the risks involved were put aside.

CHAPTER 26

All truths are easy to understand once
they are discovered; the point is to discover them.

—Galileo Galilei (1564–1642)

The next morning, they met at Herbert's. Korin brought Herbert his jelly doughnuts and cream cheese, lox, and a bagel for Alan. She knew it was a favorite that he rarely allowed himself to have. There were coffees and juice for all, and a raspberry scone for Oscar.

"These are great doughnuts." Herbert stuffed another doughnut quarter into his mouth.

"Great bagel, as well," said Alan. "Did you have it flown in from New York for me?"

"I hope you had the scone flown from London," Oscar joked.

Alan looked around the room. Herbert had white powdered sugar around his mouth, and some had fallen onto his shirt. Oscar had a cream mustache from the foam on his coffee and crumbs from the scone on his lap. Alan wiped a bit of cream cheese from the corner of his mouth and motioned to Oscar to do the same. He put his hands down on the smooth wooden surface of the table where they sat. He could tell Korin was happy. Despite his frustration that the test flight hadn't resulted in more widespread recognition of UFOs, he felt things would eventually go in that direction.

"You boys look happy," said Korin. "I am, as well. We're going to make this hoax work and have a good time doing it."

"You seem unusually positive today," said Oscar. "Are you planning to tell Alan and me what you and Herbert were up to yesterday?"

"You're looking at the first person ever to see and be in another dimensional space. It's not possible for anyone to realize how big our universe is. But yesterday I saw that everything we know is just one dimensional space. It's all just a small percentage of what exists." Korin spoke with delight and confidence. "Herbert believes I may be the first person to see dark matter, and he's working on confirming that. But I'll let Herbert tell you more about it."

"You've all heard of Albert Einstein's equation, $E=mc^2$," said Herbert. "What this showed the world was that matter can be transformed into energy. That's what makes an atom bomb—a small amount of matter is transformed into energy."

"Do you use the field to change matter into energy?" asked Oscar.

"Not at all," answered Herbert. "The field is made up of particles that are so small they allow us to slip out of our dimensional space and penetrate into other dimensional spaces. This is really not possible to comprehend, but you might try to think of it this way: if you see a telephone line strung between poles in the distance, the line appears one-dimensional. A straight line has only one dimension, and the telephone line appears as a line in space. However, if you were a tiny ant crawling on the line, then that phone line would appear three-dimensional. All three dimensions of the phone line were always there, but they weren't readily apparent to you until you were reduced to a smaller level. Many things exist and have influence over us without our recognizing they're there."

"Are you speaking about spiritual things?" asked Oscar.

"No," answered Herbert. "I'm talking about things in the material world. For example, it wasn't until very recently that science knew that bacteria caused infections. Even more recently, we discovered that viruses are the cause of many diseases. Before we knew of the damaging effect of x-rays, doctors regularly used them on pregnant women.

"But I'm getting a little off-track here. I just wanted to point out that energy and matter are interchangeable and that many things influence us greatly without our even knowing they're there. These include bacteria that we now know cause infections or a phone line that we now understand has three dimensions. It all depends on how you look at, and come to understand these things.

"Let's get back to the experiment Korin and I did yesterday," Herbert continued. He got up from the table, walked over to an old rocking chair, and sat. "One property that matter and energy share is wave function. Every particle of matter in the universe has a wave signature unique to the type of particle it is. All energy is made of waves, and each type of energy has a unique wave signature."

"Can you tell me what you mean by wave signature?" asked Oscar. "When I think of waves, I think of the ocean, not matter or energy."

"The ocean makes a good analogy," Herbert answered. "When you see waves, you see some high, some medium, and some low. The height is the wave *amplitude*. You've probably also noticed that waves can come ashore one after the other very rapidly, or be more spaced apart so they come ashore less often in a given period of time. The timing between the waves is the wave *frequency*. The particular amplitude and frequency of something gives it a unique wave signature."

"Okay, I'm following you." Oscar leaned forward in his chair and stared intently as Herbert rocked back and forth in his chair.

"By changing the frequency of sound, you'll hear different pitches," Herbert said. "By changing the frequency of light, you see different colors. You can make the sound louder or the light brighter by increasing its amplitude. The light we see is all within a very narrow band of frequencies. We can see red light, but not infrared light, at one end of the visible light spectrum. We see violet, but not ultraviolet, light at the other end. Science has known for some time that humans can't see most light or hear most sound. So the basic idea of changing frequencies to make something detectable has been around a long time.

"The field has a frequency and everything inside the field is affected by that frequency," Herbert added. "After adjustments, the field and its contents resonate at the same frequency. When that frequency goes out of sync with our dimensional space, the sphere and its contents can't be seen or detected. What we found out yesterday was that the field and its contents could be synced or brought into resonance with *another* dimension. When we did this, Korin saw another dimensional space."

Watching Herbert rock back and forth in his chair took Alan back to the days when he used to sit, content, on his grandfather's lap, listening to his stories. Later, he trusted his grandfather as no other. There was nothing he couldn't tell him when they were alone. For a long time, he had shared his homosexuality with no one else. He had found his grandfather's rocker after he had passed away and brought it back to San Francisco, although it matched nothing else in his home. At first, Jeremy despised the rocker, but once Alan had explained that only his grandfather would listen to him when he was young, he placed the chair in a prominent place in their formal living room.

"So that's what you meant when you called me yesterday and said you'd been to another dimension and back," said Oscar with a small smile.

"What did you see?" This was an enormously important question to Alan. Her answer would determine what he would share regarding his agreement with Herbert.

"I was in two different dimensional spaces. In the first, there were lots of distant stars. Many more compared to what we ever see here. In the second, I saw stars, too. But I also saw what appeared to be a planet," Korin answered.

When he heard this, Alan wanted her to add something more. He wanted her to say there must be other life there. But neither Korin nor Oscar spoke up on the topic. Alan knew that if he said something, they wouldn't understand. They would be nonbelievers until there was concrete evidence of life on other planets. "What does this all mean to us as far as the plan is concerned?" he asked.

"For one thing," answered Korin, "we have somewhere else to go if this all turns out badly."

"As much as I like the four of you, I don't want to spend eternity in another dimension with only you guys," Alan said, hoping someone would suggest that others would be there, too.

"Don't worry, Alan," said Korin. "It'll all be fine. You'll be back with Jeremy in your multi-million-dollar mansion in no time."

"Before the two of you get into a discussion about what could happen or who might have the biggest house, why don't we take a look at the videos?" Oscar carried his laptop over to Herbert. "Alan has done an amazing job at putting them together."

"Do you want me to hook this into my projection system?" Herbert took Oscar's laptop out of its case.

"Yes, please do."

"It's my understanding that while we're in the sphere, we will only communicate with the 'earthlings' by text and this video—no direct visual or audio communications from us to anyone. Is that agreed?" asked Alan. This was important to him in ways he knew Korin did not, at least at this point, understand.

"Absolutely." Korin looked at Alan and then at Oscar. "If any of us is seen or heard, no one will believe we're aliens. Because you know computers best and type fast, you should run the keyboard, Alan. Just to make sure there are no errors that will reveal us as earthlings, have Oscar check the messages before you transmit them."

"I can do that," said Alan. "Will you be reading them, as well?"

"I think we should all read and have input on what goes out," said Korin.

Alan wanted more control over the messages, but he didn't want to say that. Having Korin in charge of the messaging in real time could interfere with his plan. "What if you write up some ideas in advance, Korin? Then I can have them ready. If I have to take input from everyone in real time, it could get confusing," he suggested.

"Okay. I'll get you something. For now, let's see your videos."

Alan started the programs and sat back as they watched. The first was Blaise Pascal, and the second was the crucifixion. Everyone was pleased with the results. Korin commented that Jesus didn't look like the paintings and sculptures she'd seen. His face looked older and his body more powerful. Oscar explained that most experts agreed that he would likely have been a more powerful-looking person and that art from even a few hundred years ago usually showed older-looking faces on younger people. People, Oscar explained, didn't age well two thousand years ago. Jesus had always been shown as looking much younger than he really would have appeared.

"Korin, what's wrong?" Oscar looked over in alarm as Korin suddenly slumped in her seat. Grabbing her arms and holding her up, he asked, "Are you okay?"

"Is she unconscious?" Alan froze where he was. Korin's eyes were closed and her mouth partially open. He didn't know what to do.

"Yes, I believe she is. Get me a wet cloth, Herbert," Oscar said urgently.

Herbert was already up. He quickly moved to an adjoining bathroom, wet a face cloth, and brought it to Oscar. "Should I call an ambulance?"

Alan watched carefully as Oscar placed the cloth gently on Korin's face, pressing and removing it from her skin several times. He saw the concern in Oscar's face. The way he touched her told Alan there was much more to the relationship between those two than he had previously thought. His grandfather had once patched up the scrapes from Alan's bike crash with a similar look on his face. The memory brought him back once again to his boyhood.

"She seems to be breathing okay. Let's recline the chair completely." Oscar pushed a button on the side of Korin's chair and forced the seat back into a reclining position. "Let's give her a minute before calling 911. She doesn't seem to be in immediate danger."

"Are you kidding?" Alan's voice was loud and nervous. "She's unconscious! We should call 911 right now!" He was completely unfamiliar with anyone going unconscious. It frightened him and made him question everything they were doing.

"Calm down, Alan." Oscar paused and looked seriously at him.

"I've seen people unconscious before, and she doesn't seem to be in distress. Rushing her off to a hospital in an ambulance will just add stress to her life—and to ours as well." Oscar lovingly reapplied the wet cloth to Korin's face.

"What do you think is wrong with her?" asked Herbert with concern in his voice.

"Her breathing and heart rate seem normal. She hasn't had any convulsions, and her skin temperature is normal. She may have just fainted—maybe from exhaustion," Oscar said calmly.

Although he didn't say so, Alan was quite upset and had many other ideas about what was happening. Maybe, he thought, the field was having a belated effect on her heart rhythm. Maybe it had changed something about her body chemistry. While he was very worried, he saw that Oscar was good at calming down a stressful situation. Unlike him, Oscar seemed to excel in the most stressful times, and now was one of those times.

"Herbert, do you have any smelling salts?" asked Oscar in a steady voice. His serene nature caused Alan to put down the phone he had picked up to call 911.

"No, I don't."

Oscar maintained his calm. "Okay, you've got a small kitchen off the next room. Is there any vinegar in there?"

"Yes."

"Go and get another cloth. Put some vinegar on it and bring it back to me." Before he finished his sentence, Herbert was on his way. He rushed back and with the cloth, sopping wet. "You may have overdone it just a bit. I just wanted a tablespoon of vinegar. It looks as though you put half a bottle on this." Oscar held it under Korin's nose.

"What, uh ahh, what is that?" asked Korin in a slurred voice. "No, wait, it's balsamic, isn't it?"

A smile of relief crossed Oscar's face. "So you've still got your sense of humor. Not too many people would notice the type of vinegar after fainting."

"I didn't faint," Korin said firmly.

"It sure looked that way to us," said Alan. "I was sure something really bad had happened to you. I was just about to call 911."

"It was something different," Korin said slowly. "I know I was physically here, but my mind was not. I started thinking about what we would do while we were in the sphere showing the videos to everyone. Then I flashed back to my experience yesterday when I saw the other dimensional space. I kept flipping back and forth between those two ideas in my mind. I'm not sure how, but I lost touch with my consciousness here, and I was again aware of some other dimensional space."

Korin sat up slowly and felt disoriented. It wasn't a bad feeling, but it was different from any she'd experienced before. She remembered how drunk a small amount of alcohol made her feel the first time she drank. She wondered if she would adjust and as with the alcohol, it would be easier to orient herself next time.

"Fascinating," said Herbert. "Describe what you were feeling."

"It's difficult to put into words. I wasn't asleep, but my consciousness wasn't here. My awareness somehow focused on the dimensional space I experienced yesterday. I just didn't have a frame of reference for understanding what I was perceiving. I wish I could be more specific. It wasn't a bad experience, and, strangely, I think I could make it happen again."

"Let's not try that just yet," said Oscar. "Why don't you sit up first and then try to stand up slowly." Oscar moved the back of Korin's chair upright.

Korin put her hands on the armrests and stood up. She looked around. Alan watched her face. She seemed surprised, even a bit confused. He wondered if she appreciated what had happened and whether he would notice if something similar ever happened to him.

"I feel better now than I did when I came here," said Korin. "I feel refreshed. It's as though I just finished meditating *and* had a massage. How long was I out?"

"Not long," said Oscar. "Maybe a few minutes. I'd say it was less than five. Somehow, I knew you were fine. You seemed very relaxed."

"Don't you think it would be a good idea to take her by the hospital and have her checked, just to be sure?" Alan asked.

"I'm not going to any hospital," Korin said with conviction. "If I told anyone else what happened, they'd confine me to a psychiatric ward until I stopped talking about going to another dimensional space. I'm fine. I'm just a multi-dimensional kind of girl."

"People who do transcendental meditation learn to go in and out of a meditative state. Maybe that's similar to what you did," Herbert suggested.

"I think you're right. It was a different mental state. But without the experience I had yesterday, I don't think I would have been able to get there." Korin walked around the room, showing no ill effects whatsoever.

"Well, as they say on the prescription-drug TV commercials, you should refrain from driving or operating heavy machinery when you try this," said Oscar with a smile. "I'm joking, in part, but until you know more about this mental state, you need to be cautious."

"I understand," said Korin. "A lot of new experiences are going on. Until I better understand how they'll affect me, I'll take it slow."

"Well, slow for you, that is." Oscar knew she had no intention of slowing down.

"This just gets more and more interesting. I'd like to figure out what really happened," said Herbert. "But for now, I'll focus on making our hoax work."

"We came here today so that Herbert could tell you about my experience yesterday and see the videos. I didn't expect it all to go the way it did," said Korin. "But I'm not disappointed. I'm not sure how, but I think the ability to go into another dimension mentally might be a very handy skill to have."

"How about if I drive you home?" asked Oscar. "It's not that far, and Herbert can follow me and bring me back here to get my car. Are you okay with that, Herbert?"

"Sure, as long as you go slowly. I'm not a fast driver," Herbert answered.

"I'm sure I'm okay. But if you both think it's a good idea, that's what we'll do," Korin agreed.

"Here's a copy of the video for each of you," said Alan. "Look it over carefully. Call me with any ideas."

The four left Herbert's with Oscar driving Korin's Bentley and Herbert following.

"I want to hear more about your experience." Oscar adjusted the seat of the car. "Could you see anything?"

"Most of the time, I couldn't see a thing. But then I saw points of light moving by. Why do you ask?"

"I wondered if others may have had similar experiences from time to time," said Oscar. "We all experience normal consciousness and sleep. Alcohol and drugs alter normal consciousness and change sleep as well. But what I was really getting at is that many people claim to have spiritual or religious experiences. Native Americans induce them with a plant extract. Pentecostals claim to be possessed by the Holy Ghost. Buddhists meditate to obtain a different mental state. Throughout history, there are records of people who claim to have seen points of light moving by."

"So you think I was possessed by the Holy Ghost?" Korin asked in irritation.

"Calm down. That's not what I said. I'm raising a question. You experienced some kind of altered mental state. I haven't had the experience. I've talked to others claiming they have, but I didn't know them well. Most of them didn't know what had happened. It was a mystery to them. People want to think they're not crazy. They want to believe that their mind is working perfectly. So for them, the event ends up being described in spiritual terms. People interpret what they see based on their experience. Someone who is very religious might have interpreted what you saw as a version of God or heaven. Modern medicine makes it possible to revive people who would have died only a few years ago, and they report their 'near-death' experiences. Nearly every airport and major office complex has user-friendly devices mounted on walls that even untrained people can use to restart a person's heart. So more and more people are having these experiences. Many of them have a very different perspective on life and death after they go through one of them. I don't know if your event is related to those others, but there could be a connection."

"Oscar, you know I'm not a believer in spirits or religion of any kind. I wasn't having a spiritual event. What I had was a result of the experiment Herbert and I did yesterday."

"I believe you. But I also wonder if you could be mistaken, and that you really don't know what you experienced. That's at least a possibility, wouldn't you agree?"

"Sure, it's possible. But there was something strangely similar about the events yesterday and what happened today. I never had that type of experience before, and then the day after the experiment with Herbert, I have a very similar one. It is, you'll admit, strangely coincidental."

"Yes, but there may be a connection between your experience and what others have reported. It could be that people who had mind-altering experiences—which they believed were spiritual—weren't spiritual at all. It could be that they were momentarily connected with or perceiving another dimensional space. Unlike you, they had no frame of reference with which to associate their experience. Instead, they associated the unknown with God or some spirit."

"That's interesting, Oscar. You're actually a very smart guy—and kind of sexy, too." Korin reached across the center console to squeeze Oscar's thigh.

"You're right on both counts," Oscar said with a smile. "Another interesting fact is that many of the people who have these experiences are actually very smart. I always wonder why people who seem so intelligent can be so taken by religion. Maybe they really did experience these events. They didn't see God, but they did have a glimpse at another dimensional space. They just didn't know that's what they were seeing."

"I'm guessing you have a plan to test your theory," said Korin.

"Absolutely. I wanted Herbert to follow us here for a reason. While he's driving me back to his place, I'll talk to him about doing the same experiment on me that he did with you yesterday."

"Brilliant. I know it will work. You'll know what to watch for," said Korin.

Oscar parked the Bentley at Korin's and got into Herbert's car, having something more in mind as he said goodbye to Korin. He was dying, and his need to understand what was beyond acutely interested him.

The way is not in the sky. The way is in the heart.
—Gautama Buddha (c. 563–483 b.c.)

"Thanks for following me here, Herbert. I just wanted to be sure she got home all right." Oscar closed the door to Herbert's car and fastened his seatbelt.

"No problem. I was concerned, as well. I wouldn't want her blacking out while driving home."

"I had an ulterior motive for asking you to follow me here," Oscar said. "I want you to repeat the experiment you did yesterday on me when we get back to your place. Will you do it?"

"Let me think about that. What are you hoping to learn?" Questioned Herbert, applying his usual scientific analysis to the situation.

"I want to have the experience myself," said Oscar. "I've read a great deal about near-death experiences and talked with people who had them. I'm sure there's a connection between them and what Korin experienced today. People who've been resuscitated after a heart stoppage often refer to the same things she described. There must be some kind of connection, and I want to find out what it is."

"I think you may be on the wrong track there, Oscar. I don't think she had a near-death experience. Is that what you think?" asked Herbert with a sense of confusion and disbelief.

"No, I don't think Korin almost died. But something happened to her. It seemed that she experienced a very different consciousness. You know our brains generate electromagnetic fields. Many people believe that consciousness is created by resonance between neurons in the brain and the other cells in our body. When people have a near-death experience, both brain function and the function of other cells are interrupted. When this happens, most people actually remember nothing. But some have experiences that seem similar to what Korin described. I want that experience."

Oscar didn't want Herbert to know of his illness. But he was acutely aware of the limited time he had. As each day passed, he felt a greater need to know more about what he would ultimately experience. He was afraid of dying, and fear was not an emotion he cared for. After watching Korin today, he wondered whether the fear would subside if he made himself more familiar with the experience. Then he could live what remained of his life more comfortably.

"Interesting," Herbert admitted. "I see where you're going. Most people don't remember anything because they're out of resonance with our dimension and never reach resonance with any other dimension. They have no experience to remember. But a few actually change the electromagnetic fields of their brains so they experience another dimensional space. You just could be right." Herbert's voice became excited.

"So you'll do the experiment?" asked Oscar. From the time Korin mentioned the hoax, he had agreed largely to obtain money to support his family after his death. Regardless of how risky the plan was, he wasn't risking much even if everything went wrong. But now he also considered the plan interesting for other reasons. He could see a way to make his own life better. Perhaps he could write about it and change the way mankind thought about religion. It wasn't via the plan Korin had envisioned, but it just could change the underlying basis of all religions.

"I'm as curious as you are about how it will work out. Let's do it." Herbert accelerated the car to get back to his lab.

Oscar imagined that Herbert would be more focused on the physics and whether the science of these other dimensional spaces was the same. In Oscar's mind, physics was math, numbers, and calculations, all of which were unimportant. He wanted to know more about what he would experience, and how it might resemble or differ from the near-death experiences of others. Perhaps what he and Herbert were about to do would interconnect quantum mechanics and spirituality. "Tell me what to expect," he said, exiting the car at Herbert's place.

"First, everything will go black, completely black," Herbert explained. "At that point, you're out of sync with this dimensional space and any other. You won't be able to hear me, or I you. I'll change the frequency, and just as a radio dial tunes in on a station, you should be able to see another dimensional space."

"How many different dimensional spaces are there? Will I see more than one?"

"I can't say for sure. I don't know, at this time, how many there are. Korin saw two, and that was all I tried for. The frequencies of those two were mathematically spaced apart, based on whole-number multiples of the wave length," explained Herbert.

"If you try for a total of four, the two Korin saw and two more, what am I likely to see?"

"Almost all of our dimensional space—or our universe—is empty space. What I believe Korin saw—and you will see—is a view of a different dimensional space; that is, a different universe from somewhere in its deep space. The probability of you seeing anything other than distant stars is small—that's my best guess," said Herbert.

"If you're all set up from yesterday, I'll just get in the sphere, and we'll try it. Work it so that I end on the two frequencies where Korin saw something."

Oscar had discussed his impending death with his wife. He had held her in his arms as they both cried. She was a gentle and understanding person, but she couldn't feel what he was going through, and, for this reason, he had decided not to call her before the experiment with Herbert. He did wish she were there to hold him before he embarked on something so definitive, but her presence would make going forward with the hoax impossibly difficult. But he had to find out what would happen—what, if anything, lay beyond.

"I'm ready to go. Just get in the sphere, sit in seat number one, and put on the headphones," said Herbert.

"I'm ready."

With that, Herbert activated the field and lost contact with Oscar, as expected. Herbert adjusted the field frequency, attempting to put Oscar into resonance with a different dimensional space. The first two levels he set were levels Korin had not experienced. He held the frequency in place on each of these levels for exactly one minute. Next, he adjusted the frequency to one of the levels Korin had experienced. He had held that level for about thirty seconds when something unexpected happened.

Herbert had two cell phones. One was used only by Korin, Oscar, and Alan. It began to ring. It almost never rang. The caller ID said Korin was calling. He decided to answer it.

"Herbert, do not change the frequency. Leave it where it is," said Korin desperately.

"How do you know what I'm doing?" Herbert looked over his shoulder as if expecting to find her there.

"I'll explain later. Just trust me on this. It's important to leave the frequency where it is now," she said.

"Okay... How long do you want me to leave it there?"

"Stay on the phone. I'll let you know," she answered.

Five minutes passed. Herbert was getting impatient. He checked to see if Korin was still on the line. She was. He waited another five minutes. Still nothing.

Without realizing what was happening, Herbert had put Oscar in sync with Korin. Oscar knew Korin so well. He saw things about her she would never say. When he held her after she came back to consciousness, he sensed she would try to return to the mental state he had seen her in earlier, and she did. Once Oscar reached that frequency, he and Korin were synced together. He had wondered if this might happen and imagined that somehow the link could be broadened to answer questions about death.

"Okay, Herbert, go ahead and bring the field back to zero," said Korin over the phone.

Herbert did so, and Oscar came out of the sphere.

"What happened?" Herbert asked.

"The first part went just as you said. I saw distant stars. But then at the third frequency, I had a very different experience. I was somehow connected to Korin." Oscar's face was suffused with wonder.

"Interesting." Herbert frowned. "I have no idea why that happened or how it could have happened."

Oscar didn't care if Herbert ever found out what happened. Herbert was looking for a scientific explanation to describe something spiritual. Oscar had felt the experience, and it was the understanding he was looking for—of why humans believed in something supernatural. He had felt an energy that interconnected not only him and Korin, but all people. "You spend some time thinking about it. I'll do the same. I'm overwhelmed now. I'm going home." Oscar remained focused on the connection he had made and what it meant.

"We'll talk later, then." Herbert stood up and embraced Oscar before he left.

Oscar immediately called Korin's cell phone from the car. "Well, that was interesting," he said. "I've never had that kind of connection with anyone. I didn't know it was possible."

"I knew you loved me, but I didn't know how much. You're more romantic than you let on," said Korin.

"Don't forget, I could tell how you felt, too. I guess we both know it's not just about the sex. The experience was interesting in so many ways."

"I used to worry about you seeing me naked. But that was nothing. Being connected mentally to someone is a whole new level of exposure. It's going to take some adjusting to," said Korin.

"I think we'll both need some time to think about all this."

"Agreed," said Korin. "Let's meet tomorrow. We have some very important things to talk about."

They agreed to a time and place and hung up. Oscar wondered if the link could be reestablished. Even if it could not, he had done something no one else had ever done. He wanted to share this kind of connection with others. He wanted to write about it and tell the world his feelings. This made him wonder if, after death, he would be able to make these connections, and this thought somewhat quelled his fears.

CHAPTER 28

Between men and women there is no friendship possible.
There is passion, enmity, worship, love,
but no friendship.

—Oscar Wilde (1854–1900)

"I was thinking about what I might say to you most of the night and all morning." Korin walked into a conference room in her office where Oscar sat waiting for her.

"Really? I wasn't thinking about you at all." He ended his sentence with a smile, showing he wasn't serious.

"I should have known you weren't doing this just for the money. That just wouldn't be like you."

"The money is important. If I'm going to be dead in a year, I want Amanda and the kids to be taken care of," said Oscar.

"We were connected in a strange way," Korin said. "I understood some of your deep feelings, but no specifics. Does your family know about your illness?"

"Amanda does, but not the kids. I just can't tell them."

"There must be something I can do. I'll get you the best doctors in the world."

"My situation isn't a matter of more money and more doctors. I know I criticize Stanford all the time, but some of the world's best oncologists are here. There's plenty wrong with the health care system in this country, but you'll never see an Arabian prince going to Cuba, France, or Canada for treatment. They come here. Anyway, I'm tired of doctors poking me. I'm done with that. If you want to do something for me, don't pity me. Treat me as if you didn't know," Oscar insisted.

"Do you want to talk about your illness?"

"No. I don't, at least not now," said Oscar.

"I might be able to connect you with people who can help. New treatments—"

"I'm not interested in experimental medicine. I've wasted too much time talking to doctors about it. Let's switch the subject. Tell me how you felt about our sharing thoughts. What stood out for you about the experience?"

"I've always wondered what other people thought of me." Korin walked to the window and looked out at the tree-lined hills just west of Interstate 280. "Not just what they said, but what they really thought. I had lovers before I was married, one in particular whom I loved unconditionally. I loved him with all my heart. He told me many times he felt the same way, but in the end, he didn't. It broke my heart in a way I can't describe in words. It was as though my insides had been torn out. It took me a very long time to get over it. No, that's wrong. The truth is, I never really recovered. I let go of the pain, but it left me a different person. I never wanted to have that happen to me again. Yesterday, I understood that you have the same feelings for me as I do for you. That was nice to know."

"I didn't want you to get all mushy on me. I thought I knew before, but now I'm sure I know what you like, at least in men." Oscar stood and looked out the same window. "In fact, I think I know better than you do yourself."

"Oh, really. How so?" Korin walked away from Oscar toward the other end of the conference room.

"You know what you *think* you want," Oscar said, "but some of what you want from men stems from a lack of understanding of what men are. You want things that just aren't generally in a man's nature. Likewise, you fail to desire other characteristics because you think they're not part of what men are about." Oscar looked away from the hills and faced Korin.

"Interesting, I guess you know the same is true of you," Korin said, smiling playfully.

"Perhaps. We can get back to that. It's an interesting topic, and I'd like to hear more of what you think. But it's not what I really wanted to talk to you about. There's something more important and urgent we need to discuss." Oscar walked over and touched Korin's arm, turned her toward him, and looked directly into her eyes.

"Really? Just when I thought you were romantic, you tell me there's something a lot more important than our relationship. What is it?" Korin switched instantly from playfulness to a more typical business tone. So many things spun in her head. She wondered why he wouldn't talk about his illness. She couldn't imagine a time when he wasn't around. She was determined to change his fate even without his cooperation.

"It's about the hoax. It's about this plan to tell the world that religion is a fairy tale. I don't know that it is." Oscar felt uncomfortable bringing up the topic of religion.

Korin became even more concerned now. She wondered if he had perceived more detail in her thoughts than she had in his. "How so?"

"I know you don't believe in God. However, the vast majority of the people in the world do, at least they believe there's a spiritual entity that somehow interconnects us all. The truth is, the experience we had yesterday has shaken my atheistic beliefs. I felt there was something much more to life than I'd even imagined." Oscar picked up a silver pitcher and poured himself a glass of water.

Korin prided herself in knowing what people were about to say. Her business often relied on her being right. She hadn't expected this. It seemed so different from the Oscar she knew. She realized her own emotional involvement was affecting her perceptions. "In a way, I understand what you're saying," she said quietly. "The experience we had yesterday and the one I had the day before opened up a great deal to me. I felt outside of myself and, at the same time, more connected to everything. But Oscar, that's not God. I think you may be having these thoughts because you realize how close you are to dying."

"No. That's not it. I must admit this all seems strangely coincidental. But I've known about my illness for months."

"It's very strange that right after we start moving forward with a plan to show the world that spiritual beliefs are unfounded, you start to believe in God," Korin said coldly.

"Yes, but it's also strange that after we put together the means to convince the world there's nothing more, we suddenly find out there *is* so much more. Doesn't it seem to you that divine intervention might be responsible for showing us the way to God at this time so that we don't lead others in the wrong direction?"

"I think you're losing your nerve on this whole project," Korin accused him. "I think that if we convince the world that religion is a fairy tale, you're afraid you'll die and not go to heaven." Angry, she walked the length of the conference room away from Oscar and then turned to look at him. Different ideas came to mind now. To keep Herbert content, the religion component had to be there. If Herbert wasn't on board, she would never convince Oscar to do what she needed him to do. Everything was intertwined, and Oscar was making it impossible to make her secret plan work.

"Korin, if I didn't know you as well as I do, I'd get up and leave." Oscar spoke in a calm but stern voice, as though correcting a student who had spoken out of turn. "I'd leave and never see you again. That was completely uncalled for, and you know it. It's you who can't handle something. You're angry at me because I'm dying."

"Oscar, we're all dying. Maybe not as soon as you. But we're all dying. You know what this project means to me," Korin said, halfheartedly acknowledging that she wished she hadn't made her previous remark.

"It's not the project you're worried about. I know it's me. I understand that. I accept it now."

"I'll never be able to accept you not being with me. It's just not possible." Korin's voice cracked.

"It *is* possible. It's also possible for you to change your plan, especially in view of the experience we had. Can you do that?"

Korin looked out toward the hills. She didn't answer right away, and Oscar felt no need to fill the silence. The two of them had reached a point in their relationship in which no awkwardness arose during a long silence. They both understood that this was a difficult moment. Oscar sat down at the conference table and looked at Korin as she gazed out the window.

Korin knew they cared deeply for one another and wanted the relationship to continue. But that relationship was changing. Now Oscar disagreed with her on a broad philosophical point that would disrupt her efforts. She excused herself to the ladies room to give herself time to think. She walked to the stairs and went outside. Somehow the fresh air helped, and she returned with a thought of how to proceed.

"I had an idea," she said. "Maybe we need to divide up the topic of our conversation. There's a part about your illness. There's a part about God, and there's a part about religion. Wouldn't you agree?"

"First, I told you I'm not going to talk about me being sick," Oscar said firmly. "On the other two, I agree with you if what you mean is that a person can believe in some form of God without believing in any particular organized religion." He walked to a chair near Korin and held the back of it.

"Okay, that's part of what I meant. But I was thinking of separating the two in terms of our plan. Can you still support the plan if we focus on religion and not God?" she asked.

"I'm not sure the plan is a good one," said Oscar. "If there is a God, and I now believe there is, people will focus on some type of ritual—an organized religion—as their way to worship Him. When I first agreed to your plan, I was ninety-nine percent sure there was no God. I believed that what we see is all there is. Now I know there's a whole lot more. You know it too, and it seems to me that some entity which I'll call God directed us to discover this just before we put our hoax plan into operation."

"Do you believe in the talking serpent in the Garden of Eden?"

"No."

"Do you believe Jesus rose from the dead?" asked Korin.

"No."

"Do you believe God gave Moses the Ten Commandments?"

"No."

"I could go on and on, and you know it. You know better than I do that all religions cling to foolish myths. None of that would be so bad if the members of one religion didn't so often kill or try to kill members of another religion for not believing in the same foolish ideas they believe in."

Oscar spoke with passion. "I understand your point. I don't deny that rituals such as slicing the foreskin off of a baby boy's penis, bowing toward Mecca five times a day, or putting a wafer on someone's tongue is all nonsensical. No one would do these things if they needed a logical reason for doing it. But I had an experience yesterday that changed me. It makes me think those things are all logical if they lead the person doing them toward a greater understanding of God."

"So this is all about your experience yesterday. That's what's changed your thinking?"

"Yes. I know what you're going to say. You're going to say I'm a 'Born Again,' and you may be right. But I had the experience, and it changed me," said Oscar, almost apologetically.

"I was about to say I had the same experience, and it didn't change me, but then I realized that you and I actually had very different experiences. I didn't know what to expect when Herbert put me in the field. You did, because I had told you. While you were in the field, you connected with me. I wasn't in the field when I connected with you. You seemed to have experienced a different dimensional space than I did."

"So what's your point?" asked Oscar.

"My point is this: I can go back to Herbert and have him put me in the sphere and repeat what he did when you were in there. If I do that, and you put yourself into the mental state you were in when we made contact, then my experience should be very similar to yours. If I have the experience you had, I should come out of the sphere and be a believer. I should be born again." Korin was convinced this wouldn't happen.

"That's not a bad idea, but it will never work if you refuse to keep an open mind about how it might impact you," said Oscar.

"I can do that. You can be sure I'm doing just that—you'll be inside my head at least part of the time," Korin pointed out. "I think I know why—at least in part—we were able to connect last time. I was thinking about you. I was thinking about the last time we made love, and how good it felt to have you inside me. At the same moment, you were thinking exactly the same thing. That's when it happened, and I knew what you were thinking. The fact that we both had the same intense thought at the same time while we were tuned to the same frequency made the connection work. Do you know what I'm talking about?"

"Oh, yes. I certainly do."

"Because it worked last time when we focused on that thought, we should focus there again. But after we connect, we also need to try something different. You need to think about why you believe in God, and I'll try to understand your thinking. If I understand you, then I'll agree to change the plan. Hell, if I really understand you on that point, I'll *want* to change the plan."

"This could be the first time two people with very different positions on an issue truly have a meeting of the minds." Oscar smiled and tipped his glass toward Korin.

"Indeed it could."

They continued in the conference room together long enough to finalize the details. Korin called Herbert and arranged the proposed experiment with him. She then arranged a time to meet Oscar to travel to Herbert's place the next day. They said goodbye in Korin's car and ended their encounter with a passionate kiss, which ended with tears in Korin's eyes. She was confident that Oscar didn't know the details of her plan or even that she was planning to try something that could save his life. She didn't know all the details herself as yet, but she needed to go forward anyway in order to keep Herbert engaged. She also felt confident she could share some level of mental connection with Oscar without him knowing any details.

She thought about what he had said to her. It seemed odd that he now believed in God, and she, in part, wished she could share that belief. Maybe then she could believe He could save Oscar. But she couldn't. She could only believe in science, and the data she had seen earlier regarding the researchers' cure for cancer was compelling, even if it was only early stage.

She imagined that once the hoax was actually in progress, there would be great excitement. There would be distractions and confusion at times. In the midst of it all, there would be a realization that anything was possible. She'd seen others develop such a mentality in the early stage of company formation. It was invigorating, wonderful, and infectious. She was counting on that kind of mental energy evolving in the sphere as the hoax played out. If it did, Oscar would be caught up in it, and he would also, she believed, be caught up in the plan that would save him. Her plan.

CHAPTER 29

A coward is much more exposed to quarrels
than a man of spirit.

—Thomas Jefferson (1743–1826)

Oscar leaned against his car and waited for Korin to pick him up the next morning. He hadn't changed his position. He assumed that once Korin fully understood his thinking, they would be in agreement.

He kept reflecting on what Korin had said and wondered if he did, in fact, now believe in God due to his impending death. He thought back to his first experience with mortality. He was twelve years old and riding his bike along a two-lane road with Clarence, his best friend, the two of them talking back and forth about a girl in school. His friend rode in front, and as they became lost in thought Clarence turned into the path of an old blue pickup truck. The impact threw him over a hundred feet, killing him instantly. Although he never remembered doing so, Oscar stopped, got off his bike, and sat, stunned, on the side of the road. That same feeling had returned to him when he first heard his diagnosis. It was too awful to believe, and yet gut-wrenchingly real. The unbelievability juxtaposed against the undeniable reality had left him traumatized and unable to move. Removing all thoughts of death to an unconscious area of his mind was how he coped with it before and how he dealt with it now.

"Good morning, Ms. Prentise." Oscar got into Korin's car when she pulled up to drive him to Herbert's.

"Good morning, Dr. Cantor." Korin smiled and reached over to squeeze his hand lightly.

"Before you get in the sphere, I want to tell you a few things others have said after having near-death experiences," Oscar said.

"I'm not so sure I want to know what they think."

"Knowing what others think won't change the reality of what happens to you. Either we're limited to our earthly existence, or we aren't. In any event, if we're trying to repeat the experience I went through, you need to know at least some of what I know," insisted Oscar.

"Okay. Teach me. I'm all ears."

"Many people have what they refer to as an out-of-body experience. They see their own bodies below while their spirits hover above and look down on their bodies. I had something similar happen to me when I was in the sphere. Just be aware of the possibility of this happening."

"You didn't tell me about this out-of-body experience before."

"I don't always tell you everything, and I'm sure you don't tell me everything. I'm letting you know now so that when you're in the sphere, you'll try to imagine what might be going on back in this dimensional space. Imagine yourself sitting in the sphere and you looking down on it back at Herbert's estate."

"I can do that," said Korin.

"Not everyone who has a near-death experience has an out-of-body experience, so you may not have one. Some people come out of the experience and are very frightened and relieved to be back. They believe they were pulled back from hell. These people are very grateful to those who resuscitated them. They often try to live better lives after the experience in hopes of changing their end result from hell to heaven." Oscar looked to Korin for a reaction.

"Don't look at me. Nothing happened to make me think I was in hell."

"If you say so," said Oscar with a small smile. "Others are quite angry they've been brought back. They describe being in a place where they felt completely safe and content in every way. They often believe they were in heaven. These people often have no fear of death after their experience."

"That didn't happen to me either. I never had any belief in heaven or hell, and I never had a firm concept of what either was. It's not possible, in my mind, for everything to be perfect all the time, and if someone were placed in this perfect existence, I can't imagine him enjoying it for very long. Likewise, I don't see how it would be possible for anyone to suffer constantly forever in hell."

Oscar reflected that he had felt the same way until his experience in the sphere. He still didn't believe in a burning hell or a perfect heaven. He just somehow knew there was more than only the here and now. He wanted Korin to know this as well. The idea of there being more helped him deal with his own condition, and it made him accept what had happened to Clarence. "But you'll agree that many things you don't understand are nevertheless real. You also know that you learn new things all the time. You've learned things over the last few months that you couldn't even have imagined before. Many things are real to you now that you would have denied existed a year ago. Think about how some kind of mental change could switch your ideas about what heaven and hell represent to you."

"You have some good points," Korin admitted. "I'm not sure I can imagine heaven or hell, but I'll get in the sphere with an open mind and see where it takes me. To be sure, I expect you to have an open mind as well, and I'll know if you don't." Korin took one hand off the wheel and pointed a finger at Oscar with a gentle look of warning.

They found Herbert working at his computer, the screen filled with an equation. Herbert was deep in thought and didn't look up when they let themselves in. Not wanting to interrupt, they stood and watched for several minutes in hope of a lull when they could announce their presence. The lull didn't come.

"Herbert." Korin said his name a bit louder each time until he looked up. "Herbert. *Herbert.*"

"Oh, good to see you. I can get lost in the math at times. I'm sure you understand."

Oscar was astounded by what he saw on the screen. He wouldn't have recognized a physics equation, but what he saw was Drake's Equation, and he did know that. Was this a clue to why Herbert and Alan were agreeing to the plan? For now he thought it best to play dumb and discuss this possibility with Korin later. "Well, Herbert, I'm not so sure we do understand. I was never that interested in math and have no feel for what you're doing."

"Really," said Herbert, disappointed. "Math is such a beautiful thing. It's the perfect science. There are often no experiments, and when you have the answer, it's clear—you can prove it's correct. I'll show you sometime. But that's not why you came here, is it?"

Neither of them answered immediately. Oscar kept thinking about why Herbert would be using Drake's Equation.
He understood Herbert's love for math and his enthusiasm
for sharing it with others. But there was another aspect to
what Herbert was doing that wasn't so easy to comprehend.
Herbert had been changing some of the parameters of
Drake's Equation, and Oscar was trying to figure out why
he would do this. He wanted to ask, but didn't want to divert
them from the reason they were there today. He decided to
let Korin do the talking.

"You're right about that, Herbert," she said. "Oscar and
I have had some interesting discussions about what happened here over the last couple of days. As I explained on
the phone, I want you to run the same frequencies on me in
the same order as you did on Oscar. We're hoping it will help
us clarify a few things."

"Sure," said Herbert. "I can run the exact program, but I
can't say if it will give you the same results. You're different from Oscar, and yesterday isn't today. I'm still trying to
determine how time and space/time influence the field."

"Great. I'll get in the sphere. Oscar will sit in your mini-
theater and try to focus on what I'm thinking. Let's do it,"
said Korin with enthusiasm.

Oscar expected it would all go as it had the last time.

Herbert needed a little time to set everything up. When
ready, he activated the field and ran the same frequency
setting in the program he had used yesterday with Oscar.
Oscar confirmed with Herbert that it was all going as it had
yesterday, but he understood that Herbert didn't know what
was happening to Korin.

The program moved through the first two levels, as
before. Herbert waited one minute on each before moving

to the third level, where he would leave the frequency set for a longer period. This is where they expected Korin to contact Oscar as he sat concentrating on Korin from the next room. The field remained at the third level for just over three minutes before something happened.

"Bring her back," shouted Oscar, running toward Herbert. "Turn the field off. Get her back."

"Okay, I'm turning it off. Hello, Korin are you there?" asked Herbert.

There was no answer.

"What's wrong? She should be here," said Herbert to himself. He continued to adjust the settings in the program.

"She said she was starting to move forward straight into a light," said Oscar with controlled urgency in his voice.

"Forward you said? Did she indicate a speed?" asked Herbert.

"Well, yes. She said slowly."

"Okay, that's good. I'll run a sweep outward from her original position." Herbert entered instructions rapidly into the computer. "Korin? Korin? Come on, Korin."

"What's going on, Herbert? Can I help?"

Herbert didn't answer. He briefly held up a hand to indicate that he was concentrating on working the controls and had no time to answer at the moment.

"Korin?" No answer. "Korin, Are you there?"

"Yes, I'm here. Why did you bring me back?" Korin's voice sounded far less pleased at being back than Oscar and Herbert were to have her with them again.

"It seemed to be the right thing to do," said Herbert, confused. "We thought you might want to come back."

"Korin, we all need to talk. Why don't you come in here so we can figure out what just happened." Oscar spoke into the microphone Herbert had been using to talk to her.

"If I must." Korin got up from her seat and left the sphere to join the two men.

"It's good to see you," said Oscar, as he and Herbert embraced her together. "I thought we were going to lose you. Let's go sit down and talk about this."

As they entered the room where Oscar had been sitting, Korin turned toward Herbert. "You did something different didn't you? I wasn't in the same place Oscar was."

"Ahh, yeah, I guess I did," said Herbert sheepishly. "I kept all the frequency settings the same, but I projected the beam that generates the field a long way out into deep space—very far out into space."

"So before we get into what happened, why did you do that?" she asked calmly with real curiosity.

"I know we could have done the same experiment again," Herbert explained. "This is all so new I just had to see what would happen if I changed some of the parameters. You had already told me that you were able to know what each other was thinking. I wanted to see if that would work if you were very far away."

"It worked. I still felt a connection to Oscar. I knew his feelings. I knew where he was. But then there was this bright light, and I was being drawn toward it, and I stopped thinking about Oscar. I just wanted to move toward the light."

"That light must have been a black hole," said Herbert.

"No, it wasn't black. It was very bright. It wasn't a hole. It was a bright, glowing sphere," insisted Korin.

"Definitely a black hole," Herbert responded. "What you don't understand is that a black hole won't appear black because everything around it, including stars, is being drawn into it. A black hole is very dense matter. Imagine all the matter of planet earth condensed to the size of a golf ball. A black hole is spherical, and matter all around it in every direction is drawn into it. So it appears to be a very bright spherical light when viewed from a distance. It doesn't look at all the way they show it on the science channel. It's not a swirling vortex with matter going downward like water in a drain. When matter compresses, it always assume a spherical shape. That's why all the planets and stars are spheres. A sphere has the smallest amount of surface area for its volume. A black hole would definitely be a sphere and not a swirling vortex."

"Interesting," said Oscar. "People who've had near-death experiences describe themselves as being drawn to a bright light. One scientific explanation of this is that when we're put in a very traumatic, life-threatening situation, our minds go back to the same shared experience—our birth. We were all taken from the womb and brought into a place where we experienced light for the first time."

Suddenly Oscar no longer thought in terms of God. There could be many explanations for the white light. This realization was, for him, both enlightening and disconcerting.

"The other explanation must be spiritual," said Korin. "The light could be God."

Oscar couldn't believe this was Korin talking! "Are you saying you think the light was God? What do you mean when you say 'God'? Is it a supernatural being that's somehow interconnected to every person? Tell me what you mean," he said urgently.

"Yes, I mean a supernatural being who cares about and is connected to every person."

"That sort of being can't really exist. It would be far too complex. It's not logical," said Oscar. Korin looked at him as if he'd lost his mind. This wasn't what he'd been saying previously.

"It seemed that way to me before, but not now," she said. "Our bodies are made up of billions of cells that are interconnected for a purpose. Our brains are made up of billions of neurons that interconnect to make thoughts. It seems to me that a God could do the same thing on a much larger scale."

"You can't be serious. Herbert is right. It was a black hole," said Oscar with great confidence.

"Are you saying you're changing your position? You were the one telling me you had a spiritual experience and I needed to understand it. Now that I understand it, you switch your position. Am I hearing you right?" asked Korin in disbelief.

"You're hearing me just fine," said Oscar. "You asked me to keep an open mind on the issue, and I did. You were correct. It's all just physics. Now that I realize it, you tell me you saw God. How ironic!"

"This is amazing!" said Herbert. "It's all much better than I had hoped for. Let me see if I have this right. When you came here today, Oscar believed he'd seen God yesterday, and you, Korin, thought it was all physics. Now you've both reversed your positions. Is this right?"

"That's right," said Korin. "Oscar came up with this plan. He figured that if I had the same experience he had, I would believe in God. He was right, and now he's changed his position!"

"Yes," said Oscar. "Korin thought that if I could just understand her thoughts on this, I would see that it was all physics. She was correct. But now she's changed her mind. I'm wondering if maybe this isn't the real Korin!"

"And I'm wondering if maybe this isn't the real Oscar!"

"Settle down," said Herbert. "There's a perfectly logical scientific explanation for this. It's called 'spooky movement at a distance.' Let me explain."

"Please do." Korin glared at Oscar.

"For decades it's been known that subatomic particles have a property called 'spin.' The spin can be a labeled characteristic such as positive or negative, up or down, etc. That part isn't of concern here except to say that the sum of a positive and a negative is zero. When two particles spin together, their spins will be opposite—so a plus-one and a minus-one combine to be zero. If one is positive, the other is always negative."

"Okay, that makes sense," said Oscar.

"Now, we've known for decades that you can separate two particles that were initially together as a pair with opposite spins," said Herbert. "When you do so, they'll each maintain their original spin orientation. No matter how far apart you put the particles, the positive one will stay positive, and the negative one will stay negative, and the total will be zero."

"So what's 'spooky' about that?" asked Oscar.

"Nothing so far. Here's the 'spooky' part: If you change the spin on the positive one to make it negative, the negative particle will take on a positive orientation, and again the sum of the two will be zero. Although that's fascinating, the next part is downright astounding. Regardless of how far apart the particles are when the orientation of one is changed, the orientation of the other changes at the very same instant. So if the two particles are, say, one light-year apart, and you change the spin orientation of one, the spin orientation of the other will instantaneously change.

"This, of course, defies Einstein's Theory of Special Relativity, which holds that the speed of everything is relative to the speed of light, meaning that nothing other than light can travel at the speed of light, and certainly nothing can travel faster."

"Are you making this stuff up, Herbert? This sounds far-fetched to me," said Korin dubiously.

"It's true. I've worked with others trying to include the basic idea into computers. It would make them run much faster. Computers are currently limited by the speed of light. Go ahead and search the internet for 'spooky movement at a distance' and you'll see." Herbert motioned Korin to sit in front of his computer and confirm what he was saying.

"I think I will." Korin typed in the search, only to find that Herbert was indeed telling the truth. "Okay. It seems you're right. You can't blame me for not believing that story."

"Not at all," said Herbert. "I doubted it myself when I first heard about it, as did Einstein."

"If you and Einstein didn't get it, I'm not embarrassed about not understanding it or even believing it," said Korin.

"Einstein saw the data and studied it, but he couldn't begin to explain what was happening, so you're in good company," Herbert responded.

"I'm no Einstein," said Korin. "But I do get the concept of two particles being connected in some way and how the overall order of the universe might require them to balance each other. So it makes sense to me that when a plus-one changes to a minus-one, the corresponding particle would also switch. But Herbert, there's a big leap between that and what happened to Oscar and me."

"I'm not going to tell you that I know what happened to you two," said Herbert. "However, your brains are made of atoms interconnected by the flow of electrons. It seems reasonable that when you were connected and focused on the same thought, if one of you changed to the opposite idea, the other one would switch as well. You won't find this on the internet. But I can't explain it otherwise. Further, you both still remember that you had a different opinion before."

"I must admit," said Korin, "that your explanation does seem to fit what happened to Oscar and me. I experienced this overwhelming feeling of being connected to everything. That, together with the bright light, made me think about something greater than myself. I assumed that was God. Although I still have those feelings, I can appreciate how physics provides an explanation."

"Let me interpret that for you," said Oscar. "It means we're going forward with the hoax, and, I think, the sooner the better. I'll call Alan on the way home, and we'll coordinate on timing."

Oscar had come to Herbert's believing in a supernatural being or some kind of God. But as he'd seen so often in the study of religion, once science took the mystery out of it, the 'God' part disappeared. He'd always taught his students that the particular God you believed in depended on the knowledge you had. "Before we go, Herbert, tell me what happened just now. Why didn't the sphere come back as expected? Did something go wrong?"

"I was a bit concerned. I had put the sphere into deep space to determine if that would have any effect on the two of you being able to link," Herbert explained. "I have no way of knowing what will be at a given position in any other dimensional space. But I surmised that other universes would be similar to ours and, therefore, be mostly empty space. So I figured if you were in deep space in this universe, you would also be in deep space when you switched dimensions."

"But I ended up near a black hole?" asked Korin.

"That all depends on what you mean by the word 'near.' You ended up close enough to a black hole that you saw it and were drawn toward it. That moved you out of the position I had put you in. So when I went to get you back, you weren't there."

"So how did you find her?" asked Oscar.

"I used some of my mini-spheres. Not so long ago, Alan and I did some work for the CIA on ways to maintain what they refer to as 'informational superiority,' which of course means knowing more than your enemy knows. We helped them make components that could record everything around them—visual, sound, pressure, temperature, anything about the environment. I had made some in spheres the size of a pea. I sent these sequentially out to where Korin had been and just beyond. I brought them back almost immediately and downloaded the information the spheres had recorded. That information told me where she was relative to where I had put her initially. Once I knew that, I locked on and brought her back here."

"Are you saying I was almost sucked into a black hole?" asked Korin.

"It was unexpected. There may be many more black holes than physicists originally thought." Herbert sat down at his computer screen and brought up images taken by the Hubble telescope showing scores of galaxies. "There's a lot out there that we don't know much about."

"It's disconcerting about the black holes, Herbert. Could this be a problem for us while we're executing our plan?" asked Oscar.

"There's uncertainty in everything we do. But I believe I can control the experiment so that black holes are not an issue. I won't be projecting the sphere into deep space again—at least not until I know a lot more," promised Herbert.

"These mini-spheres sound interesting. Do you have more of them?" asked Korin.

"Sure do," said Herbert. "I lost two trying to get you back, but I still have three left. Why do you ask?"

"They could come in handy. We might want to know what others are saying or doing while we're executing our hoax," she said.

"Herbert, just promise me you won't let Korin use the mini-spheres to spy on me. She knows too much about me already," Oscar joked.

"No need," said Korin. "I already know all I need to know about you. So let's you and me get out of here."

Korin lingered behind as Oscar left the room. Once he was outside, Korin said to Herbert, "I need you to make this work. All of it."

Once Korin had gone, Herbert immediately called Alan. "Korin and Oscar just left here. When they first arrived, I didn't notice them coming in. I was working at my computer."

"Why are you calling me just to tell me that?" asked Alan.

"Because I had Drake's Equation up on the screen. They walked up behind me, and I know they saw it."

"How did they react? I mean, did they seem to recognize it for what it is?"

"They didn't seem to, but it's so well known. They must know what it's for," Herbert answered.

"Calm down," Alan said. "You and I know what it's for, but most people don't. Most people don't even know the term, let alone actually recognize the equation when it's written down. Why did you have it on your screen anyway?"

"I was trying to figure out how it would change with the discovery of other dimensional spaces," said Herbert.

"Here's what I think: We just keep moving forward. We don't know enough to change anything. At any rate, Dan's working on a backup plan," said Alan.

"Yes, but I'm not sure how far along Dan is with finalizing that."

"You need to call him and find out. If he's not ready, then we're not ready," said Alan.

CHAPTER 30

The moment a person forms a theory,
his imagination sees in every object only the traits
which favor that theory.

—Thomas Jefferson (died July 4, 1826,
on the same day as John Adams)

Before Korin could close the door on her Bentley, Oscar asked, "Did you see the equation on Herbert's screen when we came in? It was Drake's Equation."

"Whose equation?"

"Drake's Equation. It's used to calculate the potential number of extraterrestrial civilizations in the Milky Way galaxy," said Oscar.

"That's a bit curious. But why is that a big deal?"

"I told you I thought Herbert and Alan were up to something. They aren't sharing everything with us."

"Why do you think they're keeping something from us?" asked Korin.

"You presented this incredibly risky plan to two smart, wealthy men, and they agreed to it almost immediately."

"I told you, it's a good plan. Sure, it's bold, but it's exciting," said Korin.

"When I shared your thoughts, I confirmed something about you that I always suspected: You expect people to agree with you. You think you'll always get your way, and you have no real appreciation of how fortunate you are when you do," Oscar said.

"I just have a positive outlook. Yes, I expect things to go my way, and if they don't, I figure out how to change something so they will," said Korin.

"For all I know, all rich white people think that way."

"Don't give me that 'poor black guy' story. Things haven't gone badly for you, and they're about to go a whole lot better financially. Rich white people get sick and die, as well. You're not ill because you're black."

This seemed harsh to Oscar. He held back the urge to tell her so, knowing it would accomplish nothing in the end. He wanted to figure out what Herbert and Alan were up to. "We're getting off track. You asked why I thought they're keeping something from us. I told you why. They both agreed to your plan too easily. What else did you want to ask?"

"What are they keeping from us?" asked Korin.

"They aren't telling us the reason they agreed so easily."

"And what is the reason?"

"I'm not sure yet," said Oscar, "but it must have something to do with Drake's Equation."

"Okay. I'm not sure I agree with you, but let's go with that for now. You say it has to do with extraterrestrial life. Is that right?" asked Korin.

"Partially. It's a way to calculate the probability of intelligent life beyond earth."

"After we carry out our plan, there will be no need for the equation. Everyone will be certain there's intelligent life beyond earth. Isn't that right?" asked Korin.

"Not exactly. The equation allows you to figure out how many civilizations there might be in our galaxy. I'm not certain, but I believe the equation Herbert was looking at was changed from the original. Maybe he was trying to apply the equation to a new situation," said Oscar.

"Why would he do that?"

"Because even though Herbert and Alan will know the sphere isn't from some extraterrestrial location, no one else will," said Oscar. "Everyone else will rerun Drake's Equation. Having found one other extraterrestrial civilization will dramatically increase the probability of finding others."

"That's interesting. When you first brought this up, I thought you were completely off base. But I have a good memory for detail, and when I first met Alan, he mentioned something to me about life on other planets. I thought he was nuts."

"Alan also asked me what I thought would be the effects of finding life on other planets," said Oscar.

"What did you tell him?"

"I told him some facts about the effects of Europeans coming to North and South America."

"What facts?"

"Well, I'm a professor; I told him a lot of things. I said that most people don't know there were no horses in North or South America before Europeans brought them. Just a few European strays from time to time resulted in over seven million wild horses roaming the plains of North America by the 1700s. This totally transformed the lives of Native Americans. What they had always done on foot could now be done on horseback."

"Interesting. What else?"

"Another animal example is pigs in Cuba. There were no pigs there before the 1500s, when eight were brought ashore.

In less than three decades, there were 30,000 pigs in Cuba. This changed the diet of Cuban people," said Oscar.

"I remember hearing about disease brought to the New World by European explorers."

"The biggest effects were in South America," Oscar said. "In some areas as much as ninety percent of the population died. The diseases moved so fast that sometimes all the people in a given area were dead or moved on before the Spaniards arrived there. Smallpox was brought in by other natives who had contact with the Spaniards. Some diseases were taken back to Europe, such as syphilis, which didn't exist in Europe before the 1500s. It goes on and on. Potatoes weren't grown in Europe until discovered in the New World, and they then provided the food supply that made larger European cities possible."

"It's clear the effects were dramatic."

"But the four of us are *faking* everything. There's no real spaceship. Why would any of this matter to Herbert and Alan?" asked Oscar.

"I don't know. But somehow there's a connection. It was Herbert who led me toward a 'spaceship' idea."

"Really? I thought that was all your idea."

"Herbert mentioned he could make something hover the way a spaceship does. I just filled in the rest," Korin said.

"Maybe the spaceship part is all that's important to Herbert and Alan."

"I don't think that's the case. But even if it were, why would a spaceship component be important?"

"And why would they want to keep that from us?" asked Oscar.

"We're now back to my original question, except you're asking it now. I don't think we can come up with an answer.

But I think we should address a separate question. Herbert told us about his mini-spheres. Those spheres present a lot of possibilities. I don't think he would have used them on us, but I don't know if he has," said Korin.

"Good point. I don't know why he would have, but if he did, he would know about my illness. I should just be up front about it and tell him." As he said this, his cancer seemed more real to him. He'd felt that not telling others kept them from treating him differently. Now he wondered if he'd kept it a secret to make it seem less real to himself. He now understood why he never wanted to talk to anyone about Clarence.

"It's your call," Korin said. "We're going to see them tomorrow. Think about it overnight."

CHAPTER 31

*He who knows nothing is closer to the truth than
he whose mind is filled with falsehoods and errors.*

—Thomas Jefferson (1743–1826)

Alan, Korin, and Oscar met the following day at Herbert's. Herbert and Alan sat on one side of a rectangular conference table facing Oscar and Korin.

Oscar looked at the wall behind Herbert and saw a mounted, handwritten note that read, *"Make voyages. Attempt them. There's nothing else,"* signed by Tennessee Williams. Oscar didn't need to ask Herbert if it was an original, but he did wonder if it was a recent addition to Herbert's collection. He hadn't seen it before, and it seemed to fit the circumstances so well. Something about it gave him comfort.

"I'm going to put my cards on the table," said Oscar before anyone else could speak. "I've got about twelve to eighteen months to live. Cancer. This is an exciting plan, but there's no way I would have consented to be part of it if I were expected to live out a normal life. The long and short of it is that I want the money for my family. I'm not interested in your sympathy or in talking about my illness. I've shared my motivation for participating. Now I'm interested in knowing why the two of you would do something so risky."

"First, I won't lie to you," said Herbert. "I was aware of your illness. I knew you didn't want to tell others or talk about it, and I respected that. I have many reasons for wanting to perpetrate the hoax, but I'm not going to share them. Let's just say I have some issues with organized religion. Specifically, I have some issues with the Catholic Church. If we can do this, I feel it would make things right. I'd like to leave it at that. It just may be that not talking about the details is how I deal with it."

Immediately Oscar understood. He'd done the same thing, first with Clarence's death, and then with his own diagnosis. Still, he thought Herbert's approach was ill-conceived. Not talking about his problem didn't make it less real. But looking at Herbert and sensing his pain, he decided to say very little. "I understand," he said simply.

"I guess that leaves me," said Alan. "It's odd how we're all so different, yet so much the same. You're right in guessing that I have another motive for joining such a risky endeavor. It's been my experience that when I tried to share this information, no one believed me. They thought I was crazy, or, at best, thought I was mistaken about what I saw. I wasn't mistaken, but like you, Oscar, I didn't want people to think of me differently, so I just kept it to myself."

"Interesting," said Oscar. "Knowing what I've been going through with my illness and knowing what all of us have been working on, I think you've got a very receptive audience here. Could you share what you saw?"

Oscar sat back and listened as Alan started by painting a picture of Santa Barbara, California, where he and Jeremy had gone for a long weekend vacation. Located just over a hundred miles north of Los Angeles, Santa Barbara is known for its mild temperatures, college-town atmosphere, and gourmet restaurants. Oscar could see in his mind's eye the image of Alan and Jeremy walking out on a pier late at night. They sat down at the end on the wooden boards and looked out across the water toward the uninhabited island just off the coast. Up to this point, all seemed just as Oscar had experienced the place himself.

Alan's voice changed, and he looked at the faces of his friends as he described seeing an orange glow under the water. At first, he thought it might be an explosion of some sort. He and Jeremy looked on with increasing curiosity as the size and intensity of the glow grew. They looked around for other people, but they were alone.

Alan had difficulty repeating the story. His voice cracked as he described a tubular-shaped object over a hundred feet long erupting from the surface of the sea. The tube was orange, translucent, and glowing brightly. Both ends of the elongated structure expanded, with the expansion moving toward the center of the tube until the object formed a sphere that hovered over the surface of the water. As orange light continued to radiate from the sphere, it moved straight up and was gone from sight.

"That's quite a story, Alan," said Korin. "I'm not questioning you, but I can see why no one would believe it. Most folks think you're nuts if you say you had a near-death experience and saw God or were out for a walk and saw a UFO. I've never seen a UFO, but I can relate. I can see how you want others to believe in UFOs."

"Well, UFOs or UUOs—that's unidentified underwater objects. Either or both would work for me," said Alan.

"Now I have a better idea where the two of you are coming from," said Oscar. "It seems that both of you moved Korin toward this hoax and got me involved in order to smooth out the edges of the plan."

"Is that true?" asked Korin.

"It is, in part," said Herbert. "But there's more to it. I picked you for this, Korin, because I understand how you think, and, in some areas, it's very similar to how I think. You and I have both been very successful. With each success, we've wanted more. It's become an addiction. We both need to try something new, different, and very bold. When that need is met, we're good for awhile, but the urge returns again and again. It never stops. It must be at least as intense as the need a heroin addict feels. You and I share that, and very few others would understand what I'm talking about, but I know you do."

"What about you, Alan? Are you addicted as well? Do you need something different and bold in your life?" asked Oscar.

"Oscar, you once told me that I was crazy. I said I wasn't, and you said everyone was crazy or mentally off. Do you remember?" asked Alan.

"I say many things. I hope you weren't offended," said Oscar.

"Not at all," said Alan. "You said everyone understands that their body isn't perfect — too fat, too tall, too short, nose or ears too big, whatever — but most people think their brain works perfectly. You said it's a ridiculous assumption, considering that the brain is thousands of times more complex than the body."

"I think you've said something similar to me before. But since my body is perfect, I didn't understand," said Herbert with a smile.

"We're all nuts, or mentally ill, in some way," said Oscar. "It just shows up at different times and in different ways. Right now, on the issue of mental health, I'm not doing well. I'm not doing well at all. I'm dying, and working on this project has been a distraction. I keep telling myself I need to do it for the money—you know, money for my family. But I also need to do it to stop thinking about dying."

"We came here to figure out if it was worthwhile to go forward with our hoax," Korin summed up. "It seems we've locked onto a path that we can't change. I don't think there's anything more to discuss. We're going."

Having agreed with this, they decided to take the next day off and go ahead with the plan the day after, weather permitting.

Oscar had come that day thinking Herbert and Alan had something to hide, but he never imagined that learning their motivations would change how he thought about them and about himself. He now saw them as driven by events, and less able to control their lives than he'd thought. It made him think he might at least try to control his own life. He didn't want to be dominated by a fear of death. He wanted to be the best he could with the time he had remaining.

CHAPTER 32

The greatest danger, that of losing one's own self,
may pass off quietly as if it were nothing; every other
loss, that of an arm, a leg, five dollars, a wife, etc.,
is sure to be noticed.

Søren Kierkegaard (1813–1855)

Korin hated waiting, and a whole day off seemed a very long time. She had such confidence not only that they would be able to fool the world, but that their event would be a positive event for civilization. Ever since Korin was a little girl, she'd believed she could and would change the world. She didn't know when or how, and before this project began, she'd wondered if perhaps the only way to do it would be through her children. Sitting in her living room, she watched Camille and Evan as they did their homework. Jim sat there as well, and although there were occasional interactions, it was a quiet time.

She used some of her mental energy to jot down thoughts about what might happen the next morning. She found it impossible to imagine how she might feel then. She recognized that what Herbert had said was correct. Something was compelling her to go. She needed it, but she was going for Oscar's sake, and she had no reservations.

She'd told her family she was leaving tomorrow morning on a business trip to New York and that she would return in a day or two, depending on how the meeting went. Strangely, she thought, everything she said to them was true.

She called Oscar, who was also spending the day at home. He said that his anticipation of the trip helped him deal with his fears, and that he wanted to squeeze all he could out of his remaining time. She imagined him in his garage, working on his 1955 Porsche Speedster. He loved cars, and had put a lot of work and money into restoring this one. She knew he would be thinking about many things—his wife, his children, his students and colleagues at Stanford. She could see him in her mind's eye chuckling about how his fellow professors would react to what was about to happen the next day. Oscar had told them he expected to be in New York a day or two to meet the publisher of a new book he was writing. He said he wished he could see the faces of his colleagues, and hear them speculate and pontificate on what the "aliens" would say and do.

Korin also called Alan. He was spending the evening out at a restaurant in San Francisco. He didn't bring up his own UFO story, but he did say he had concerns about what might happen after people thought they'd made first contact with an alien civilization. Still, he had the greatest hopes about the good the hoax would ultimately do. He'd been with Jeremy for over twenty years; during half that time, fear had kept both of them from telling their families they were gay. He would overcome his fear about hovering over the UN building with a vision of a world where people didn't need to hide who they really were—even from their own families—and what they believed in.

When Korin called Herbert, he was going to get a good beer and a burger after testing the sphere and the field several times. He said the most beautiful thing about the field was its simplicity. The sphere itself was a bit more complex, but Herbert had simplified that as well.

During the call, she felt Herbert had wanted to open up even more than he had, but it seemed too impersonal to do it on the telephone. She somehow knew he was having sexual thoughts and not negative ones, but desires. The thrill of the test run had done something to him. She'd first noticed these thoughts coming to him as he watched her walk out of the sphere. She wasn't the focus of his desire, but the excitement of the test flight, combined with the image of her figure at just the right moment, had somehow initiated sexual desire in him.

Herbert wanted to talk to her about something else. He said he envied people who believed in God and had a religion that brought them comfort. It was a false comfort, but nonetheless they had it, and it bothered him that he didn't. Creating the idea of alien life in the minds of others might change everyone's perceptions of religion, God, and our place in the universe. In the words of Vice President Joe Biden, it would be a "Really fucking big deal."

The four of them had planned to meet the following day at six o'clock at Herbert's. They were all a little early, and it was still dark and cool outside when they arrived. It was very quiet as they each drove into Herbert's oversized garage. Herbert was already there, and, without saying a word, they linked arms and looked at the sphere.

"What was that?" asked Alan suddenly. "Did you hear that?"

"I sure did," said Oscar. "It was over there in the trees. Something was moving around."

"Calm down. It's only Quark, my dog." Herbert pulled a small flashlight from a case on his belt and shone the light to show the yellow Lab moving through the bushes, stopping to look back at Herbert, and then moving on.

"Perhaps we're all a bit more sensitive to everything. There's a lot about to happen, and the whole world will be a different place when we get back here," said Korin.

"And we will be different as well," added Oscar.

"I'll open the door, and we'll get going," said Herbert.

They entered the sphere and sat in seats as before. Everything had been checked, and they were ready to go.

"Okay, Herbert, I think we're all ready. Put us over the UN building, and we'll see if your 'one great mouse click for man' is a 'great mouse click for mankind,'" said Korin.

"Roger that, Houston," joked Herbert. He clicked his mouse on an icon on his screen, and in an instant they were over the UN building in New York, where it was nine o'clock in the morning.

Korin scanned the screens, and although she had long anticipated this moment, she found it difficult to comprehend that they were really there. It was surreal and unimaginably exciting. She wanted to get up and look out a window, but she didn't. They had agreed that doing so could expose them. Someone could take a picture, and those outside might see them for who they really were.

She thought about what Herbert had said about her. She was a risk taker; she was addicted to risk; it was always about the next challenge. She was delighted with what she was doing. "The weather is as predicted. It's clear and sunny. It's a great day to change the world."

"As we expected, no one seems to notice a thing," said Oscar. "Some tourists are taking pictures, but as far as they can tell, we're nothing more than a decorative globe over the UN building."

"The New Yorkers don't even look up." Korin glanced over the different screens showing pedestrians in the surrounding area.

"I'm turning on the outer screen," said Alan. "Perhaps that will get their attention." He activated the screen and his program, which brought up brightly lit images of religious symbols of every type. Because Oscar had given him so many symbols, he decided to have only a subset of the total appear on the sphere's surface at any one time. Each symbol projected a white light outward as it moved around the circumference of the sphere three times before being replaced by a different one. The order of the symbols was random, but the time each was projected onto the outer screen was proportional to the size of the religious group associated with it. Alan had, with the approval of the others, also included symbols of various gay and lesbian groups worldwide.

Oscar commented that there would be a big market for miniature toy versions of the sphere as soon as someone could get them to market. "Look, that woman's dog is barking at us," he added. "Dogs really are smarter than people. The woman just keeps trying to pull the dog along without even looking up to see what the little mutt is barking at."

"There are two more dogs barking," Korin said. "Look at screens three and five. I know our dog always notices anything different. If I put my briefcase down in a different place from usual, he goes over and walks around it several times, smells it, then looks over at me as if to say 'it's in the wrong place, stupid.' People just aren't as aware of changes in their surroundings as dogs are."

"You were absolutely dead-on right about this, Oscar," said Alan. "No one has noticed anything unusual. It's as though we're a new decoration on top of the UN."

"Sometimes I'd rather be wrong. We got much more attention at Groom Lake. People see what they expect to see, nothing more, nothing less." Oscar leaned back in his chair and scanned the different screens.

"Perhaps I should have brought Quark along," said Herbert. "He would appreciate all the attention from these other dogs."

"Wait. Look at screen seven. That guy on the sidewalk is pointing at us. He looks excited. Can we get any audio on him, Herbert?" asked Korin.

"Well, some. It won't be clear, though."

Sounds from the surrounding area started coming through their speaker system. Herbert focused the sound reception on the man Korin had pointed out. The best they could tell was that he was upset because the UN had put a symbol of Christ next to the Star of David. He didn't seem to like any of the other symbols either, but apparently didn't know what any of them represented.

"Well, that's less interesting than I thought," said Korin. "By the way, Oscar, I told you almost no one would know what all those symbols represented."

"Give it time. Others will figure it out," said Oscar calmly.

Time passed, and they continued to observe the people below, hoping to be noticed.

"I feel as though we've only been here a few seconds. But it's been forty-five minutes, and we've only been noticed by a few dogs and a religious nut. I'm going to send the text message we agreed on." Alan followed their agreement to send a text message to the Secretary General of the UN if no one noticed their presence after forty-five minutes.

The message read:

> IMPORTANT: DO NOT PANIC. SEND SECURITY TO THE
> ROOF OF THE BUILDING AND ASK THEM TO REPORT
> BACK TO YOU ON WHAT THEY SEE.

The Secretary's phone was on vibrate when the message came in. He signaled his assistant and asked him to notify security. He asked that they proceed immediately, and with caution, as he couldn't identify the sender, and only a few people had his cell phone number.

In just under ten minutes, three security guards exited a door on top of the building with their guns drawn.

"That worked," Korin said. "I see the guards. But they haven't seen us yet."

"I'm not sure I want them to see us. They could start shooting at us," said Alan.

"Not likely, Alan. But I do think they're about to see us. Two more guards are coming out the door, and one of them has a dog," said Oscar.

Transfixed by the screens, Korin watched the guards as they looked around and appeared to see nothing out of place. Then the dog noticed the sphere and started barking and pointing upward with his nose. The guards looked up. A screen camera zoomed in on their faces, and they appeared to react with surprised curiosity, first pointing their guns, but then lowering and holstering their weapons.

"That's it. We've been spotted. It took just under an hour, and we had to help them. It would have been longer if the dog hadn't barked at us," said Korin, as they all watched the guards staring upward in amazement.

"I'm not sure what we're seeing," radioed one of the guards. "There's some kind of large sphere hovering above the building. Over."

"What do you mean by 'hovering'?" came back as an inquiry on his radio.

"Well, there's a sphere. It's maybe a hundred feet over the top of the building, and it doesn't appear to be attached to anything or have any wings or propellers. Over," said the guard on his radio.

"I see it," said another guard. "I'm on the ground out in front of the building, and I see the sphere. It's got symbols of some kind moving over its surface."

Other guards made similar reports. As the number of reports increased, the level of excitement rose. The presence of the sphere was conveyed back to the Secretary General. He had security notify local law enforcement. He called Susan Rice, the U.S. Ambassador to the United Nations.

"Hello, this is Secretary-General Ban Ki-moon."

"Yes, good to hear from you," said Rice.

"I'm calling to make a brief inquiry. Do you know anything about the sphere hovering over the UN building?"

"A sphere you say? Could you be more specific? I don't know what you're referring to."

"I'll take that to mean you don't know anything," said Ban Ki-moon.

"I'll have to check and get back to you."

The plan was to send the Secretary General a second text message fifteen minutes after the first one. In putting the schedule together, Korin had calculated that he would be aware of the sphere at this point, and would have checked logical sources to determine if anyone could explain it. At this point, he would be concerned, but not panicking, and might be close to ordering evacuation of the building.

"Okay, it's been fifteen minutes. I can't wait any longer. Alan, please send him the second message," said Korin. She and the others saw more and more people notice the sphere over the UN building as word spread from the guards to people in the building and then to others in the street. The second message read as follows:

> WE HAVE COME HERE FROM ANOTHER DIMENSION. WE
> MEAN YOU NO HARM. WE WILL WAIT HERE ONE HOUR.
> AT THE END OF THAT HOUR, YOU CAN ASK US TO STAY
> OR LEAVE, AND WE WILL COMPLY.

Korin knew the Secretary General would have previously received false information of all sorts, including false threats. This message had to be different so it would seem they weren't asking for anything, which is why she went so far as to offer to leave if he wanted them to.

Her plan worked. The Secretary General went to the roof of the building, accompanied by two security guards.

"Look," said Korin. "It's Ban Ki-moon, and he's waving at us. Send him another message, Alan. Tell him, 'Yes, we see you waving.'"

Korin focused one of the cameras directly on the face of the Secretary General, who looked down at his phone, read the message, looked back up at the sphere, and said, "Holy shit! I think they're aliens. I mean, they're from another world. Radio the Head of Security and tell him to evacuate the building and the surrounding area. Tell them to do it now."

Suddenly, everything was changing. Facial expressions, body language, and the speed at which people moved were all dramatically different. Korin wondered how history would record these moments of first contact. For different reasons, the excitement level was also changing inside the sphere. Korin strained to stay focused and methodically execute the plan. "Send him a message saying he can text us back," said Korin.

The message was sent, and as fast as the Secretary General could punch in a message, he asked:

> HOW DO I KNOW YOU ARE REALLY ALIENS FROM
> ANOTHER WORLD?

"That's a fair question. I say we answer him with a question. Ask him, 'How do we know you are the leader of this planet?'"

The reply came back:

> GOOD POINT. YOU NEVER SAID YOU WERE ALIENS
> FROM ANOTHER PLANET, AND I NEVER SAID I WAS
> THE LEADER OF EARTH.

"We need to get him off that point," said Oscar. "Herbert, can you put us directly in front of him on the roof, hold us there for five seconds, and move us back up here?"

"Sure, just give me the word," said Herbert.

"I think you're right, Oscar," agreed Korin. "He's headed in a direction we don't want. Do as Oscar suggested, but instead of immediately bringing us back up here, put us just above the ground in front of the building and then back up. Sound good to you guys?"

"Yes, but what if I change the screen on the outer shell to read, 'Please stand clear,' while we're on the roof and near the ground?" suggested Alan.

"A warning sign is a good idea," said Korin. "We don't want anyone hurt." She put her hand on Herbert's shoulder to provide a degree of comfort, sensing he was tense. He looked up, touched her hand, and, without saying a word, she felt his appreciation. With everyone's consent, he set the coordinates and repositioned the sphere first directly in front of the Secretary and then near two guards standing on ground level at the entrance of the building. Korin watched the screens, and wished she were outside to see it actually happen. There was no sound, no feeling of movement—just an instantaneous repositioning of the sphere from one place to another. Anyone seeing it would immediately appreciate it was different in kind from any technology on earth.

"I think that worked. That's the reaction I was hoping for." Korin viewed the screens to see large numbers of people looking up in wide-eyed amazement. Some, but not all, seemed scared. Others seemed curious, and still others looked stunned and immobilized as they looked up at the sphere. The dogs continued to bark, and the air was filled with sounds of sirens from approaching law-enforcement vehicles.

"A text message just came in," said Alan. "He wants to know if he can speak directly with us."

"Send our planned response," said Korin.

Alan sent a response that read:

WE DO NOT SPEAK THE WAY YOU DO.
COMMUNICATIONS WILL BE LIMITED TO TEXT.

A reply came back:

Understood.

"It's been ten minutes since we gave him an hour to get back to us. Send the next planned message," said Korin, and the following message went out:

We have come here from another dimension. We mean you no harm. We will wait here another 50 minutes. At the end of the 50 minutes, you can ask us to stay or leave, and we will comply.

A large digital clock with bright green numbers was set over the screen directly in front of Korin. It continued counting the seconds backward from one hour as she watched the Secretary General on the roof. He looked at the screen on his phone, at the sphere, and at the stream of law enforcement arriving below. He punched the keys on his phone and sent the following message:

Can you send your text messages to me at my office computer?

"Good. That works for us. I'd rather have him inside," said Korin. "Send a reply."

Yes.

Korin's screen showed the Secretary looking back up at the sphere. He waved somewhat sheepishly and started walking toward his office with both security guards in tow.

The cameras of the sphere scanned the surrounding area, and the level of interest from onlookers rapidly increased. The United Nations security officers and NYPD were there, but not in force as yet. Some people continued with their

normal business as though nothing of significance had happened. All four inside the sphere watched the screen images
and saw excitement building in the surrounding area.

"This is working out well." Korin leaned back in her
chair. "We'll just repeat the last message in ten minutes, as
planned. For now, we wait and see what they do. We'll keep
monitoring their communications as we can, but we'll go
silent for now." She took a drink of water and breathed a
sigh of relief.

Intellectually, she understood that this long-awaited
event was underway, but it seemed so unreal. The clock
counted off the minutes faster than expected, and the large
screens positioned around the inside of the sphere were
no substitute for the real, three-dimensional world outside.
She felt claustrophobic, and only the text messages seemed
real.

CHAPTER 33

Rather than continuing to seek the truth,
simply let go of your views.

—Gautama Buddha (c. 563–483 B.C.)

Forty minutes passed, and the office of the Secretary General had become the center of the universe. Text messages let Korin know the U.S. Ambassador, the NYPD Chief of Police, and the mayor of New York were there. The tenor of their messages suggested that each of them expected this event to provide a political springboard that would dwarf the effect Rudy Giuliani got from the 9/11 attacks. The bureau chief of the FBI in New York arrived to be briefed. From the screens, the four in the sphere saw security working with the NYPD to evacuate the UN building and the surrounding area. Local news reporters started to arrive, and national reporters were on their way.

Korin's desire to see the real world grew, but the window openings on the sphere remained closed. The four of them separately monitored radio, television, and the internet, all of which were consumed with reports and pictures of the sphere and speculation about its origin and what it would do.

"The stock exchanges opened this morning, but they're all closed now. They were all headed sharply down at closing," said Alan.

"Yes. I saw, and the price of gold went up tenfold while the electronic exchange was open." Korin scanned various financial internet sites. "The price for actual gold bullion and other metals will be much higher by the end of the day. I so wanted to buy gold last week, but I knew any big purchases could lead investigators to me."

"I saw a story on the internet that people are emptying out grocery stores. I'm really glad you brought me some jelly doughnuts this morning." Herbert put the last quarter of one of them in his mouth. "Thanks, Korin."

"You're welcome. I bet my family is worried, but I hope they feel good about my having stocked up on lots of food the day before I left," she said.

"Here's an interesting and unexpected benefit to this," said Oscar. "Apparently, the story got out that dogs noticed the sphere first. Now many people believe that aliens are already walking around on earth, and that only dogs can tell humans from aliens. Pet shops and the animal shelters already have lines of people waiting to get any animal they can."

"Interesting," said Herbert. "Quark will be pleased."

"Perhaps we can shift people from worshipping Jesus, Mohammad, and God to worshipping dogs," said Oscar. "Why not? The Egyptians worshipped cats."

"Here's another interesting story," said Alan. "Stores that sell knives and swords are doing a lot of business. In states where you can't easily buy a gun, the knife stores are packed, and camping equipment is going fast."

"Not unexpectedly, medicine is in big demand. Drugstores are being cleaned out," added Korin. "But overall, there doesn't seem to be a destructive level of panic."

"Let's hope it stays that way. That's a lot to happen in the short time since we've been noticed," said Oscar.

"Also, remember that not all of the news we hear will be correct. Remember the 1989 earthquake. If you watched the news, it looked as though all of San Francisco was burning, when in reality there wasn't that much damage beyond one section of the Bay Bridge and the Cypress structure highway collapse," said Alan. "For now, it seems that people are reacting with surprise and curiosity, but not with terror and panic."

"Good point, Alan," Korin agreed. "Of course, the news reports will exaggerate everything. They also know almost nothing about us at this point, so speculation is rampant. One commentator said he believed it was all a hoax devised by the UN to make itself seem more relevant in the world. His opinion was that without a major event of this type, the UN would close its doors in under five years. Another commentator said he was sure it was either some kind of advertising scam or a plot by the Christian Right to scare people into believing that the Rapture was upon us."

"We're at forty-five minutes from our initial one-hour count-down message, and, as planned, our message is now going out every five minutes," said Alan.

"This has been the most interesting hour of my life, and I can tell it's going to be a lot more exciting before it's all over," said Herbert.

"I feel the same way. It's going to get better, a lot better," said Korin.

"Perhaps you're right," said Alan. "Look at the incoming message."

WE DO NOT NEED MORE TIME TO DECIDE. WE WANT YOU TO STAY. WE WOULD LIKE TO ASK YOU SOME QUESTIONS. WOULD THAT BE ACCEPTABLE TO YOU?

"Alan, type this for our reply," said Korin. "'Confirmed. We will stay. We have found that we are very good at providing information to others about themselves. Do you have questions about yourselves?'"

"Sounds good to me," said Oscar. "Let's send it."

"One thing's for sure—they won't be expecting that. They'll want to know all about us. I'll send it," said Alan.

"While they're thinking that over, perhaps you can bring back the mini-sphere you sent to the White House earlier. I think we're about to be in a position to make use of it," said Korin.

"Will do. I'll bring it back and download the information," said Herbert.

Just under ten minutes passed before the next message came in. Herbert had had time to retrieve the micro-spheres, download, and scan the information. The next message read as follows:

WE ARE UNCLEAR ON WHAT YOU MEAN BY TELLING US ABOUT OURSELVES. COULD YOU EXPLAIN THIS FURTHER?

"Perfect! It couldn't have played out better," said Korin with an expression of delight. "Have you picked out a good segment for me, Herbert?"

"I have President Obama on video," Herbert answered. "The pictures and the sound are good. The White House

Chief of Staff is there along with the Secretary of Defense. They're advising the President against coming to the UN building until they know it's safe."

"That should shake them up a bit," said Oscar. "Especially since they've probably been told he's on his way."

"How long is the segment?" asked Korin.

"It's exactly two minutes, fifty-seven-point-six seconds," Herbert said.

"That'll work. Send it to them, and play it on one of our screens while we wait for their reaction," said Korin.

On first seeing the mini-spheres, Korin had understood how they could play a critical role in the hoax. The "aliens" would need to convince the world that they could make recordings. Showing a verifiably real recording of the world's most secure location would be compelling evidence that they had both the means and the desire to record important events. However, it came with a risk. The ability to record anywhere secretly could seem to be a serious security risk to earth. She paced back and forth nervously as she waited for a message.

> IT APPEARS YOU CAN MONITOR US. CAN YOU MONITOR EVERYTHING?

"That's a safe question," said Korin. "They have to be interested in knowing the scope of the sphere's ability to watch them. That's very close to what I wanted them to ask. Let's lead them a bit more. How about this for a reply?"

She stepped to Alan's keyboard and typed:

> WE HAVE RECORDED A GREAT DEAL OF INFORMATION OVER TIME. WE WILL BE HERE LONG ENOUGH TO SHARE ONLY A TINY FRACTION OF THAT WITH YOU.

> CHOOSE AN EVENT YOU WANT TO KNOW ABOUT. WE
> CAN SHOW YOU A RECORDING OF THAT EVENT. HERE
> IS AN EXAMPLE WE PICKED FROM YOUR HISTORY.

"We could send it with the video of Pascal," she added.

"No, no, no," said Oscar. "That's way too much, too early. It will seem to them that we're leading them toward questions about God. Right now they only want to know if we're spying on them. I say we send them this…"

He took a turn at the keyboard while the others looked on.

> WE ARE NOT RECORDING YOU NOW. WE HAVE
> RECORDED SOME OF YOUR IMPORTANT EVENTS OVER
> THE CENTURIES, AND THE VIDEO WE SENT YOU WAS AN
> EXAMPLE.

"I can go with that," said Korin. "If that works for all of you, let's send it."

The response was sent. The Secretary General might not believe the response was truthful. However, Korin thought he would consider that aliens who had been perceived as potential evil spies could also be interesting historians. She hoped he would feel he'd made the right decision by asking them to stay. She wanted him to realize that with videos of actual events, the world could truthfully examine actual historical events and learn from that examination.

The Secretary General could obviously hardly wait to hear more. He tapped out a new message.

> CAN YOU SEND US A VIDEO OF SOME SPECIFIC EVENT
> THAT TOOK PLACE DECADES OR EVEN CENTURIES AGO
> ON EARTH?

"Oscar, you were right! Your message has them thinking the way we want," said Korin.

"Now let's try sending a portion of what you sent before," said Oscar. "I suggest this."

He typed:

> WE WILL BE HERE ONLY LONG ENOUGH TO SHARE
> AN EVENT OR TWO WITH YOU. FOCUS ON WHAT'S
> IMPORTANT TO KNOW ABOUT.

"That works for me," said Korin.

"Me, too," said Alan.

"Sure," said Herbert, and the message was sent.

By monitoring the internet and news shows fed by rumor and leaks, they determined that the message had created direct confrontation inside the Secretary's office. The FBI felt they should take more time, and get input from others before asking the next question. The Secretary thought it would be best to get some answers immediately. After all, he argued, the aliens could be gone in an instant, and the opportunity to gain important information would be lost forever.

Unable to decide on an action, they agreed to do what all politicians do in a difficult situation—have a press conference. The Secretary General presided. It was the first time that so many people had ever listened to and actually cared about what he said. The four watched from the sphere as he described the first contact by the aliens and the sphere's instantaneous movement from place to place around the exterior of the UN building.

The FBI bureau chief explained that the aliens appeared to have considerable intelligence-gathering abilities. He didn't reveal that the sphere had sent a video of recent events inside the White House. They had all agreed that disclosing this might create more alarm.

The Mayor praised the NYPD for its work in controlling panic in the city. He had very little idea whether they were, in fact, controlling panic, but this seemed to be an appropriate message. Without being specific, he indicated that the aliens seemed to know a great deal about us, and he joked that he hoped to ask them how to balance the city's budget.

There were questions, and the answers were, as usual, so vague as to provide virtually no useful information. When someone couldn't quickly formulate a vague answer, he didn't admit to ignorance but said, "We're not at liberty to share that information at this time."

Although the public got few genuine facts from the press conference, a great deal of information was getting out in other ways. Korin had correctly predicted that every computer hacker on the planet would focus on the Secretary General's computer once it leaked out that the aliens were using it to communicate with officials in the UN. She'd asked Alan to facilitate this unauthorized access. Before the conference was complete, all the communications between the sphere and the Secretary General were on the web. Almost instantly, the world knew the aliens had the power to answer questions about historic events, which was exactly what Korin and the others had hoped for. While the "aliens" appeared to focus on communicating with the world leader, they were now connected to millions of ordinary people, and most of them had their own idea of what questions to ask.

The Secretary General and the others returned from the press conference to the Secretary's office and found his computer inoperative. As they started blaming this on one

another, the FBI bureau chief's cell phone rang. The sphere
had sent a text message:

> Go to the Security Counsel main meeting room.
> Log onto the computer assigned to the French
> Ambassador.

The officials all did so. When they logged onto the French
Ambassador's computer, a message appeared:

> Hello from the sphere.

The Secretary typed a reply.

> Hello from earth.

"The next communications are important," Korin said.
"We need to convey the idea that we want to answer a question on the minds of most people. Based on the group we're
dealing with, do you guys have any thoughts on this?"

"Why don't we turn it around?" Oscar walked along the
outer perimeter of the sphere and hesitated slightly each
time he passed by a closed window. "They don't agree and
don't seem headed for agreement. If we ask them if they
want an answer to a question on the minds of most people
on earth, they'll struggle and come to no conclusion about
what that is."

"That makes sense to me. How about something simple
like, 'Should we answer the question most people on earth
want answered?' Would that work?" asked Korin.

"Change it just a little," said Oscar. "Try this: 'Would you
agree that we should answer the question most people on
earth want answered?'"

"If that works for all of you, send it," Korin said.

Alan typed and sent the message. Korin counted on the officials knowing they were being monitored. Since they were all politically astute, none of them would want to take a controversial position. They would agree there was no way to know what the question would be.

The following came to the sphere:

> WE AGREE THAT ANSWERING THE QUESTION MOST
> PEOPLE WANT ANSWERED WOULD BE IDEAL. HOWEVER,
> WE HAVE NO WAY OF KNOWING WHAT MOST PEOPLE
> ON EARTH WANT TO ASK.

"I believe you have them where you want them," said Alan.

"I believe I do," said Korin. "Let's send them this: 'We are capable of determining the question most people on earth want to ask us.'"

An insignificant exchange of messages continued. The officials asked where the aliens were from and why they were here, and Korin gave little information in return. She tolerated the exchange for some time to give the impression the "aliens" were willing to try to understand earthlings. Finally, they sent the following message:

> MORE THAN ANY OTHER QUESTION, PEOPLE ON EARTH
> WANT TO KNOW IF THEY SHOULD BELIEVE IN GOD.
> THIS QUESTION WAS ADDRESSED BY BLAISE PASCAL,
> ONE OF EARTH'S GREAT THINKERS, AS SHOWN IN THE
> VIDEO.

They sent the video of Pascal speaking French to acquaintances in an outdoor setting where there were no furnishings to be scrutinized by the officials later. One of

Pascal's friends was sufficiently well known that portraits had been made and survived until the present, and he would be recognized. Pascal spoke passionately about Pascal's Wager. As Oscar had previously explained, Pascal reasoned that regardless of the odds that God existed, a prudent person would believe in God because there are only four possibilities:

(1) you believe in God and you are wrong;

(2) you believe in God and you are correct;

(3) you do not believe in God and you are wrong; and

(4) you do not believe in God and you are correct.

Of those four possibilities, Pascal believed you would be a big winner if (2) turned out to be true—there is a God, and you believed in God.

A message came back:

> IT WILL TAKE TIME FOR US TO REVIEW THE VIDEO YOU SENT.

"Well, Oscar, I told you no one would know who Blaise Pascal was. And the French is from the 1600s, so it's not clear," Korin said.

"That's not a problem," said Oscar. "Once we're gone, others will figure that out. Meanwhile, it gives us a basis for commenting." He'd prepared basic background information on Pascal as well as an English translation of Pascal's Wager, and both attachments went along with this message:

> SEE ATTACHED. DOES HIS REASONING APPEAR LOGICAL TO YOU?

The Secretary General and others took time to consider the translation and sent a reply:

> WAS THIS THE ANSWER TO THE QUESTION ABOUT
> WHETHER WE SHOULD BELIEVE IN GOD?

"Korin, I think I can answer that," Oscar said. He typed the next message:

> IT'S NOT FOR US TO SAY WHAT YOU SHOULD BELIEVE
> IN. HOWEVER, TO US, BLAISE PASCAL'S STATEMENTS
> ARE COMPLETELY ILLOGICAL.

The Secretary typed and sent a question:

> WHY DO YOU FIND THEM ILLOGICAL?

Oscar typed a reply:

> PASCAL'S STATEMENTS ASSUME ANY GOD WOULD
> REWARD PEOPLE WHO BLINDLY BELIEVE IN GOD,
> AS OPPOSED TO THOSE WHO USE THEIR MINDS TO
> QUESTION THE EXISTENCE OF GOD. PERHAPS MORE
> IMPORTANTLY, IT SEEMS MANY PEOPLE ARE ONLY
> ACTING AS THOUGH THEY BELIEVE IN HOPES OF
> PLEASING GOD. THEY HAVE NO REAL BELIEF. THEY
> ARE FAKING. IF THIS ENTITY YOU REFER TO AS GOD
> EXISTS, WHY WOULD HE APPROVE OF FAKING A BELIEF
> IN HIMSELF? IF THE PEOPLE ARE NOT FAKING, THEN
> THEY ARE USING THEIR MINDS (WHICH GOD MAY
> HAVE GIVEN THEM) BY QUESTIONING HIS EXISTENCE.

The main meeting room fell into complete turmoil, but it wasn't caused by Oscar's reply. A second object had appeared over the sphere, and renewed fears of alien invasion ran through the room. No one in the main meeting room knew what to do at this point. The object hovering above the sphere didn't appear on the screens inside it.

Korin was delighted at how the hoax was unfolding. She watched Oscar closely, and he seemed completely engaged in sending the messages. He wasn't even thinking about his illness—but she was. She wondered if the rest of her plan would work and thought it was ironic that its success depended so much on belief—Oscar's belief. She understood that this was an enormously unusual situation and that all of them, including Oscar, were completely caught up in the moment. She counted on that to change Oscar's mindset. If he believed the second sphere was a real alien spaceship, her secret plan could work. If he didn't believe it, the plan would fail.

CHAPTER 34

Fix reason firmly in her seat, and call to her tribunal every fact, every opinion. Question with boldness even the existence of a God; because, if there be one, he must more approve of the homage of reason, than that of blindfolded fear.

—Thomas Jefferson (1743–1826)

Korin continued to feel closed off from the world outside. She wanted to be out there—or at least see something other than a two-dimensional screen. She joined the others in monitoring TV, radio, and internet communications. The world had focused its attention on the UN building and the sphere positioned over it. Communications by text had slowed, and Korin surmised that those in the main meeting room were overwhelmed with instructions, messages, and suggestions from the outside. She waited impatiently and then received the following message:

> OUR EARLIER INVITATION TO ALLOW YOU TO STAY WAS
> BASED ON YOUR VESSEL ALONE. WHY HAS A SECOND
> VESSEL BEEN BROUGHT HERE?

"This is interesting," said Alan. "What second vessel are they referring to?"

"Herbert, did you make a second vessel?" asked Korin.

"Fascinating," said Herbert. "Take a look at screen one. I just re-aimed the camera so that it's looking directly overhead."

"Could it be a blimp or some other kind of manmade object?" asked Oscar.

"It's no blimp. I doubt that it's earth-based, because no one in the main meeting room seems to know what it is," said Herbert.

"Oh, come on, Herbert," Oscar protested. "You're putting us on. There's no way that's an alien ship. The probability that a real alien ship arrives the very same day we bring out the sphere is astronomically high. I just can't believe it."

"I agree," said Alan. "There's no way this is a coincidence. There must be some other explanation."

"I'm not sure what you two are saying. Oscar, you're not going back to your idea that somehow God is intervening to disrupt our plan, are you?" Korin spoke with exasperation in her voice. She was acting a role in order to get Oscar thinking in a different direction. He simply had to believe that the sphere above them was a real alien spaceship.

"Well, that depends on what you mean by God," said Oscar.

"Oh, please, Oscar. This isn't a lecture at Stanford. We need to find out what that object is and deal with it. Let me ask you this, Herbert, is it possible some other physicists somewhere came up with the same idea you did?" asked Korin.

"Yes. It's not only possible, but from the looks of that object and its positioning, I'd say it's almost a certainty. The only question is whether that other physicist lives on earth," said Herbert.

"If I'm not mistaken, Herbert, you and I are both sug-gesting the same thing," said Oscar. "Maybe there are real aliens inside that object, and perhaps they're not here by coincidence. They're here now because of us. They noticed something we've done, either now or before, and they're here because of some connection they've made with us."

"To be honest, Oscar," said Herbert, "I hadn't thought about how we might be connected to them. Maybe they noticed when we moved the sphere between different dimensional spaces. Moving from one dimensional space to another might create ripples in space. It could well be similar to a stone moving from air into water and creating ripples on the surface. Those ripples could be detectable."

Yes. We detected your ripples.

Korin saw the new message and knew where it came from. Herbert had a response before she could speak:

"Do you guys have a good place for a burger and a beer?" he asked.

Indeed we do, Herbert. Great jelly doughnuts,
as well. Maybe not as you imagine them, but
just as wonderful to us.

The four of them looked at the screen and at each other. They all smiled, laughed a little, and made some sighs of relief. Korin was pleased with how this was going. Oscar's suspicions had been diverted by lightening things up with a sense of humor.

Because the second sphere had answered Herbert's question without a text message being sent, it was also clear to Oscar that whoever was in the other sphere could hear them speak and understand them.

"Where are you from?" asked Oscar.

A DIFFERENT DIMENSIONAL SPACE. WE ARE NOT
UNLIKE YOU.

"Why are you here?" Oscar persisted.

WE HAVE KNOWN HOW TO MOVE ACROSS DIMENSIONS
FOR AS LONG AS YOU HAVE BEEN SAILING SHIPS.
WHEN SOMEONE SAILS THROUGH OUR DIMENSIONAL
SPACE, WE VISIT THEIR DIMENSION OUT OF CURIOSITY.

"That's interesting. Have you been here before?" Alan
asked.

NO, BUT WE MAY COME AGAIN. NOW THAT YOU HAVE
THE TECHNOLOGY, YOU CAN VISIT US, AS WELL.

"I need a favor," Korin stated. "Oscar is very sick with pancreatic cancer. Your medicine must be far more advanced
then ours. Can you help?"

THAT DEPENDS LARGELY ON DR. CANTOR. DO YOU
WANT TO GET BETTER?

"Now more than ever," Oscar affirmed. "I want to live. But
there's no cure for what I have. I don't want to be poked
and prodded like a piece of meat if I'm just going to die
anyway."

"Can you make him better?" Korin asked.

WE CAN.

"Do it then. Make him better. Please make him better,"
Korin pleaded.

ARE YOU BE WILLING TO BE TREATED BY SOMETHING
WE SEND, DR. CANTOR?

"Tell them 'yes,' Oscar. Tell them you want their help. I need you to get better." Korin's voice was desperate.

"I don't understand what you're offering, but I do want to be well. Yes, send me something to heal me."

LOOK INSIDE THE COMPARTMENT UNDER YOUR PANEL.

Oscar opened the compartment door to see a container of orange liquid and a pamphlet entitled, "Instructions for the Treatment of Pancreatic Cancer." As Oscar picked it up, a tear rolled down his cheek. "Thank you."

There was no reply, and the object they'd been communicating with was no longer on any of the screens.

"Where did they go? Can we get them back on the screen?" Oscar asked anxiously.

"They're gone. I believe they've gone where we can't communicate with them," said Herbert.

WHERE DID YOUR OTHER SHIP GO?

"It's the Secretary General. What should I answer him?" asked Alan.

Korin was distracted. She was holding Oscar, tears running down her face. She was shaking and hadn't even heard Alan.

"Let's send this," said Herbert as he typed:

IT HAS RETURNED TO WHERE IT BELONGS.

"Okay, it's been sent," said Alan.

Oscar gently pulled away from Korin and said, "That won't satisfy them, and we need them off the topic of the second ship. Ask them if they received our comments on Pascal's Wager."

Alan sent the inquiry and a reply came back, saying:

Your message was received. Pascal is not
widely followed. Do you have a recording of
a significant event in our history you could
share?'

"Oscar, it seems that your main reason for coming along
has evaporated. And just by us being here, Alan has accomplished his goal. Would all of you be okay with sending the
video of the crucifixion?" Herbert asked.

They agreed and sent the first portion of the crucifixion
video with the following message:

Do you recognize this important event?

The time-stamped video showed portions of the crucifixion. It ended with Jesus being removed from the cross
after workers noted that His breathing had stopped, and he
hadn't reacted when a Roman Centurion soldier stabbed
him. They wanted to take the body down immediately in
order to observe the Saturday Sabbath by stopping work
before sundown on Friday.

"It will take them awhile to watch the video and get back
to us." Oscar stared at the container of medication he had
removed from the cabinet. "I'm not quitting on you. I'm fine
with waiting and sending the two additional videos."

"Thank you," said Herbert. "I appreciate that. Especially
since sending only one or two videos would be worse than
sending none at all."

In less time than expected, a message came back as
follows:

We recognized Jesus being crucified. Nearly
everyone on earth would recognize this event.
Can you send more?

"This is perfect. Send the second video with our planned message," said Oscar.

The message asked that close attention be paid to the face of the man on the cross and the face of the man in the second video. The second video also included what appeared to be an indication of time days later, and showed the man on the cross walking with two women.

"I'm going to move us, as planned." Herbert adjusted the controls, and in an instant, they were hovering above the plaza of Saint Peter's Cathedral at the Vatican. Thousands had gathered there shortly after the news of the sphere's presence over the UN was confirmed. It was already dark in Rome, and Alan lit up the outside of the sphere with a single religious symbol—the cross.

They continued to monitor broadcasts and ensured that the videos they had sent to the Secretary General were available on the internet.

"As expected, everything we sent out is being seen by virtually everyone, and closely examined by a range of different experts," said Alan.

"I'd really love to know what my colleagues back at Stanford are saying," said Oscar. "I know that's not what we're looking for right now, but it would be great to see some of those guys making fools of themselves."

"If I pick up on something out of Stanford, I'll record it for you," said Alan.

Monitoring became more difficult due to the vast amount of information circulating around the globe. Never before had the world focused to this extent on a single event. Although communication systems were overloaded, there was communication, and more of it than ever before. The collective consciousness of the world was forming. Korin felt both disconnected from it while inside the sphere, and at the same time largely responsible for its birth. It was clear that people were now thinking of everything differently—their governments, their religions, and even themselves. The communications discussing religion indicated that many people were reevaluating the validity of their current religions. Then she noticed something of particular interest. "I think I have what we're looking for. It's on CNN."

The CNN announcer indicated they were about to broadcast a message from the Vatican. The message was in English as follows:

> THE HOLY FATHER HAS SEEN THE VIDEOS FROM THE
> SPHERE. HE HAS AUTHORIZED AN EXAMINATION OF
> THE EVENTS SHOWN. ALTHOUGH THE HOLY FATHER
> NEEDED NO VERIFICATION TO KNOW THAT OUR LORD
> AND SAVIOR JESUS CHRIST ROSE FROM THE DEAD,
> THE FIRST VIDEO HAS BEEN VERIFIED BY WORLD-
> RENOWNED EXPERTS AS SHOWING THE CRUCIFIXION
> WHERE CHRIST DIED ON THE CROSS FOR OUR SINS.
> THE SECOND VIDEO SHOWS CHRIST AT A POINT IN
> TIME AFTER HE DIED ON THE CROSS, WALKING WITH
> TWO WOMAN WE HAVE REASON TO BELIEVE WERE
> MARY MAGDALENE AND HIS MOTHER THE BLESSED
> VIRGIN MARY.

"It's an absurd statement in many ways, but they had to do something," said Oscar. "They were losing followers by the millions. Let's send the third video while the Church is finishing its statement."

The message accompanying the third video requested that images taken from a different angle be examined more closely. The third video showed the same scene as in the first. However, now a close-up view of the man's throat was visible. As the image became larger, a beating pulse could be seen. The video then switched back to the ending of the second video, where the younger of the two women spoke to the man and said, "They believe you died on the cross. You need to leave this area and never return. Your followers will handle the rest."

"It will take them a while to translate that and broadcast the translation, but I believe we're finished." Herbert manipulated the controls, and in an instant, the sphere was back in its place on Herbert's estate in Woodside, California.

CHAPTER 35

There is nothing of significance
that will not have some unfortunate,
uncontrollable, and unintended consequences.

—Herbert Sedlack (b. 1952)

Hovering above the plaza of St. Peter's Cathedral, Hebert had wondered if they even needed to send the third video. He had created more doubt in the Catholic Church and religion in general just by showing the world there was more to the universe than they had previously imagined. Still, they had sent the third video. Herbert realized he'd changed as a result of the day's experiences. Maybe he'd changed by unloading his subconscious resentment against the church. Or perhaps his mind changed after doing what he'd felt he needed to do. He had been successful. He wasn't just leaving behind a dead cardinal shot with a BB gun. He'd used his mind and the technology he created to change everything. Surprisingly, as he watched Korin walk out of the sphere, he felt something sexual. He had no specific interest in Korin, but he saw in the outline of her figure a desire for females that he needed to fulfill.

Herbert had struggled with whether they should leave something behind to commemorate the "visit" to earth. It was risky. Anything left behind would be closely analyzed and would have to create no suspicion that the sphere was earth-based. He settled on leaving a sphere identical to their own in size, but made completely of salt from an underground mine located on Avery Island, Louisiana. The salt sphere consisted of crystalline NaCl, and a quote engraved on its front, outer surface read:

> *The day will come when the*
> *mystical generation of Jesus, by*
> *the Supreme Being as his Father, in*
> *the womb of a virgin, will be classed*
> *with the fable of the generation of*
> *Minerva in the brain of Jupiter.*
> —Thomas Jefferson

The message engraved on the back of the sphere read:

> *The way to silence religious disputes*
> *is to take no notice of them.*
> —Thomas Jefferson

From his work with the Hackers, Herbert had learned that any good hoax needed a "leave-behind," and the salt sphere was perfect. Thomas Jefferson was highly regarded by most Americans, but nearly everyone would be surprised that these words came from him. Herbert placed the salt sphere at the base of the Jefferson Memorial in Washington, D.C.

Herbert, Korin, Alan, and Oscar remained friends and continued to communicate with each other, but they agreed never to mention the hoax again.

Korin had arranged for Oscar to be treated in a hospital with the strange orange liquid they took from the sphere. In three months, he showed no sign of cancer. She told Herbert that saving Oscar wouldn't have been possible without him believing the liquid came from an advanced civilization in another universe. She also told him something else — something that surprised Herbert. She confided that she would never tell Oscar the truth. In part, his ignorance might be important to his continued health; he needed to believe the source of his cure in order for it to work. But she also understood that her relationship with Oscar would change if he knew the truth. He would never trust her completely if he knew she'd deceived him. Although she never said it, Herbert understood that it was primarily that she didn't want Oscar to feel he owed his life to her. Once Herbert understood for the first time the importance of her relationship with Oscar, he also realized how deprived he had been himself.

Herbert met with Alan, who, at first, had been delighted with the hoax. Now that everyone had seen not just one, but two spheres, the world accepted UFOs as real. This gave Alan and others the "green light" they needed to go public with their prior UFO sightings. In only a few days, however, he and others were again labeled mentally disturbed. People thought those earlier sightings were fake, even though they universally accepted the two spheres as real spaceships. Herbert never told Alan the second sphere was his own creation. Alan wanted to believe, and it never occurred to him to ask. It didn't matter. He believed his earlier sightings were real UFOs and that alien life existed elsewhere. Because Alan's credibility had been so compromised, Herbert felt the secret of the hoax was safe with both him and Jeremy.

Thinking about Alan's situation, Herbert drew a comparison to religion. People saw past religions and "gods" as false whenever a new, "true" religion caught hold. Herbert looked on with great amusement—and a degree of frustration—as a new "Followers of the Salt Sphere" group formed. They designated the sphere left at the base of the Jefferson Memorial as the holiest of all shrines. Members of this new FSS religion were already planning pilgrimages to the shrine on the anniversary of the sphere's first appearance. Herbert referred to the date as the new Christmas.

Pete and Dan were the only other people who knew the truth. While the others knew that Pete, Dan, and Herbert had met at MIT, they didn't all know the three had all been part of the Hackers together. The three of them had carried out pranks since their college days. They had secretly helped each other accomplish some rather astounding—but harmless—pranks over four decades. This one made them the proudest, and finding another to top it would be most difficult.

But already Herbert had a new idea.

ACKNOWLEDGMENTS

....

MANY THANKS to all those who played a part in turning *Cardinal Hoax* into a finished novel. Some contributed directly, others indirectly and unknowingly.

My parents Sadie and Andrew Bozicevic certainly provided a colorful childhood, rich with material for stories. My siblings Mark, Karen, Andre, and Tena have always urged me to retell those stories when we get together.

My law-school professor Irving Kayton beat me up regularly at George Washington School of Law when I tried to get by without reading all the cases. He also shepherded me further down the path of becoming a patent lawyer.

My partners Bret Field, Carol Francis, and Eddie Baba made our law firm so successful I had some time to write.

Fellow students in my writing classes at Stanford—as well as Deborah Pappas, Judith Gerleman, and Kevin Carpol—all offered helpful comments and corrections on my first draft.

Linda Foust did a great job with the final editing. Developmental editor Lydia Bird helped not only with sentence structure and voice, but with truthful criticisms about parts of the story that just didn't hold together and needed to be reimagined, rewritten, or deleted.

Of course my loving wife Paula not only encouraged me but read and helped revise the many drafts. Throughout the process, she kept telling me the one thing all writers want to hear—that she enjoyed reading the story. My daughter Lauren helped in the same way.

Lastly, there is a person I worked with every day for eight years, rarely exchanging more than a sentence about life beyond work, before we realized we both wanted to write. At that point Kimberly Zuehlke and I took a novel-writing class together at Stanford, and I began this project. Kim typed my manuscript over and over (thanks to her husband Mike for giving her up from time to time), and not only helped with the revisions but encouraged me every step of the way. I am forever grateful to her for all she's done, and hope the publication of *Cardinal Hoax* encourages Kim to finish her own novel—I'd like to read it!

Made in the USA
Lexington, KY
22 August 2011